LONNIE GENTRY

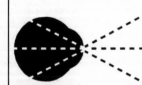

LONNIE GENTRY

PETER BRANDVOLD

THORNDIKE PRESS

A part of Gale, Cengage Learning

GALE
CENGAGE Learning·

Farmington Hills, Mich • San Francisco • New York • Waterville, Maine
Meriden, Conn • Mason, Ohio • Chicago

LIBRARY OF CONGRESS CATALOGING-IN-PUBLICATION DATA

Brandvold, Peter.
    Lonnie Gentry / by Peter Brandvold. — Large print edition.
       pages ; cm. — (Thorndike Press large print western)
    ISBN 978-1-4104-7690-6 (hardcover) — ISBN 1-4104-7690-1 (hardcover)
    1. Cowboys—Fiction. 2. Outlaws—Fiction. 3. Large type books. I. Title.
  PS3552.R3236L68 2015
  813'.54—dc23
                                                        2014042229

Published in 2015 by arrangement with Peter Brandvold

Printed in Mexico
1 2 3 4 5 6 7 19 18 17 16 15

This book is for my friend
Jason Bruner—
Wild Man of Mount Milner!

CHAPTER 1

Something screeched through the air about six inches in front of Lonnie Gentry's face. Lonnie felt the warm curl of air against his nose.

The fast-moving object made a loud *whunk!* as it crashed into a tree ahead and left of the thirteen-year-old. The shrill crack of a rifle cut through the afternoon silence of this high mountain forest and flattened out over the valley below, chasing its echoes like a rabid dog trying to bite its own tail.

Lonnie shouted a curse as he leaped back along the cattle trail he'd been following on his search for calves that might have gotten bogged in mud or entangled in brush. He stumbled back so quickly, his heart turning somersaults in his chest, that he got his boots and spurs tangled up and went down hard on his butt.

His hat went flying.

He cursed again. The pain of the fall felt

like an ax handle slammed against his rear end. This time the curse was drowned by another bullet screeching in from his right to ricochet loudly off a mossy, gray boulder on the upslope to his left.

"What the *hell*?" exclaimed the boy, who reserved his "barn talk," as his mother called it, for when he was in the company of only his horse . . . or when someone was trying to drill a tunnel between his ears with a bullet!

Lonnie grabbed his hat, scrambled off the trail's downslope side. The rifle crashed again on the heels of a dull thud, which was the bullet plowing into the pine-needle-carpeted slope on the other side of the trail.

That shot was well shy of Lonnie, which told the boy that the shooter had lost track of him. Holding his hat as he lay belly-down between two tall pines and staring along the slope in the direction he'd been heading, hot fury washed through Lonnie Gentry. His first thought had been some cork-headed fool had mistaken him for a deer or an elk, but the persistence with which they'd continued shooting had made him ponder other possibilities.

Now a man's voice yelled from the densely forested upslope, "You git him, Willie?"

And another man's voice answered, "Not

sure! Seen him go down, but he might've hotfooted it!"

The rage in Lonnie turned to fear.

Nope, they hadn't mistaken him for game. They'd known he was two-legged, and they were either after money, which he didn't have, or his horse. Possibly the Winchester .44-40 repeating rifle riding in the scabbard attached to his saddle. Which, in turn, was attached to his horse, General Sherman, whom he'd left down trail a ways to forage for himself along Willow Run, a cold mountain stream cutting straight down out of the mountains.

"Let's move in slow-like and check it out," called the man on the upslope. "Take care — the rest are prob'ly close!"

The hair along the back of Lonnie's neck pricked. They were heading toward him, and he hadn't liked the sound of their voices. They were pinched voices. The voices of determined men. Likely, desperate men.

Probably outlaws on the run from some posse. Maybe in need of guns, ammo, and horses.

Lonnie lay frozen in fear, his mind and heart competing with each other like two horses running a Fourth of July race, for nearly a minute. Then he saw movement through the trees on the upslope. He heard the crunch of pine needles of someone moving along the trail he'd been on himself a few minutes ago. The trail angled down from a low ridge. Lonnie couldn't see over the ridge, but his bushwhacker must be coming from the other side of it.

Lonnie's mind continued to churn. His hands were sweating and his toes felt like mud inside his boots. If he continued to lie here, shivering, he'd be wolf bait. No one would ever see him or hear from him again. He'd be one of those legends that streak these Never Summer Mountains of northern Colorado Territory — mysterious legends of those who'd simply disappeared.

What happened to such lost souls, no one knew. But it sure was fun to speculate around lonely campfires on a cold mountain night during roundup, say, or on an elk-hunting trip. Lonnie had to admit he'd enjoyed such stories himself. They'd given him an odd thrill. This one, however, wouldn't be nearly as thrilling. At least, not to him. Not to his mother, either. She'd likely spend the next several years bawling her eyes out and sobbing herself to sleep at night.

Men were after him. Bad men. Men who'd likely kill him as soon as they saw him, and turn his pockets inside out. They'd find nothing in there but lint, but they'd eventually find General Sherman and the rifle . . .

The rifle.

Lonnie scrambled to his feet, turned, stuffed his hat down tight on his head, and ran at a crouch downslope through the columnar pines. He ran hard, his pointed-toe stockmen's boots slipping and sliding on the thin, needle-strewn dirt. His spurs rang with every step. He leaped deadfalls and ducked under those that had fallen against other trees. He was angling down the slope, in the direction from which he'd come.

Behind him, a man's voice echoed eerily through the silent forest. "See him?"

The reply was a little louder: "No, but I can hear him. He's hotfooting it, all right! *Git him!*"

CHAPTER 2

A rifle barked loudly. Lonnie jumped with a start. He thought for a second he'd been shot, but then he realized that he'd just imagined the bullet.

The sudden punch of cold terror had caused him to lose his footing again. He fell on the downslope, and rolled. Again, he lost his hat as he continued rolling down the steep slope and into a snag of willows lining a rocky spring. The willows stopped him.

A weird, terrified energy was coursing through him. He had to get to his horse and his Winchester — his prized Winchester '66 Yellowboy repeater that his father had left him when he'd died. Between imagined images of the devilishly grinning men stalking him, all he could see was General Sherman and his rifle.

If he had the Winchester, he'd have a way to defend himself, possibly even discourage his stalkers.

In a blur, he gained his feet, retrieved his hat, stuffed it down on his head again, ran through the willows and the little trickle of water gurgling out of the rocks, and continued running toward the pulsating rush of what he knew was the stream tumbling out of the mountains ahead of him, farther on down the slope.

He scrambled up and over a low ridge. As he ran down the other side, he saw the rush of water tumbling down the slope from his right to his left. Willow Run was about thirty yards across, but even now in mid-summer the spring-fed stream was a rushing torrent as cold as hell was hot. It was sheathed in ferns and willows.

On the other side of the white roil of spraying water, near a low stone escarpment, Lonnie's buckskin stallion, General Sherman, stood tied to a root angling out of the scarp. The horse was staring toward Lonnie and twitching his ears curiously, probably wondering what the shooting had been about. Horses' ears were keen. He would have heard the shots even above the roar of the stream.

Lonnie glanced over his shoulder as he continued running toward a fir tree that had fallen across the stream, providing a natural bridge. He could see nothing behind him amidst the murky, dark-green forest, but when he was halfway across the stream, carefully negotiating the half-rotted pine, a bullet slammed off the escarpment near General Sherman. The rifle belched behind Lonnie. The horse whickered and backed away, his eyes growing large and round. He pulled at the reins that Lonnie had tied to the root.

"No, wait, General!" Lonnie yelled, holding his arms out as he set one slippery boot down in front of the other, on the pine's spongy trunk bristling with lance- and dagger-like broken branches.

The water roiling over and between the boulders littering the stream sent mare's tails of water splashing and spraying at Lonnie, filling the damp air with the wet smells of mud, stones, ferns, and cold mountain water.

Another bullet screeched off a rock to Lonnie's right, on the bank of the stream. The General whinnied and shook his head, gave the reins a hard tug, pulling them free of the root. Lonnie hadn't tied the reins very tightly; he'd just looped them over the root.

Lonnie had gentled and trained the stallion himself, and, like most western riders, he'd taught the General to remain with his bridle reins, even if they just hung to the ground. The looping over the root had only been a precaution. The General had not been trained to remain with his reins when he was being shot at, however, and now he began to turn away and to ready himself for a run to safety.

Lonnie leaped off the end of the fir and made a mad, scrambling dash toward the horse. The twin bridle reins were two snakes twisting and sliding along the ground in front of him. They slithered away faster . . . too fast. He wasn't going to catch them.

Then the General's hindquarters slid up hard and fast on Lonnie's right. Lonnie glimpsed the walnut stock of his Winchester protruding from the old leather scabbard strapped to the saddle. The gold plate at the end of the stock glistened in the sunlight filtering through the forest canopy.

Leaving the reins, Lonnie reached for the rifle. He wrapped his left hand around the stock and pulled. The rifle had just come free of the boot when the General's left hip slammed into Lonnie like two barrels tumbling from a beer wagon.

Lonnie left his feet and flew sideways. He saw the horse galloping down the slope, away from him. The General was shaking his head as though at a swarm of stinging yellow jackets. Lonnie momentarily had the wind knocked out of him, but when his senses returned, he found that he was holding his Winchester carbine across his sharply rising and falling belly with both his gloved hands.

At least, he'd gotten the rifle.

Dust and pine needles plumed in two places around him, blowing grit over his right boot. The rifles of his stalkers echoed softly above the thunder of the stream.

Lonnie lifted his head from the dirt. Two men were running down the slope on the stream's far side. They were both bearded and wearing Stetsons, bright neckerchiefs billowing down their chests. Leather chaps flapped against their denim-clad legs.

The man on the right, shorter than the other one, and with long, dark-brown hair, stopped suddenly to pump another cartridge into his rifle's chamber while the one on the left continued running toward the stream.

Lonnie cursed, heaved himself to his feet, and ran downslope as fast as he could, squeezing the carbine in his hands.

"There he is, Willie!" one of his pursuers shouted behind him. *"Git him!"*

Another bullet nicked Lonnie's right boot heel. It nudged his foot wide and sent him flying. He rolled toward the stream, felt the

Winchester leave his hands. He heard the plop as the rifle hit the water.

Mindless of his aches and pains, fear a living, panting beast inside him, Lonnie made a mad dash for the stream. The Winchester lay in a side eddy that was about two feet deep. The brass butt plate flashed.

Glancing once upstream and seeing the two men running toward him, on the same side of the stream as Lonnie, he dipped his hands into the water, and pulled out the Winchester. His hands shaking from the hot blood of terror flowing inside him, he pumped a cartridge into the chamber, twisted around, and fired without aiming.

He'd just wanted to slow his pursuers' pursuit.

He slowed it, all right. He stopped one man altogether.

The one who'd stopped was a short hombre with longish brown hair and a thick mustache and goatee. His head snapped violently back on his shoulders as he continued running toward Lonnie. Then the man's arms dropped. He released his rifle, which clattered to the ground in front of him. He kicked it.

Then he fell to his knees. He had a funny, dull look on his face, which was pink with sunburn. His head wobbled until his dark-brown Stetson tumbled off his shoulder.

As he knelt on the thick, green grass about six feet away from the stream and on the other side of a deadfall pine from Lonnie, Lonnie saw a red spot in the dead center of the man's pale forehead, where his hat had shaded it from the sun. He also saw something bright and shiny on the man's brown leather vest, beneath the green neckerchief that hung down over his heart.

A badge. A five-pointed lawman's star.

As the man stared toward Lonnie, his eyes rolled back into his head, until all Lonnie could see was eggshell white. Then the man fell forward and hit the ground flat on his face.

CHAPTER 3

"Willie!" the other man yelled, running toward his partner.

Lonnie looked at the smoking Winchester in his own hands. It was as though he were seeing the rifle for the first time. It was like suddenly realizing that what he'd been holding wasn't a rifle at all but a deadly diamondback rattlesnake. But he did not drop the weapon. That diamondback might very well have saved his life.

Lonnie rose stiffly, as though his joints had become fouled with mortar, and ran in a shambling gait on down the slope toward his horse. He didn't see much of anything before him.

All he really saw was the bearded face of the man with the red spot in the middle of his forehead.

Lonnie didn't know how far he'd run, for his head was swimming, when he dropped to his knees and the jerky and baking-powder biscuits that his mother had packed for his lunch came roaring up from his guts, and splattered onto the rocks before him.

He vomited once more, and ran the sweaty, dusty sleeve of his shirt across his mouth. As he did, he squeezed his eyes closed, trying to wipe from his brain the memory of the man he'd shot. Of course, it did not leave but became even more vivid for his wanting to forget, tightening his guts in a knot that would have driven more food out of his stomach if there had been more in there.

There was nothing left but bile, and, swallowing hard, he managed to keep it down.

His knees were weak and his hands were trembling.

Killer. He was a killer. And he hadn't killed just any man. He'd killed a lawman. He had not intended to, but he'd killed the man, just the same, and if he was caught he'd likely hang.

Lonnie looked behind at the forested ridge he'd run down from several minutes ago. Now he was in Wolf Creek Valley, which, running north to south in the shape of a dogleg, was carpeted in short blond grass, mountain sage, and willows, with Wolf Creek running down its middle. The creek lay another hundred yards beyond, sheathed in dense, green willows.

But Lonnie's attention was on the steep, forested slope he'd just left.

An ominous silence hung over the ridge. There was no movement amongst the trees that formed a gauzy, dark-green carpet shrouding that long hogback mountain. The only movement in the area was a bird of some kind, circling the ridge crest from high in the cobalt sky above, beneath a couple of thin, ragged-edged clouds that were as white as fresh linen against deep, dark blue.

The dead lawman was still up there in those trees. And so was his partner, who was most likely also a lawman. So far, the dead man's partner didn't appear to be following Lonnie, but Lonnie wasn't taking any chances. He didn't want to hang any more than he wanted to have his young hide perforated with lead.

He got up, holding his carbine with one hand, ran a grimy sleeve across his mouth once more, and continued running. He figured that General Sherman had headed for the creek, and he was right. He spotted the horse's back end sticking out of the willows, the buckskin's black tail switching at blackflies.

Lonnie slowed when he was fifty yards from the creek. The horse had heard Lonnie coming, and he'd turned his head sideways to look askance at his rider. Water dribbled from the horse's leathery, black snout. The General twitched one ear and then the other in dubious greeting.

Lonnie walked slowly forward so the horse wouldn't spook. The General wasn't normally the spooky type, but he didn't normally hear as much gunfire, either. Lonnie didn't want to chance the horse galloping off and leaving him out here on foot, with a crazed lawman dogging his heels.

Why the men had been after him, he had no idea. All he knew is they'd been shooting first, apparently content to ask questions later, and now that Lonnie had inadvertently shot one of them, he was probably more wanted now than he'd been before.

He wanted to get home — back to the relative safety and comfort of the ranch. Not that the law couldn't follow him there, but where else could he go?

He managed to walk up on General Sherman without unduly frightening the horse. When he had a hold of the reins that were dusty and cracked from being dragged and stepped on, he adjusted the saddle, which had slipped onto the horse's left side during the General's run out of the mountains.

"Thanks a bunch for leavin' me up there,

General," Lonnie said, grunting as he pulled the latigo tight. He glanced toward the eerily quiet ridge bathed in golden, late-afternoon sunshine. "Really appreciate your loyalty in extreme circumstances, you ole hayburner."

The horse whickered and testily stomped its front left hoof down close to Lonnie's right boot. The horse had a jeering cast in the big, brown eye it was directing at Lonnie.

"You step on my foot, galldangit," Lonnie said, talking only because he was nervous, his blood still surging, "I'll bite one of your ears off. How would you like that, you old cayuse?"

The General gave another testy whicker.

Lonnie toed a stirrup and, grabbing the horn with his left hand, the cantle with his right, heaved himself up into the leather. He turned the horse and headed south along the willows lining the gurgling stream. The General bounced into a spine-jarring trot. Glancing once more toward the ridge, Lonnie touched his spurs to the horse's flanks, and the General shook his head again testily and lunged forward into a rocking lope.

He and the horse ate up the ground, making their way along Willow Creek for two miles before Lonnie turned the horse across the shallow stream and followed Wolf Creek, which fed Willow Creek from the north, toward a distant ridge. His ranch lay at the foot of that ridge. He considered it his since only he and his mother lived there now, his father having died so long ago that Lonnie couldn't even remember what Calvin Gentry had looked like.

Three years was a long time to a thirteen-year-old boy.

Lonnie couldn't see the cabin and barn until after he and the General had ridden hard another twenty minutes, rising and falling over a couple of low hills stippled in pines and aspens, following a two-track wagon trail. Dropping down off the shoulder of the last hill, he saw smoke lifting from the cabin's stone chimney and making a soft, gray wash against the pine- and fir-cloaked ridge behind it. The ridge was turning darker and fuzzier now as the sun fell behind the shadowed, western mountains.

The General followed the trail through the ranch portal, which was a stout birch log stretched between the tops of two peeled pine poles driven into the ground on each side of the trail. The birch plank had the Gentry Circle G brand burned into it. The name GENTRY had been painted in an arc over the brand, but the paint had long since faded so that you could only make out the name if you were right up on it and were looking for it.

Beyond the portal, the General shook his head and whickered disconcertingly. The horse stopped, and Lonnie tensed as he stared over the General's head and into the yard, which consisted of the one-and-a-half-story, shake-shingled log cabin, sitting with its back to the ridge, on Lonnie's left, and the barn and corrals on his right, across the yard from the cabin. There were a few out-buildings, including a keeper shed for meat and vegetables, as well as a small bunkhouse used by the two or three hands Lonnie's mother hired during the spring and fall roundups but which sat empty for most of the summer and all of the winter.

As Lonnie looked around, he saw that what had troubled the General were the three strange horses in the pole corral on the near side of the barn, standing separately from the half dozen horses in the Gentry remuda. The horses were eating the fresh hay that had been forked to them from the crib fronting the corral.

They were what bothered the General. What bothered Lonnie, however, were the men the horses obviously belonged to —

the three men sitting on the cabin's long, brush-roofed front stoop.

CHAPTER 4

The man on the porch who bothered Lonnie the most was the big, rangy, hawk-nosed, blond-headed man on whose knee Lonnie's mother was sitting, though, seeing Lonnie, she climbed awkwardly to her feet and cast sheepish glances toward her son, grinning with embarrassment and swatting at the blond gent's grabby hands.

Maybelline Gentry apparently hadn't seen her son ride up. She'd been too busy making time with Shannon Dupree, the big blond gent who was funning with Lonnie's mother, grabbing at her skirts and apron while casting his jeering, hawkish gaze into the yard at Lonnie.

The other men sat around Dupree — two dull-eyed tough nuts Lonnie recognized from previous visits. The short, stocky man with long, black hair and wearing a necklace of wolf teeth over his buckskin shirt, which was open halfway down his chest, was a man whom Lonnie knew only as Fuego. Fuego was half Indian, probably Arapaho. He rarely smiled or even spoke, and the few times Lonnie had seen him, he'd reminded the boy of a dangerous, wild beast who always smelled so strongly of sour sweat that it had made Lonnie's eyes water.

The other, younger man wearing a thin, sandy-colored mustache and sideburns and whose pale-blue eyes were set too close together, was Childress. Childress smiled a lot but in a mocking way, not in a friendly one. It was as though he were always thinking about a joke he could play on someone else. Lonnie thought his first name was Jake, or something like that. Dupree, Childress, and Fuego all rode together.

A Winchester rifle leaned against the front of the cabin, between Dupree and Fuego. The three were passing a bottle around and staring at Lonnie with expressions stretching the gamut from bland indifference to sneering condescension.

Those snakes formed knots again in Lonnie's gut. Everything was coming clear, and he was fighting not only fear of who might be following him, but fury at the men sitting so casually on the stoop of his own cabin. Yes, *his* cabin. He may have only been thirteen, but the cabin was half his, because he did the work of a full-grown man around the place, and without him, there would no longer *be* any ranch in the wake of his father's passing.

Without Lonnie, his mother would have headed back to Arapaho Creek. Shannon Dupree came by every once in a while. He'd play at being a rancher for a few days or weeks at a time, but mostly he'd play at being Lonnie's boss while he caused more work than he accomplished and spent most of the day drinking and eating or "taking naps" with Lonnie's mother.

Lonnie booted the General ahead, turning him toward the barn. He kept his eyes off the men on the cabin's porch, as though his not seeing them meant they were no longer there.

He knew they were still there, though. He also knew that their presence here at the Circle G meant trouble. Probably *had already meant* trouble. Everybody knew that Shannon Dupree and the men with him were outlaws. They'd likely robbed a stagecoach or a bank or something, and that's why the lawmen had been on the ridge earlier. The lawdogs had probably lost Dupree's trail and had been looking around for him when they'd run into Lonnie, and, not getting a good look at him, probably thought he was one of Dupree's bunch.

Because of Shannon Dupree, Lonnie Gentry was a killer.

Lonnie trembled as he swung down from the General's back. The barn doors were standing partway open. He swung them wide and led the General inside.

As he reached under the buckskin's belly for the latigo, footsteps sounded behind him. He glanced through the barn's open doors and out into the soft saffron light mixing with the deepening shadows and the cottony smoke from the cabin's chimney. The smoke was perfumed with the tang of burning piñon. Lonnie's mother, Maybelline Gentry, was walking toward the barn, holding her yellow skirt and the hem of her white petticoat above her black patent, side-button shoes.

Lonnie's mother was a pretty woman. She turned heads everywhere she went. Lonnie didn't like that about her. He didn't like the way men looked at her, the way Shannon and the other men on the porch were looking at her now as she strode toward the barn, her yellow-blonde hair hanging in a strategically messy braid down the right side of her head, with many vagrant strands sliding against her peach-colored cheeks. She'd gussied herself up for Dupree in a fresh yel-

30

low housedress, which hugged her a little too tightly, with white lace collar and sleeve cuffs. Lonnie thought she'd added a little blush to her face and red paint to her lips.

Lonnie often wished he had a fat, ugly mother like Oscar Lomax's mother on Dead Mormon Creek, so that men would leave her — *and Lonnie* — alone.

Lonnie turned back to his work as she entered the barn. He considered whether he should tell her about the trouble — about his having killed the lawman. He wanted to tell her. He wanted to get it off his chest in the worst way.

At the same time, it felt like too much of a confession right now, in light of the presence of Shannon Dupree. He didn't want Dupree to know. He thought his killing someone might cause Dupree to think that he, Lonnie, now had some sort of kinship with Dupree, a known outlaw. But nothing could be farther from the truth. Dupree had likely killed many men though Lonnie didn't know that for sure.

Lonnie had shot that lawman accidentally, and he just wanted to forget it had happened. It sure as hell didn't mean that Lonnie was anything like that cross-grained, bottom-feeding trash, Dupree.

"What's he doing here?" Lonnie said,

reaching up to slide the saddle off the General's back.

May Gentry stopped inside the barn door. "He rode in this morning, right after you rode out."

She had a light, free and easy tone, and Lonnie turned to see that her cheeks were flushed and that her blue eyes were fairly glowing, as though a lamp inside her head had been turned up bright. The sick, shaky feeling inside of Lonnie, the feeling that he'd been stabbed with a rusty knife and that the blade was still in there, twisting, got even worse.

It was the look on his mother's face that had made it worse.

"Oh, no," Lonnie thought, feeling his knees quake. "Oh . . . *no* . . . !"

His mother was smiling and fiddling with her hair. As she glanced back toward the cabin where the three outlaws were passing the bottle on the porch and laughing and talking in secret, jovial tones, she said in a quiet, delighted little voice that made Lonnie want to vomit again — "Lonnie, honey — I have most wonderful news. Shannon's asked for my hand!"

CHAPTER 5

A hard knot formed in Lonnie's throat. His head was swimming. So much to take in: killing a lawman only hours earlier, Dupree here at the Circle G with Fuego and Childress. Now, on top of all that, Dupree had asked his mother to marry him.

A man Lonnie hated above any other he'd ever known — even more than he hated the Devil — had asked his mother to marry him.

Lonnie already knew the answer to his next question, but, hell, things really couldn't get any worse than they already were. So he drew a deep, calming breath, and asked, "What . . . what'd you say, Momma?"

May Gentry smiled down at Lonnie angelically. He could tell it was not only her love for Shannon Dupree that made her look that way. She'd probably taken a couple of nips from Dupree's bottle. But she blinked, and the angelic smile lost some of its luster. She wrinkled the skin above the bridge of her nose and stepped toward Lonnie, turning her mouth corners down and tilting her head to one side.

"It'll be all right, Lon. Really, it will."

"What'd you tell him, Momma?" Lonnie couldn't help the way that had come out. His nerves were jumping around beneath his skin like the baby snakes he'd once seen writhing around inside an old cabin wall, and he hadn't been able to keep himself from practically shouting the question.

His mother's face turned sunset red. She bunched her lips, then her arm swung up and forward, and *crack!* The palm of her right hand smacked Lonnie's left cheek. It felt as though she'd laid a hot iron against that side of his head.

Lonnie grunted and stepped back. Tears welled in his eyes and a sob was rising in his throat like a slow croak, but he fought back both the tears and the sob, blinking his eyes and swallowing hard. There was a toughness in Lonnie Gentry that sometimes surprised even him. He wasn't sure where it had come from. It was sort of like realizing your hands were no longer sore after a hard day's work, because they'd acquired a hard layer of calluses.

That's kind of what had happened to Lonnie's heart over the past three years, since his father had died and he'd had to take over responsibility for the bulk of the outdoor work around the Circle G, knowing that if he couldn't keep up, he and his mother would either starve or they'd have to head to Arapaho Creek and maybe live in a boarding house.

Lonnie wasn't sure which would have been worse. He just knew he wouldn't want to do either. So he worked twelve, sometimes sixteen hours a day during the busy seasons — during spring calving, the summer hay cutting, and the fall branding and roundup. And somehow, doing a man's work at thirteen had given the boy a working man's thick skin that only a few things could penetrate.

A slap wasn't one of them.

That seemed to puzzle his mother, who stared down at him, frowning, until she glanced toward the cabin, and said in a hard, accusing voice, "You never have liked Shannon." She turned back to Lonnie, lines of anger cut across her lightly tanned forehead. "No, he's not your father. But he could be, if you'd let him. You probably don't remember, since you were so young, but your father was no saint. No man is. There is no such thing, Lonnie. But we

35

could use a man to take charge around here — you an' me."

"Leave me out of it." Lonnie knew he'd crossed a line there, but there was so much fear and anger surging inside him, he couldn't hold it all back. "We're doin' fine, Momma."

"We've done all right, but we need help."

"I don't need no help. All Dupree ever does when he's here is suck on a bottle the way the calves suck the heifers' teats. Besides . . ."

Lonnie glanced toward the cabin. One of Dupree's "boys" — he always called them "the boys" though they were as old as Dupree, well into their thirties — walked around the front of the cabin and headed toward the privy flanking the place. Jake Childress's feet looked a little light and unsteady. He had to reach out and grab the cabin wall to establish his balance.

Dupree and Fuego were still on the porch, smoking and taking turns with the bottle, as they stared toward the barn, their seedy eyes glued to Lonnie's mother, who was only twenty-seven. She'd had Lonnie when she was fourteen. Fuego had the Winchester across his knees now, and he was rubbing it down with a rag, a quirley smoldering between his lips.

36

"Besides what?" Lonnie's mother said.

Lonnie licked his lips and canted his head in the direction of the cabin. "Besides, you know what they been up to? Before they came here? You know where they were?"

"They were working over at the Fifty-Five Connected for Mort Bradley in the Mummy Range. Why?"

"Do you know that for sure?"

"What are you saying, Lonnie?"

"How do you know they didn't rob a bank or somethin'?"

"Because Shannon told me months back they were through with all of that. Shannon did his time. He's a changed man. I don't like how you're talking to me, Lonnie. I hate that tone. You know that." May Gentry glanced toward the cabin and lowered her voice. "And I will not have you talking Shannon down to me anymore."

"I saw some lawmen up Willow Run," Lonnie blurted out, his knees feeling weak again. He could not confess the killing. Not to his mother, not to anyone. It was just too awful. "I seen some lawmen . . . from a distance. They wore badges, and they were carryin' rifles and they were looking around at the ground like they were trackin' someone. Outlaws, maybe."

A dark cloud of apprehension scudded

across May Gentry's face. She studied Lonnie pensively, then she said in a quiet, defensive tone, "There's plenty of outlaws in these mountains," she said. "You know the Never Summer range is their favorite place to hole up after they committed some robbery in Cheyenne or Julesburg. There aren't enough lawmen to cover all this country . . ."

Mrs. Gentry let her voice trail off and she glanced back at the cabin. Shannon Dupree lifted his head to peer over his boots resting on the porch rail, and called, "When's supper, May? Me an' the boys are so hungry our bellies are startin' to think our throats have been cut!"

Lonnie's mother forced a smile and waved. "Comin' hon," she yelled. To Lonnie, she said, "Supper's ready. Get washed up."

"I ain't hungry," Lonnie said, pulling a curry brush off a nail.

"Finish with the General and get washed up," his mother said firmly, and headed back to the cabin. "Scrub beneath your fingernails and comb your hair. Like it or not, this is a special night."

CHAPTER 6

Lonnie took his time with the General, first wiping him down with a scrap of burlap sacking and then slowly currying his coat. He checked all four hooves to make sure they hadn't picked up any sharp rocks or thorns, and cut burrs out of the General's tail. When he was sure the horse had cooled down enough, he brought him a bucket of water, and when the General was finished drawing water, Lonnie looped a feed sack of oats over the horse's ears.

When he'd turned the stallion into the corral with the other horses, he forked some hay from the crib and turned to the cabin. Lonnie gave a ragged sigh. It was nearly dark now, only a little green light left in the sky. The high, forested ridges that rimmed the ranch yard were black as ink. A lone wolf was howling somewhere on the mountain behind the cabin.

The cabin's lower story windows were all

lit. Through the sashed window right of the door, Lonnie could see his mother sitting at the kitchen table with Shannon Dupree and "the boys." Lonnie glanced back along the trail that was a faint, butterscotch line in the darkness. No movement out there. Not yet. There was a chance the law would not come for him. There was a better chance that they would. Maybe not tonight or to-morrow. Maybe not for a few weeks. But eventually they would.

A posse, probably — five, maybe ten men.

If the dead lawman's partner came for him tonight, what would Lonnie do? Would he confess his sins, or run? He'd heard that when you killed a lawman, you were done for. Other lawmen took the killing of one of their own personally. So did judges. That it had been an accident wouldn't matter to anyone. Especially not to the partner of the lawman Lonnie had killed.

Besides, who would believe him? His mother was known by some in the Never Summers to "cavort with owl hoots." They'd see Lonnie as an owl hoot, too. A thirteen-year-old murderer.

Lonnie would drop through a trapdoor and hang by his neck, kicking and dancing in midair, until he was dead. He'd seen a man do that in Cheyenne once, in front of a

40

crowd who'd gathered to watch, and the image haunted Lonnie to this day. The boy shuddered as he remembered how the hanged man had kicked so hard that he'd kicked off one of his boots.

Lonnie considered saddling a fresh horse, packing a cavvy sack and a war bag, and riding out. All hell had broken loose. But the cabin door opened, throwing a wedge of yellow light across the porch, and his mother called impatiently, "Lonnie? Supper's gettin' cold!"

Lonnie made a sour face. Oh, well, he was too tired to ride out tonight. He'd fill his belly, get a good night's sleep, and consider his options again in the morning.

He headed back to the cabin and washed up at the tub perched on a wooden stand on the porch, against the cabin's front wall, beneath a cracked mirror a little larger than Lonnie's hand. His father used to shave in that mirror. From the rain barrel standing in a corner of the porch, he dippered up tepid water and thirstily drank several dippers full, then raked his fingers through his close-cropped brown hair that wore the shape of his hat, and stepped to the cabin door.

Reluctantly, he drew it open and stepped tentatively inside.

41

"Hey, Squirrel!" intoned Shannon Dupree, who rose from the near end of the table, where Lonnie's mother usually sat. His wet, longish blond hair showed the lines of a comb, and he wore a checkered oilcloth bib tucked into the collar of his rand-and-black-plaid work shirt. He also wore a pistol on his hip.

"How you doin', Squirrel?" Dupree said, turning to Lonnie and punching him twice lightly in the belly.

They were soft punches but in Lonnie's mood, and in light of his feelings toward the outlaw, they might as well have knocked the wind out of him.

"Come on, kid," the outlaw persisted, feinting like a boxer and wagging his big, red fists in Lonnie's face, swiping at his chin. "Come on! You got some sand, don't ya? Let's see what you got, Squirrel!"

Lonnie exploded, and though Shannon towered over him, over six feet tall, the boy lurched forward and drove both his fists into the big man's hard, flat belly. It was like hitting a side of beef hanging in the keeper shed.

The big man roared with glee, blowing his sour whiskey breath. "There ya go, Squirrel. Don't take nothin' off'n nobody. Hah!" He bent down, wrapped his arms around Lonnie's waist and picked him up as though the boy weighed no more than a bucket of water. Lonnie felt his boots rise up over his head until he was upside down and facing the open front door, punching only air.

Fury boiled even harder. Fury fueled by helplessness and humiliation. He heard himself sob and his fury doubled. Flailing with his fists and feet, Lonnie screamed above Dupree's loud guffaws, "You go to hell, you gutless, raggedy-heeled outlaw!"

Dupree stared down at Lonnie. Lonnie glared up at him and Dupree opened his arms, dropping Lonnie straight down to the floor.

Lonnie's mother screamed, "Oh, Shannon!"

Lonnie hit the floor on his shoulders, the back of his head taking a glancing blow. He was on his back, gasping, trying to force air into his lungs. He wasn't on the floor long, however, before Shannon Dupree, his long, slanted, gray demon's eyes looking flat and dead and mean as a rattlesnake's, reached down and picked Lonnie up and threw him up against the wall between the window and the door.

The eerie, menacing flatness in Dupree's eyes told Lonnie that he was about to die.

CHAPTER 7

Dupree held Lonnie against the wall with one hand wrapped around the boy's neck, digging his long, thick fingers into Lonnie's windpipe.

"Oh, Shannon, no!" Lonnie's mother beseeched, running around the table and throwing herself against Dupree.

Dupree stood like a brick wall. Lonnie flailed at the man's sun-browned, muscle-corded arm, trying to work the iron grip free of his throat. He felt like a bug on a pin, at the big man's mercy. When the room started to grow dim around Lonnie, and his knees started to buckle, Dupree removed his hand from Lonnie's throat.

The boy dropped to his knees, sucking air down his aching throat and into his lungs. His head throbbed, ears burning. He felt as though his eyes would explode from their sockets.

"Shannon, that was mean!" May Gentry

admonished Dupree as she knelt beside Lonnie and placed a hand on his back. "Lonnie, honey — are you all right, son?"

"Ah, hell," Dupree said, all fun and games again. "I was just funnin' with the boy!"

He wrapped a hand around Lonnie's arm. Lonnie fought against the man, but there was no use. Dupree was four or five times stronger than the thirteen-year-old. Dupree pulled Lonnie to his feet and patted his head, laughing. The other two men sat at the table, regarding their gang leader and the boy uncertainly. Childress chuckling, close-set eyes glowing from all the whiskey he'd been drinking.

The stocky half Indian, Fuego, kept shoveling food into his mouth.

"You all right, son?" Dupree said. "Sorry if I hurt ya. I was just funnin'. Oh, come on — you can take a joke, can't ya? Why, I got no respect for a man who can't take a joke. Sit down, and I'll buy ya a drink!"

"Shannon, let him go," Lonnie's mother implored as Lonnie jerked his arm free of Dupree's loosening grip, and stumbled out onto the porch. He was still trying to work the kinks out of his windpipe with his fingers as he stumbled down the porch steps and started dragging his boot toes across the yard toward the barn.

45

"Ah, come on, Squirrel!" Dupree yelled behind him. "Get in here and eat your supper." More quietly, he said, "Ah, hell, May — I was just havin' a little fun with the boy. I thought we were just horsin' around. You know — like a boy and his pa!"

Mrs. Gentry said something that Lonnie couldn't hear beneath his own choking as he continued toward the sanctuary of the barn. But her voice rose in the quiet night behind him, "Lonnie, come back. Shannon didn't mean it. Son, you have to eat!"

"Ah, that's too bad," Lonnie heard Dupree say inside the cabin. "I thought the boy had a thicker hide than that. I was just horsin' around, May!"

Lonnie fumbled one of the two big barn doors open, and slipped inside. It was almost dark outside, and it was even darker inside the barn. It smelled of hay and horses and moldy tack leather and of the milk cow that was out in the rear pasture. Lonnie knew the layout by heart, so he didn't bother to light a lamp.

He stumbled back into the rear shed addition, which served as a tack room and an extra sleeping area for a hostler. Lonnie slept in the tack room whenever his mother was "entertaining" Dupree. Fuego and Childress sacked out in the bunkhouse, and

Lonnie didn't want to be around them, so he stayed in the side shed, where he had some gear including a bedroll.

His rifle was in there.

Lonnie fumbled around until he got an old hurricane lamp lit. The lamp's glow revealed the cramped quarters stuffed with shelves overflowing with tack of all kinds — harnesses, hames, bits, saddles of all ages and states of disrepair, and even some horseshoes. There were ropes, one wagon wheel, and odds and ends of Lonnie's father's gear from before the Civil War, which he'd fought in. Cobwebs hung everywhere, and mouse droppings littered the place.

There were two old Civil War–model Confederate pistols that Lonnie kept clean and enjoyed shooting from time to time, when he was caught up on his work. Shooting the old pistols made him feel a little closer to his father, whom Lonnie had never really known and now, of course, never would.

If Shannon Dupree thought he was going to become Lonnie's father, Dupree had best think again . . .

Lonnie had set his Winchester '66 against the tack room wall. Now he picked it up, brushed his hand down the fore stock that still had some mud on it from its bath in the creek, and he racked a shell into the chamber. Lonnie's heart was racing. Bells of fury and humiliation continued to toll in his head.

"One shot," he seethed through gritted teeth. "One bullet to Dupree's black heart, and that would be the end of him."

Lonnie moved to the tack room door. He stopped suddenly. In his mind, he saw the lawman he'd shot earlier — the man's head snapping back with the red spot on his forehead.

Again, Lonnie's belly writhed as though he'd slugged a quart of sour milk.

A sneering voice inside his head said, "Two men in one day? Sure you got it in you, Killer?"

Dupree's cold, dead, menacing eyes flashed in Lonnie's mind. He could do it. At least, he thought he could now, with the rage coursing through him. He could burst into the cabin and shoot Dupree in the heart. But what, then, about Dupree's "boys"? Surely, they'd kill Lonnie.

And what about Lonnie's mother?

Could he put her through all that?

Lonnie felt his grip on the Winchester loosen. He slammed the tack room door, threw his back against it, and loosed a mewling wail of frustration. Tears streamed down his cheeks. He hastily leaned the rifle

48

against the wall and threw himself belly-down on the cot. He mashed his face against the musty, cornhusk pillow covered with blue-striped ticking that smelled of old sweat. He felt the dam inside him break, loosing a veritable earthquake of pent-up emotion.

He hadn't cried in a long, long time. In fact, he couldn't remember the last time he'd cried. But now his body was racked with wails that the pillow muffled. He writhed on the cot, closing his hands over the wooden frame, kicking his booted feet against it, ramming the pointed toes into the bedroll covering it.

He was not crying about Shannon Dupree. He was not crying about the man he'd killed earlier that day. He was crying about all of it together and about his seeming powerlessness to do anything about this mountain of trouble that had suddenly grown up in front of him.

He had done so much to keep the ranch going, to make it possible for him and his mother to remain here on the range. He'd done the work of two men. Three, maybe four men. But now he'd hit a mountain wall. All his hard work and determination were like spent cartridges in a gun's cylinder.

The gun was empty.

And, to top it all off, he was lying here crying into his pillow as though he were still in rubber pants!

That thought sobered him. He gave one last, shuddering sob, and rolled onto his back. He drew a couple of deep breaths, kicked out of his boots, curled onto his side, and closed his eyes.

It took a while, but he managed to sweep all the shrieking, razor-clawed demons from his mind, and the gauzy sanctuary of sleep closed over him like a favorite quilt.

CHAPTER 8

"Lonnie?"

His mother's voice came as though from the far end of a long tunnel. Lonnie groaned, smacked his lips. Then there was a light, wooden knock, and he recognized the creak of the tack room door's rusty hinges.

"Lonnie?"

He didn't want to reenter the horrific world he'd fled, but his mother's voice tugged at him as though it were the hondo of a lariat looped around his neck.

"Son, wake up. I have to talk to you."

Her hand was on his shoulder and he heard the cot creak as she sat on the edge of it. He smelled food. His stomach reacted to that, and he lifted his head from his pillow.

Mrs. Gentry had a steaming tin plate in her hand — slow-cooked steak smothered in onions and dark-brown gravy. The gravy also covered a helping of mashed potatoes and green beans from a can. A chunk of his mother's crusty, dark-brown bread teetered on the edge of the plate.

The fragrant steam bathed Lonnie's face. His stomach opened its mouth and roared. He hadn't realized how hungry he was. He sat up against the wall flanking the cot, drew up his knees, and took the plate from his mother.

He saw that there was a tray on the bench running along the wall opposite the cot. On the tray was a glass of milk. His mother fetched the glass, and set it on the backless chair beside the cot.

"I thought you might be hungry," she said softly. He could tell from the glitter in her eyes and the paleness of her drawn cheeks that she'd been crying.

"Obliged," Lonnie said, instantly forking a heap of gravy-drenched potatoes into his mouth, and chewing as he cut into the meat.

"I'm so sorry, honey," his mother said, running a hand through his short hair, and pressing her lips to his temple.

Lonnie canted his head away from her. He wasn't in the mood for apologies. In fact, he wasn't in the mood for *her.* Only the food she'd brought. He wished she'd leave, go back to the no-account scoundrel she was going to marry. Soon, she and the no-account scoundrel would ruin everything Lonnie had worked so hard for.

He had no doubt about that. None at all.

"Did you hear me, Lonnie?" she asked again, again running her hand back from his forehead.

"I heard."

"He'd been drinking," she said, as though that explained or excused Dupree's behavior.

"Yeah, I s'pect so," Lonnie said curtly, continuing to shovel food into his mouth. Shovel and chew, shovel and chew. God, he was hungry!

May Gentry removed her hand from her son's head with a sigh. She had a blanket over her shoulders. She sat on the edge of the cot, holding the blanket closed at her throat, staring down at the wooden floor beneath the deerskin slippers she was wearing. She seemed to be waiting for something, or maybe thinking intently.

When Lonnie was nearly done with the meal but still shoveling and chewing, she turned to him, and her eyes were large and grave.

"Lon?"

Lonnie stopped shoveling. Chewing, he looked at her, frowning. "What?" he said around a mouthful of food.

"I need a favor."

Lonnie swallowed and sat staring at his mother, puzzled. Apprehension raked the back of his neck. He rested the plate atop his upraised knees, and waited.

May Gentry rose from the cot and walked to the door, which was closed. On the floor beside the door was a pair of saddlebags that hadn't been there before. She picked up the saddlebags, slung them over her shoulder with a grunt, her blonde hair spilling across her shoulders, and sat down on the edge of the cot once more.

"What're those?" Lonnie asked.

His mother stared at him, her eyes still wide and grave, fearful, hesitant. She closed her upper teeth over her bottom lip and opened the flap of the pouch hanging down her right shoulder. She reached into the pouch, withdrew something, and showed Lonnie the two-inch wad of paper money resting in the palm of her open hand.

Lonnie's eyes snapped wide. "Holy cow!"

The smell of ink and paper mixed with the leather smell of the saddlebags pushed against his face, nearly taking his breath away. It was an exhilarating smell. Even more rich and intoxicating than the food had been. Lonnie's heart hammered as he stared, his lower jaw hanging nearly to his chest, at the wad of what appeared to be ten-dollar greenbacks secured with a paper band in his mother's open hand.

He slid his gaze from the single wad of bills to the bulging pouch. "There's *more?*"

"Oh, yes," his mother said grimly. "Lots more."

Lonnie laughed and slid his hand toward the wad of bills, but before he could touch it, his mother returned the wad to the pouch hanging down her chest. And then, through the knee-jerk glee of seeing that much money and semiconsciously speculating on what could be bought with it — how easy a fellow's life could suddenly become! — Lonnie was assailed with what felt like the blow of an ax handle.

The money was not his and would never be his. Dupree had brought the money.

Speechless, Lonnie looked into his mother's dark eyes.

"Shannon's asleep in the cabin. Earlier, I saw him shove something under the bed. When I was sure he was dead asleep, I dragged it out." Lonnie's mother's voice broke. Tears rolled down her cheeks. "It's stolen money." She paused, swallowed. She swiped the back of a hand across her cheek as she stared down at the pouch in shame. "They robbed a bank. Or a payroll, maybe.

I don't know."

Her lips quivered. She turned her face away and cleared her throat.

"Holy cow," Lonnie said numbly, without the delight with which he'd said it before. He'd suspected that Dupree was on the run from a robbery of some kind. But now, seeing the concrete proof of it . . . not to mention that much money . . . Lonnie felt like he'd been dropped on his head all over again.

"I knew it," he whispered, thinking back to the two lawmen.

"Yes, you did," his mother whispered, hanging her head in shame. She sniffed.

Lonnie felt sorry for her. "What're you gonna do, Ma?"

Mrs. Gentry turned to him again gravely. "Not me, Lonnie. *You.*"

CHAPTER 9

Lonnie said, "Me?"

"Son, I want you to do your mother a big favor. I want you to saddle General Sherman before dawn and take this . . ." She let her voice trail off as she looked distastefully down at the bulging saddlebag pouch, as though she wasn't sure what to call it. "This *money* . . . this *loot* . . . to the town marshal in Arapaho Creek. Say you found it out on the range somewhere, maybe in the line shack."

Lonnie scowled, incredulous. "Why in hell should I do that?"

Under the circumstances, he thought he was due a curse or two. His mother seemed to agree, because she ignored it, saying, "Because I want you to."

"He's a bank robber, Momma," Lonnie said. "Why should I help him?"

"Because by helping Shannon, you'll be helping me."

Lonnie found his tongue tied for nearly a minute as he stared in bafflement at his mother. May Gentry couldn't hold his gaze for even half that long. She lowered her eyes in shame.

"Momma," Lonnie said gently, her miserable expression touching his heart. "You aren't really thinkin' you're still gonna marry him, are you?"

"Lonnie, we all make mistakes."

"You think robbin' whatever bank he and them other two men robbed was just a *mistake*?"

"He'd been drinking," Lonnie's mother said, her eyes desperate, pleading. "When Shannon drinks, he does things he wouldn't do otherwise. I think those other two men, Fuego, especially, got him drunk and then, once he was good and pie-eyed, talked him into stealing this money. I don't think Shannon would have done such a thing otherwise. He promised me he wouldn't!"

Lonnie didn't know what to say to that. What his mother was spewing was nonsense. But she was not usually a nonsensical woman. The fact was she was lonely. So desperately lonely that she was sitting here spewing nonsense in defense of the bank robber she'd fallen in love with.

Lonnie had known she was lonely. Until

now, he hadn't realized how lonely and sad she really was. A hand reached into the boy's chest and twisted his heart counter-clockwise, and he had to swallow the hard knot in his throat to keep from sobbing.

He set his plate on the floor and dropped his boots down to the floor, as well. He sat beside his mother, wrapped an arm around her waist. "Momma, I —"

He stopped when she turned her fear-bright eyes on him. "Lonnie, if lawmen come for Shannon, they'll take me, too."

"No, they won't."

"Lonnie, word has gotten around about me an' Shannon. Folks know he comes by here from time to time. The lawmen who come for him will think I provided a place to stay for him and the other two, knowing what they'd done. They'll think I'm part of it. They might even think you are, too."

Lonnie shook his head. "We'll tell them otherwise, Momma." But then he remem-bered the lawman he'd killed, and fear jolted him like a lightning bolt striking a lone pine on a high mountain ridge.

He looked toward the night-dark windows reflecting the wan lantern light, and he saw the twisted, thick-lipped, black-eyed faces of a thousand demons staring in at him, laughing. Silently teasing, jeering. A shudder racked him.

His mother wrapped an arm around him and gave him a squeeze as she said, "Please, Lonnie. Before first light, ride on out of here and deliver these saddlebags to the marshal in Arapaho Creek. Tell Marshal Stoveville you found them along the trail or in the line shack up on Eagle Ridge. It's not right to lie, but under the circumstances, I don't see any other way."

Lonnie brushed a tear from his cheek. His mother's desperation deeply pained him. "Are you sure you're not just doing this for Dupree?"

"For him," she said, smiling thinly and giving a slight nod. She knew how lame it was to feel something for a worthless owl hoot, but because of her loneliness, she couldn't help herself. "But for us, too."

"He'll find it gone first thing in the mornin'."

"He won't stir till noon. None of them will. Not after all they drank. It'll be all right."

"No, it won't. He'll be mad. He'll hurt you."

Lonnie's mother gave a weak smile and placed a hand on her belly. "He won't hurt me, son. I'm carrying his child."

That was like a fist buried deep in Lonnie's gut. He gaped at his mother. He felt the blood rush to his face. He was at a total loss for words.

"I can handle Shannon, Lonnie," she said. "You worry about gettin' to Arapaho Creek. Once you've returned the money, don't come back to the ranch right away. Spend a night or two at the line shack."

"What are you gonna do, Momma?"

May Gentry sighed as she set the saddlebags on the floor and slid them under Lonnie's cot. On one knee, she squeezed her son's hand reassuringly. "Like I said, I know how to handle Shannon. When he gets all that poison out of his brain, he'll come around. He'll know he done wrong. He doesn't want to lose me. He doesn't want to lose our child."

"Momma," Lonnie said, slowly shaking his head, dead certain that she was wrong but knowing he couldn't convince her.

His mother picked up his plate and glanced at the untouched glass of milk on the chair. "Finish your milk, son. I'll fetch you out a bag of biscuits and jerky for the ride to Arapaho Creek. I'll throw in some food to tide you at the line shack. There won't be time for breakfast tomorrow."

And then she left. She returned a few minutes later with a small croaker sack of trail

61

food, which she set on the counter. She kissed Lonnie's forehead, and left again, and Lonnie turned down the lamp and lay on the cot, staring at the dark ceiling, thinking.

When the maniacal thoughts in his head finally tired themselves out, he drifted off . . . only to be awakened by what felt like a blackfly stinging the underside of his chin.

Instantly awake, he swatted at the unseen insect.

The back of his hand hit something un-yielding before him. The blackfly stung him a little harder, then he smelled the stench of sweat and whiskey. In the wash of pearl moonlight angling through the tack room windows, Lonnie saw the silhouetted face of Shannon Dupree hovering over him.

The moonlight winked off the wide, silver blade in Dupree's fist. That's what was stinging Lonnie. Not a blackfly. Dupree was holding the up-curved point of a bowie knife against the underside of Lonnie's chin.

CHAPTER 10

Dupree's eyes, framed by his blond hair, were as black as black marbles. He stretched his lips back from his teeth that appeared unusually large in the darkness, and he said quietly, "You call out, I'll cut you from ear to ear."

Lonnie lay stiff as a board, head tipped back and away from the razor-edged point of the massive blade. The blade looked as wide as Lonnie's thigh. The boy drew shallow breaths, felt sweat bead on his upper lip.

The money, he thought.

Dupree had seen Lonnie's mother remove the money from under the bed in the cabin. Lonnie saw no reason to be a hero. Dupree would find the money on his own if Lonnie didn't tell him, so Lonnie was about to tell him it was under the cot, when Dupree said, "Wanted to have a little chat with ya, Squirrel. About tomorrow."

Lonnie was puzzled. Mostly, though, he was horrified, and the point of the knife digging into his jaw wasn't helping matters.

He waited, drawing shallow breaths as he stared into the cold, black, dead eyes of Shannon Dupree.

Dupree said, "Tomorrow, me an' the boys are gonna ride on out of here . . . with your mother. She don't know it yet, but she will in the mornin'. I wanted you to know so you don't make no trouble, understand? You stay out here in the barn and keep your mouth shut."

"Why . . . why're you . . . takin' . . . M-Ma?"

"Insurance," Dupree said, spreading his mouth with self-satisfaction. "You make any trouble, I'm gonna take out this big ol' bowie knife and cut your throat from ear to ear. Nice wide gash, understand?"

Lonnie stared at those dead eyes, speechless. His heart sputtered, hiccupped.

Dupree said, "And then I'll kill her, too. Same way. Hate to do that, her bein' such a fine-lookin' woman. But I'll do it. You know I will." That grin again. "So you just stay out here until me an' the boys an' your ma have rode away. All right?"

"All . . . all right," Lonnie said, wincing as Dupree pressed the point of the blade a little more snugly against the underside of Lonnie's chin. Lonnie felt the point pierce the skin. He felt a blood drop grow around the stinging point. The blood was cool and wet.

Dupree pulled the blade away, and straightened his legs. He was so tall that his head disappeared into the darkness above where the moonlight was angling through the tack room window behind him. He hiked a boot onto the chair beside the cot, and there was the soft screech and snick of the bowie knife being returned to a sheath inside of the boot.

"Good boy, Squirrel. Play your cards right, you might make a man someday."

Dupree tussled Lonnie's hair with menace. Turning, he stumbled drunkenly, and for a second Lonnie thought the man was going to fall on top of him. There was a sharp, sickening stench of whiskey and sweat. Lonnie slid to one side and threw up his hands to shield himself from the big man's body. Then Dupree got his feet beneath him and, chuckling, stumbled on over to the door and went out without closing the door behind him.

Lonnie heard the outlaw chuckle once more, and his stumbling footsteps dwindled away until for a time there were no more sounds except for a slight breeze pushing against the barn and the frogs croaking down along the creek.

Lonnie lay frozen, bathed in cold sweat, staring up at the dark ceiling relieved in shadows cast by the pearl moonlight. When he heard the faint, muffled scrape of the cabin door closing, he scrambled up out of the cot, stepped into his boots, donned his hat, and grabbed the Winchester. Vaguely, he noted the sting on the underside of his chin, and brushed a couple of knuckles across it. They came away lightly blood-smeared. He'd live.

At least, the slight cut beneath his chin wouldn't kill him. If Dupree looked beneath Lonnie's mother's bed to reassure himself the loot was still there, and he was given no such reassurance, Lonnie and her mother were likely wolf bait.

That's why Lonnie rummaged around for a box of .44-40 cartridges, and loaded the carbine. When he had it fully loaded, he pumped a cartridge into the action and po-sitioned the hammer to off-cock. All he had to do was pull the hammer back, aim, and fire . . .

He drew a light denim jacket on over his shirt, and left the barn. He closed the doors behind him and stood with his back to them, where the barn's shadow concealed him. He stared toward the cabin. No lamps were lit. All was dark and quiet.

So far . . .

Lonnie had to make sure his mother was safe.

To that end, he ran at a crouch across the yard, trying to stay out of the moonlight as much as he could. When he gained the foot of the porch, he moved around to the cabin's left side and hunkered down outside the window of his mother's bedroom. He was in the moonlight here, but Dupree's men were in the bunkhouse on the other side of the cabin, so there was no one out here to see him skulking around.

Lonnie pressed his right shoulder against the cabin's rough log wall. He held his breath and pricked his ears, listening. Inside, there was nothing but silence. Dupree must have gone back to bed as soon as he'd gotten back inside the cabin. Lonnie's mother was likely asleep. She was a sound sleeper, always had been.

But Lonnie wanted to make sure Dupree didn't check under the bed for the stolen money. If he did, things would go even farther south around the Circle G than they already had. If he did find the stolen money, Lonnie would enter the cabin and shoot the man before he could harm May Gentry. Then he'd likely have to deal with the other two men — Fuego and Childress.

Probably easier thought about than done . . .

Lonnie looked down at the rifle he held in his hands. It quivered slightly. Could he shoot straight if he had to? If he had to, by criminy, Lonnie would shoot Shannon Dupree like he was nothing more than a Thanksgiving turkey that Lonnie had come upon in the forest.

If he had to . . .

But it looked like he wouldn't have to shoot tonight. After he'd been outside the window no more than two minutes, Lonnie heard Dupree's long, raking snores. He listened for a time, making sure they continued, and then he hotfooted it back to the barn, and sat on a saddle tree, thinking through his options.

His main concern was for his mother. What would happen to her if Lonnie did her bidding and hightailed it with the stolen money? Dupree had threatened to kill her if Lonnie impeded the plans of Dupree and "the boys" in the morning.

What would stop him from killing Lonnie's mother when he found out she'd tricked him and sent Lonnie to Arapaho

68

Creek with the money? Likely, the child she was carrying. Despite his threat earlier, no man could harm a woman carrying his child.

Still, to be sure, Lonnie's best option would be to go into the cabin and shoot Dupree as he slept. But what if he missed Dupree and shot his mother instead? And even if Lonnie was able to kill Dupree — which was a long shot, for he'd never intentionally shot another man before today and he wasn't sure he really had the nerve to do such a thing — what about Fuego and Childress?

Lonnie paced in front of the barn doors.

After he mulled the situation over for a good twenty agonized minutes, he decided to follow through with his mother's plan. He just had to hope Dupree didn't kill her when he discovered the ruse. Chances are he wouldn't because there would be no point except revenge. And, again, she was carrying his child. Besides, Dupree would want to come after Lonnie as fast as he could, and overtake the boy before he reached the marshal in Arapaho Creek.

There seemed no risk-free solution to the mountain of trouble before the boy. But heading to Arapaho Creek seemed his best bet. He'd recognized neither of the lawmen up on Willow Run, so he didn't think they were from Arapaho Creek. He didn't think that Marshal Stoveville had any deputies, as the town was small and relatively quiet. Without a doubt, Dupree would follow Lonnie there — possibly all the way to the town and maybe even right on up to the doorstep of Marshal Dwight Stoveville, whom Lonnie would warn ahead of time.

Lonnie looked out between the barn doors.

It was still good dark. Maybe around three, three thirty. It wasn't safe to ride out in the dark, but he was too eager to get to Arapaho Creek to wait around for dawn. He certainly wouldn't be able to sleep anymore tonight. Besides, the moon would light the northeastern trail until the sun rose in a couple of hours.

As quietly as he could, his heart drumming anxiously in his ears, Lonnie saddled General Sherman. He set the saddlebags filled with Dupree's precious loot over the top of another pair of saddlebags filled with trail supplies. Lonnie hung his cavvy sack, filled with cooking paraphernalia, from his saddle horn. There was no telling how long he'd have to be away from home.

Lonnie led the General out of the yard, wincing with each of the big horse's heavy

70

footfalls. When he was a hundred yards beyond, he mounted up and put the horse into
a spanking trot. Lonnie headed along the
northern trail while casting anxious glances
behind at the eerily silent ranch yard growing smaller and smaller until it disappeared
altogether, and he was very much alone.

CHAPTER 11

Later that day, after he'd ridden a good ten miles from the Circle G, Lonnie sat on a rock by the small fire he'd built.

He fished a blackened tin cup from the canvas cavvy sack on the ground by his feet and used a small leather swatch to pad the hot handle while he poured coffee from the dented pot. The dark-brown brew sent its fragrant steam wafting into his face with small white ashes from the burning pine branches.

The smell was one of the best Lonnie knew. It complemented the forest smells. He sipped the coffee and then opened the two-pound bag of jerky his mother had packed, and started eating. When he finished a ragged strip of jerky, he ate a biscuit. When he'd had two strips of jerky and three small biscuits, he poured a fresh cup of coffee.

The General whinnied. Lonnie jerked

with a start, and the hot coffee sloshed over the brim to burn his hand through his leather glove.

He winced as he jerked his head up, looking around.

The General was craning his neck to look behind him, edgily switching his tail.

Lonnie had left the main trail that ran through the bottom of the canyon to set up camp here on the side of the ridge, out of sight from the trail. He hadn't wanted to be pestered. The trail was a hundred yards back down the slope, but now Lonnie heard what the General's keen ears had picked up — the slow thuds of approaching horses.

A man said something. The thuds grew louder. There was the clang of a shod hoof kicking a rock. Still looking behind him through the trees toward the bottom of the canyon, the General whinnied again. Lonnie reached for the carbine leaning against a tree to his left, and, rising from the rock, slowly levered a live cartridge into the action.

He glanced at the saddlebags containing the stolen money. They sat at the base of a tree on the other side of the fire, near the General, one pouch slumped against the other. Both pouches bulged curiously. Lonnie wanted to run over and hide the bags in some shrubs, but he could see three horse-back riders approaching along the shoulder of the slope behind the General. If Lonnie tried to hide the bags now, they'd see him and grow suspicious of what he was hiding.

Lonnie's pulse throbbed in his fingers.

Three riders . . .

He stepped back away from the fire and over to where he could get a better look at the men approaching. His knees were warm and weak. For a second he thought they would buckle from the overwhelming wave of fear washing over him. Then he saw that it was not Dupree. The lead rider had long, dark-brown hair and a mustache. The man behind him was older and potbellied and he wore an old, ratty, bullet-crowned, broad-brimmed hat. He was old — maybe in his fifties, even older.

The man behind the old one was younger. He was older than Lonnie but not by much, and he was blond and wild-looking, with bright green eyes and thick lips stretched back from small, brown teeth. His face was heavily freckled. He looked like he might have been soft in the head.

Lonnie knew most of the men who lived and worked in these mountains, but he'd never seen these three. When he'd first seen that they weren't Dupree's bunch, he'd

74

been relieved. Now that relief was tempered by a healthy, natural apprehension.

All types moved through the Never Summers, including cutthroats on the run from the law. The mountains were a haven for cattle rustlers who preyed on the ranchers' herds, like human coyotes. And that's what these three appeared to be — even the young, freckle-faced one.

Coyotes. Only more dangerous because they all wore at least one holstered pistol. Rifles jutted from leather sheaths strapped to their saddles. Lonnie thought he could see the glint of a running iron strapped to the third rider's horse, partly concealed by the young man's bedroll and saddlebags.

That marked them as rustlers, sure enough. Running irons were used to doctor cattle brands.

The first man, the one with the long hair, stopped his horse about twenty yards from Lonnie. The man looked Lonnie up and down, paying special attention to the cocked rifle in the boy's gloved hands. The first man glanced behind at the old man, who reined his sorrel gelding to a halt about five yards behind the first man.

"It's a kid," the long-haired man said.

Then he turned his attention to General Sherman. So did the old man. There was a conniving hunger in their eyes. And Lonnie felt a rock drop in his gut.

The three newcomers, looking around curiously, let their gazes linger on the General, shrewdly appraising the valuable stallion.

The old man said, "You alone, boy?"

"Nope."

The three looked around again from the backs of their horses. The long-haired man said, "Who's with you?"

"That horse and this rifle," Lonnie said, resting the Winchester on his right shoulder.

He eyed the three strangers directly, keeping his expression bland, his gaze resolute. There was no point in letting them know they'd spooked him. He wanted them to ride on. If they saw the saddlebags containing the money, all hell could very well break loose.

Lonnie wasn't about to turn the money over to them. It wasn't theirs any more than it was Dupree's. Besides, he wouldn't be robbed. Of his horse, the money, or of anything else. He considered the money his own until he could turn it over to the town marshal in Arapaho Creek, who would make sure it was returned to wherever it had come from.

The long-haired man, who looked particu-
larly mean, grinned and looked at the old
man and the blond young man. They all
laughed, their eyes glinting at Lonnie holding his carbine on his shoulder, as though
he'd told a joke they'd found amusing. The
old man looked at the fire behind Lonnie
and to his left. Lonnie wondered if the
man's eyes had found the bulging saddlebags, as well.

His chest was tight with the possibility.

"Say, now, you got a pot of coffee on.
Mind if we join you?"

"Sure smells good," said the blond young
man, cutting his eyes devilishly between the
old man and the long-haired man. Then he
looked at General Sherman. For the time
being, the young man's main concern was
Lonnie's horse.

Lonnie felt another cold rock drop in his
gut. It was the custom of the country to allow men to join you around your cook fire,
and to share food as well as coffee. Not to
allow it would be to commit an unforgive-
able sin and to beckon trouble.

These men knew it. And Lonnie knew it.

They had him.

Lonnie faked a welcoming smile but he
opened and closed his hand around the
neck of the rifle resting on his shoulder as

he said, "Light and sit a spell. I've a pot of coffee on the fire, and you're welcome to what's left. When that's gone, I'll make more." He was saying the words automatically. They were the words he'd heard over and over again, and he'd been expected to say them, so he'd said them.

But if these men thought they were going to rob him of his horse or anything else, they had a big surprise in store.

At least, that's what he told himself.

"That's mighty kindly, partner," the old man said, grunting as he swung heavily down from his sorrel's back. "We'll take you up on that."

He tied his horse's reins to a branch sticking up from a deadfall tree. As he did, he cut his eyes again toward General Sherman, who was eying all three strangers and their horses cautiously, twitching his ears and stomping his right front foot. The old man's sorrel returned the General's belligerent look with ears up and his tail curled.

When the other three had tied their own horses, they reached into their saddlebags for tin cups, and Lonnie met them at the fire, standing near where he'd been sitting on the rock, holding his rifle across his knees and continuing to gaze at the newcomers blandly. He felt a hard defiance and a cold anger, for he knew what they were after, and he kept telling himself over and over they weren't going to get his horse or the saddlebags.

He wasn't sure any of the three had seen the bags yet, but they were bound to. The strangers were within ten feet of where the pouches leaned against the tree near the General. They'd see Lonnie's second set of bags near the fire, and they'd wonder about that. It wasn't common to carry two sets of saddlebags.

Lonnie silently cursed himself for a fool for not having hidden the saddlebags before he'd built the fire. The fire is likely what had attracted these men. They'd likely smelled the smoke from below though Lonnie had chosen this place because he'd thought it was upwind from the canyon floor.

The old man grinned at Lonnie, said, "Much obliged, boy."

He reached down and with the leather swatch lifted the pot off the rock Lonnie had placed it on near the flames, and splashed some into his cup and then into the cups of the other two.

He grinned again at Lonnie as he shook the pot, and said, "Reckon we cleaned ya out," and then set the pot on one of the rocks forming the ring around the fire.

"Like I said," Lonnie said, "I'll make more."

But he merely sat down on the rock he'd been sitting on before and held his carbine across his thighs. He had no intention of making more coffee because that would mean he'd have to set his rifle down.

The three strangers, each holding a smoking cup, squatted on the other side of the fire — the old man to Lonnie's right, the young, blond-headed man in the middle and a ways back, and the long-haired gent on Lonnie's left. They formed a half circle around Lonnie, on the far side of the fire.

The long-haired man had two pistols holstered on his hips. The old man wore a big horse pistol in a holster over his belly. The blond young man wore what appeared to be a Remington .44 in a holster thonged low on his right thigh, as though he fancied himself a gunslinger.

Maybe he was . . .

Lonnie stared at the men. He didn't bother trying to make conversation, and neither did his new camp mates, who merely hunkered on their haunches, blowing on and sipping from their steaming cups and regarding Lonnie with expressions ranging from blandness to cool disdain.

The old man glanced over at the bulging saddlebags, raised his brows knowingly, and said, "Lookee there! Them bags is mighty full. You must be on a long trip! Say, what you got in there, anyway?"

CHAPTER 12

The other two strangers kept their eyes on Lonnie. The blond young man grinned, showing his small, rotten teeth. The old man cut his eyes at the bulging saddlebags again, and said, "What you got in 'em?"

"Ain't none of your concern," Lonnie said, his cool, even voice belying his trepidation. He'd found, however, that when he was his most fearful, acting brave edged him in bravery's direction.

He was getting sick and tired of sparring with trouble not of his own making. Sick, tired, and more than a little angry. The anger also helped push back some of the fear. He knew he couldn't take all three of these men if they started shooting, but if they started fiddling, as the saying went, he'd have no choice but to dance.

He'd dance one of them right on over the divide before the others took Lonnie out in a hail of lead . . .

"Well, I'm right curious," the old man said, glancing at the other two on either side of him, still sipping their coffee. "I'm so curious I think I'm going to go over and have a look inside them bags."

Lonnie's heart thudded.

He ran his tongue along the underside of his upper lip and said, "Those are my bags. Stay out of 'em." He drew a deep, calming breath and, squeezing the carbine in his hands, said, "Or you'll be sorry."

The old man laughed. "I'll be sorry, will I?" He glanced at the other two in turn. "What do you fellas think? Will I be sorry?"

"Nah," said the long-haired man whose cold eyes reminded Lonnie of Shannon Dupree's eyes. "Go on over and have a look inside, Wade. See what the kid's carryin'. See what's so valuable he's willin' to die to hold onto it."

Lonnie grew dizzy. He fought against it. He also fought against involuntarily spurting pee down his leg. He drew another breath, said, "Them's my bags. Stay out of 'em. I gave you coffee. Finish it and skedaddle."

"Skedaddle, huh?" the blond-headed young man said, chuckling through his teeth. "I like that. *Skedaddle!*"

"Your ma teach you that, boy?" said the

long-haired gent, scowling over the small, leaping flames at Lonnie. He gave his left hand a sudden flick, tossing coffee out of his cup. It splattered over a rock.

In a near tree bough, a squirrel began chittering angrily. For some reason, the squirrel's reprimand caused Lonnie to feel ever more nervous. Cold sweat was dripping under his arms.

The long-haired gent dropped his cup straight down to the ground between his brown boots, rested his wrists on his knees, and said, "Skedaddle on over there, Wade, and see what the boy's carryin' that's so precious."

"Should I?"

"I said you should, didn't I?"

"Well, okay, then," Wade said, rising slowly, staring directly into Lonnie's eyes.

"I wouldn't," Lonnie said, keeping his voice hard and cold though every fiber of his being was trembling like an autumn leaf in a chill wind.

The squirrel was chittering loudly now. The unceasing sound seemed to fill Lonnie's head.

Keeping his eyes on Lonnie's with open challenge, the old man began sidestepping toward the saddlebags. His heart banging inside his ears, Lonnie watched him. He

84

cast frequent glances toward the other two, in case they should suddenly pull their guns.

But as the squirrel kept reading them all the riot act, those two remained on their haunches, both staring at Lonnie — the long-haired gent's eyes dark and threatening, the blond-headed young man's eyes brightly mocking but also threatening in their own way.

The old man continued holding Lonnie's gaze as he edged slowly over to the saddlebags. As Wade began to reach down toward the flap of the first pouch, a rifle crackled loudly, shutting the squirrel up and tearing a fist-sized chunk of bark out of the tree about six inches left of the old man's shoulder.

Lonnie blinked as the old man yelped and hooked an arm up as though to shield himself.

Lonnie glanced down in surprise to see that he was holding his carbine straight out at the old man, and that gray smoke was curling from its barrel. Then he remembered squeezing the trigger, but it felt as though someone else had squeezed it. Automatically, he pumped a fresh cartridge into the chamber, but before he'd even gotten the cocking lever rammed up against the underside of the rifle's breech, the two men by the fire jerked to their feet and reached for their pistols.

Lonnie knew instantly he was a goner. They were both fast, and Lonnie was still turned toward Wade. When the shooting started, Lonnie felt himself being punched back — either by bullets or fear of bullets — until his boots clipped a log and he fell hard on his butt.

He glanced to his right, to where the old man was pulling the big horse pistol out of the soft, brown leather holster over his belly. As he stared at something above and behind Lonnie, Wade got a weird, terrified look on his face.

He dropped the pistol and went dancing off down the slope as though with some invisible partner before dropping to the ground and rolling.

The shooting stopped.

Lonnie blinked. He shifted his gaze from where Wade had fallen toward the other two men. They were down, as well. Dark-red blood oozed from several places in both of them.

Lonnie looked down at himself, expecting to see red oozing from his own body, as well. But he saw no such thing. He wasn't so much grateful at that instant as he was surprised. And then he remembered that

Wade had been staring at something behind Lonnie, who twisted around to gaze up the wooded slope toward the ridge.

A man in a broad-brimmed hat was straightening from a crouch and slowly lowering the smoking rifle in his hands.

CHAPTER 13

Lonnie looked around him at the dead men once more. He looked at himself, wondering if he, too, was dead but for some reason didn't know it yet. But, no, there was no blood on him. His heart was still beating and he was still raking air in and out of his lungs.

He felt as disoriented as if he'd been hit in the back of the head with a two-by-four. But he was alive, all right.

He looked behind him. The man who'd shot the three strangers was walking down the slope toward Lonnie's smoldering fire. He carried what appeared to be an old-model rifle in both hands up high across his chest.

He was a medium-tall, bandy-legged man wearing a broad-brimmed gray hat so old and weathered it appeared a dusty cream color. It was torn, and the brim flopped. It looked like the kind of hat Lonnie had seen some Confederate soldiers wearing when they'd returned home from the War Between the States. The man's badly faded and patched gray trousers were from the same type of uniform, though the man's calico shirt and his boots appeared newer. He wore a brace of old pistols in soft, black holsters on his hips.

"Any of 'em still movin'?" the man asked as he approached the camp, staring beyond Lonnie at the men he'd shot. He waved a gloved hand at a fly buzzing around in front of his face, which was lean and craggy and trimmed with a thick, salt-and-pepper goatee and mustache.

He spat a wad of chaw on a rock to his left, brushed a sleeve of his shirt across his mouth, and continued moving forward, his pale-blue eyes dancing around deep in their bony, heavily ridged sockets.

"Who . . . who are you?" Lonnie had climbed to his feet and was staring in awe at the man who'd saved his life, still trying to work his mind around all that had happened.

The man walked past him, not saying anything. He walked around the fire, the mule ears of his boots flapping, audibly sucking and working the wad of chaw bulging out his left cheek. He looked down at the long-haired gent, then moved to the young, blond-headed man. Apparently satisfied he'd get no more trouble out of either of those two he walked down the slope a ways to where the old man lay tangled up against a pine stump.

Lonnie's most recent visitor stared down at the old man, spat a wad of chew to the side, wiped his mouth, and leaned his rifle against a tree. He dropped to both knees beside the old man and started rummaging around in the old-timer's pockets. He grumbled and muttered unhappily to himself, apparently not satisfied with anything he found, until he pulled a knife out of a sheath strapped against the old man's hip.

The newcomer studied the knife, pooched out his tobacco-brown lips, and nodded his approval. Turning to Lonnie, he held up the knife and said in a thick Southern accent, "This might be worth a spud or two. You want it?"

Lonnie shook his head.

The newcomer frowned and then poked his knife in the direction of the other two dead men. "You might as well check 'em out, pull anything off 'em you can use. They won't be needing it where they're headed, and they were within about one blink of reintroducing you to your Maker."

"Were you a Confederate soldier?"

The newcomer stared at Lonnie, mildly befuddled. He rose to his feet and shoved his new knife down behind his cartridge belt. He picked up his rifle and walked up the slope toward the other two dead men.

"I reckon you could say that," he said with a dry chuckle. "Once a Grayback, always a Grayback."

"My pa fought in the war," Lonnie said. He supposed it sounded like a stupid thing to say under the circumstances, but it was the only thing his brain could spit out. It still hadn't quite wrapped itself around the three dead men, nor around the fact that he very nearly had been, as the Confederate had said, reintroduced to his Maker.

Twice in twenty-four hours. Three if you considered Dupree's nearly strangling him the night before.

"What side?" the Confederate asked as he poked around in the pockets of the blond-headed young man.

"What's that?"

"What side did your pa fight on during the War of Northern Aggression?"

"Oh," Lonnie said, his thoughts still sluggish. "He fought for the North."

"Figures."

The Confederate pulled a gold-washed

watch out of the breast pocket of the long-haired man's bloody shirt. He wiped the watch on the dead man's denim trouser leg, and flipped the lid and held the piece up to his ear. "Still runs," he said. "I reckon I'll take it. First come, first served is how I see it. Besides" — the Confederate gave Lonnie a slit-eyed grin — "your old man's a blue belly."

He stood and looked around. His gaze caught on something, and he turned to Lonnie. "Them's yours?"

Lonnie followed the man's gaze to the overstuffed saddlebags. The boy's heart gave a hiccup. Amidst all the gunfire and death and destruction, he'd forgotten about Dupree's money. When Lonnie started to wonder if he'd been thrown out of the frying pan and into the fire, the Confederate grinned and came around the fire to stand in front of Lonnie. He whistled.

"You're stocked for a long trip." The man's smile faded from his deep-set, dark-blue eyes. "You best keep those hid if you aim to make a man one day."

"Yeah, I reckon," Lonnie said with chagrin.

The Confederate pocketed the watch, rested his rifle on his shoulder, and began slouching up the slope in the same direction from which he'd come. Lonnie watched him, puzzled. He wasn't sure why, but he was reluctant for the man to leave him alone with the three dead men.

The man had saved Lonnie's life, after all.

"Hey," the boy called. "What's your name?"

The Confederate stopped and slanted a wily look over his shoulder and down the hill. "What's yours?"

Lonnie got the message.

The Grayback winked and then continued trudging up the hill through the trees.

CHAPTER 14

When the Southerner was gone from view, Lonnie turned reluctantly toward his camp littered with dead men. Though he still felt as though he'd been kicked in the belly by an angry mule, and the dead repulsed him, he couldn't help walking over to the other side of the fire and having a look.

There was something oddly fascinating about the dead. Fascinating as well as horrifying. Lonnie had seen his father after he'd died in bed of an apparent heart stroke, Calvin Gentry's face twisted in horror, his slitted eyes downcast.

Lonnie had also seen a young man Lonnie's own age after the boy had been kicked in the head by a calf he'd been trying to brand. The calf's hard, sharp hoof had cracked young George Perry's skull above his right ear, and Lonnie and the others had gathered around the branding fire to pay their respects to the dead youngster. Young

George had seemed to be smiling up at those gathered around him, his upper lip curled, eyes heavy-lidded but open, almost as though he now knew the answer to a secret that the living could only guess at, and he was gloating about it.

That would have been just like George.

Lonnie stared down at the long-haired gent who appeared to have learned no such secret. His eyes were bulging in their sockets, and his tongue was poking out the right side of his mouth. He looked as though he were strangling. His face was pale, turning blue at the nubs of his cheeks. The sight of him and the blond young man made Lonnie feel wobbly-kneed and heavy-gutted, and he turned away quickly.

He kicked dirt on his fire and packed up his gear. He set the moneybags over General Sherman's back, tightened the buckskin's saddle cinch, and pushed the bridle bit back into the General's mouth. When he had the horse ready to go, Lonnie unsaddled the dead men's three horses and turned them loose. They ran off down the slope toward the canyon bottom, buckkicking and shaking their heads, eager to be a long way from the smell of their dead, bloody riders.

Lonnie didn't blame them. He stuffed his

carbine down into the General's saddle boot and headed the buckskin in the same direction.

It was dusk when Lonnie reined General Sherman up on the crest of a hill and stared toward the north.

The town of Arapaho Creek was a fuzzy gray mass at the bottom of a rise of snow-tipped mountains. The snow shone brightly against the otherwise dark ridge crest, the edges of the glaciers limned in the salmon rays of the fast-falling sun.

The only way that Lonnie could tell that a town lay a half mile ahead was by the cluster of yellow and orange lights flickering against the velvet brown ridge beyond it. And by the occasional whoops and yells of men as well as women, by the barking of a dog, and by the jocular fiddling emanating from that direction, as well.

Arapaho Creek wasn't much of a town, but it was a mining town that also provided supplies for local ranches, and while Lonnie had never visited the settlement at night, it obviously came alive when the sun went down. He glanced over his shoulder to make sure the saddlebags filled with loot were still draped across the General's hindquarters, over Lonnie's own saddlebags.

Riding into town with as much as he was

carrying made him nervous, but he had to get the loot to the town marshal some way, and how else could he do it? He supposed he could hide the saddlebags out here somewhere, and lead Dwight Stoveville out for it later, but the way Lonnie's luck was going, he'd probably forget where he hid it. Or someone would come along and take it.

Lonnie glanced behind him. At no time during the day had he detected sign of anyone following. That made the boy uneasy for his mother, but it had made getting to Arapaho Creek a whole lot easier despite his run-in with the three men who were now most likely feeding the wildcats and wolves.

Uneasiness like a heavy, laughing monkey straddling his already burdened shoulders, Lonnie touched spurs to the General's flanks. Horse and rider trotted on down the hill and along the trail that was a fast-dimming butterscotch line before them. They crossed Arapaho Creek via a wooden bridge, the General's hooves clomping hollowly on the planks. The bubbling stream was a black-and-silver skin flashing beneath Lonnie, the water chuckling and gurgling.

The air over the river was humid and sweet-smelling.

And when they left the bridge, they were in the town of Arapaho Creek itself where the sweet smell was gone, replaced by the smell of fires and the stench of privies and rotting trash heaps.

Lonnie reined up at the edge of the business district and looked around, getting his bearings. The main street was broad and dark, but the lamplight pushing through the windows of saloons and the still-open shops helped. Silhouetted men shifted around the streets, crossing and recrossing to saloons or to the mercantile or drugstore or to one of the several bawdy houses that were usually shuttered and silent when Lonnie and his mother had journeyed here for supplies or to sell their eggs.

Remembering that the town marshal's office sat on the far side of the town, on the street's west side, Lonnie gigged the General out from under the sprawling cottonwood he'd stopped under, and headed into the fray.

CHAPTER 15

As Lonnie passed saloons and parlor houses, he heard men laughing and women singing.

The fiddle music seemed to be coming from somewhere on Lonnie's left. Men and women were clomping and clapping to the raucous music. They were having a good time. Lonnie found himself absently envying their lack of care as he put the General ahead, trying to avoid the largest clusters of men along the street, trying to ride through the town as inconspicuously as possible, hoping that no one would see the over-stuffed saddlebags resting behind the cantle of his saddle.

He didn't want to have to explain anything to anyone except Marshal Stoveville. And when that was done, he'd ride back out of town the way he'd come and head for the line shack, as his mother had instructed, and wait for his trail to cool.

A couple of dogs were fighting over a bone

in the street before the jailhouse, so Lonnie swung the General wide around them and put the horse up to the hitch rack to the right of the steps that climbed the dilapidated front stoop. The jailhouse itself was a rectangular, block-like stone barrack behind the wooden stoop. A sign over the veranda announced simply TOWN MARSHAL.

The front door was propped open with a rifle.

Lonnie looked around him. There were only a few men on this end of the street. One of the fighting dogs gave a sudden yip and wheeled away from the other one, a German shepherd, with its tail down. Lonnie swung down from the General's back. He tied the reins around the worn hitching post and then went back and pulled the saddlebags down from the General's hindquarters.

He slung the bags over a shoulder, tipped his hat down low over his eyes, and mounted the porch steps, his spurs ringing, the rotting steps creaking beneath his boots. He paused at the top of the steps when he heard a woman chuckling from inside the place, the laughter echoing faintly off the stone walls. A man said something that made Lonnie's ears warm, and the woman laughed harder.

Lonnie cleared his throat to give the pair ample warning and walked across the stoop, loudly stomping his boots and ringing his spurs, before stopping just outside the front door and glancing inside.

The office was lit by a couple of lamps, one on a cluttered rolltop desk left of the door, another bracketed on the back wall in which three jail cells were set. A long wooden table stood in the middle of the room beyond a potbelly stove that pushed its large, tin pipe through the ceiling above Lonnie. At the table cluttered with the paraphernalia of a recent meal as well as bottles, glasses, and playing cards, a man was sitting with a large, dark-haired, brown-eyed woman wearing a red dress. The woman was perched on the man's knee and she was lolling back against the man's shoulder.

The dress revealed as much of the female form as Lonnie had ever seen, and more, and it was startling as well as shocking to see so much exposed flesh. The woman's eyes snapped wide at the boy in the doorway, and she scrambled off the man's knee to drop into a chair beside him, flushing and laughing and saying, "Looks like you got a customer, Chase!"

She glanced at the man, who was wearing a five-pointed star on his blue shirt. The

101

man was not Stoveville. That puzzled Lonnie, touched the boy with apprehension. He'd thought there was only one lawman in Arapaho Creek, and that lawman was Marshal Stoveville. Though he was sitting down, this lawman appeared tall and lean, with a high forehead from which thin strands of sandy-brown hair were swept straight back. He had a black mole as large as a silver dollar on his left cheek.

Scowling at Lonnie as though peeved at the interruption in his affairs, the lawman — Lonnie saw that his badge said "Deputy Town Marshal" — removed a smoldering cigarette from between his teeth, and blew smoke at the open doorway. "Hey, kid, I think I heard your mom callin'. Suppertime!"

The large woman in the skimpy red dress closed her upper teeth over her bottom lip as though to stifle a snicker.

Lonnie looked around the room. They were the only two here.

The boy adjusted the heavy bags on his shoulders and said, "I'm lookin' for Marshal Stoveville."

The woman looked at the man, who took a drag from the quirley, slitting his eyes against the rising smoke, and said, "Over at the Ace of Diamonds." He blew out another long smoke plume toward Lonnie. His eyes, which were the same color as the mole on his cheek, glittered with mockery.

The boy said, "Obliged," and, anxiety eating at him — he hadn't thought Stoveville *had* any deputies — turned and walked back down the porch steps. Behind him, the woman snickered. The boy looked down the street on his right, saw a collection of jostling shadows in a large pool of light spilling out of a building a block away, and patted the General's wither.

Quietly, he said, "Stay, boy. I'll be back soon. I'm gonna get shed of these bags, and we'll get shed of this trash heap."

He could have left the bags with the man who was presumably Stoveville's deputy, but Lonnie didn't trust anyone except the town marshal himself. Besides, he hadn't liked the look in the deputy's eyes. They'd been cold and cunning, sort of like Shannon Dupree's eyes.

Dupree . . .

Lonnie looked around for the outlaw and his "boys" once more. He couldn't see much of anything except shadows on the street, but none appeared to be moving toward Lonnie. He adjusted the saddlebags on his shoulder again, and drew a deep breath, steeling himself for his journey into the crowded saloon but also buoyed by the thought that Stoveville would soon relieve him of his burden.

Lonnie moved through a cluster of men gathered in front of the saloon's batwing doors. The men looked at him strangely, frowning curiously at the bags on Lonnie's shoulder. Lonnie kept his head down and kept moving, pushing through the doors and into the saloon which assaulted him instantly with the nearly overwhelming stench of alcohol and tobacco fumes laced liberally with the smell of unwashed bodies and stale sweat and women's perfume.

There were between a dozen and twenty men in the place, and three or four ladies . . . if you could call them ladies, dressed as they were. They were all obscured by dull light and shadows and the wafting webs of tobacco smoke. Lonnie couldn't pick Dwight Stoveville out of the crowd.

Several faces turned toward Lonnie as he made his way over to the bar. The man behind the bar was large and as round as a rain barrel, with a soiled green apron straining across his waist. He'd been drawing beer from a tap and frowning curiously at Lonnie, who stopped between two men much taller than he at the bar, and stretched his gaze over the edge of the bar to meet the barman's quizzical gaze.

"I'm lookin' for the marshal."

The barman couldn't hear above the din, so Lonnie had to repeat himself. Deep lines stretched across the barman's forehead. He glanced at the two men nearest Lonnie who were staring down at the boy with expressions similar to the barman's.

Then the barman said, *"Stoveville?"*

"That's right."

"Stoveville's in the gamblin' den," the barman said after glancing once more at the two patrons standing in front of Lonnie, both now smirking down at him. "Gamblin' den," the barman repeated, canting his large head toward the back of the room.

Lonnie moved off down the bar. He didn't look at any of the men lined up to his right, leaning against the bar top. All were glancing back and down at the boy with the bulging saddlebags draped over his right shoulder. Lonnie was going to feel light as a feather as soon as he turned Dupree's loot over to Stoveville. He was so eager to do that, in fact, that he had to fight off the urge to sprint to the back of the room and into the gambling den, where Stoveville was likely playing poker with his cronies.

The closed door at the back of the room, behind the stairs that climbed to the saloon's second story where only God knew what went on, opened suddenly. Two well-dressed gents stepped out, both setting their bowler hats on their heads. They had grave expressions and they were talking amongst themselves, both shaking their heads, but they stopped the instant they saw Lonnie.

CHAPTER 16

The two well-dressed gents scowled down at the boy, who ignored them as he stepped around them and strode through the half-open door.

He vaguely heard several snickers behind him, but he couldn't hear much of anything above the ringing in his ears as he stared into the gambling den that was rife with the stale smells of tobacco smoke, liquor, and varnish and was furnished with several baize-covered tables and a roulette wheel. What had caught the brunt of Lonnie's attention, however, were the two pine coffins sitting on either side of the room, each straddling two abutting billiard tables.

A girl in a black dress and a small straw black hat with a veil of black lace sat near the coffin on the right. She had her head down and she was quietly sobbing into a white handkerchief. She wore black gloves, and her hair was pulled behind her head in a thick braid of sorts. A French braid, Lonnie thought it was called.

On the floor to her left, a man's dark-green Stetson sat crown down. Green bills poked up around the sweatband. A collection hat.

Lonnie again felt his blood quicken and his throat turn dry. He stood frozen inside the doorway, looking around for Stoveville, the ringing in his ears gradually growing louder as he started moving slowly forward. He tried to step as lightly as he could, so that his heels wouldn't thud too loudly on the wooden floor, and his spurs wouldn't ching.

He stared into the casket nearest the girl. When the corpse's face became visible, Lonnie stopped and stared, aghast. The man in the casket was Marshal Stoveville. The marshal wore a dark-blue suit over a white cotton shirt with a celluloid collar and a string tie, and his light-gray hair was combed sideways across his head. His brushy mustache nearly hid the thin, purple line of his mouth. His large hands that looked waxy beneath their deep tan were crossed on the bulge of his belly.

Most startling to Lonnie were the two large silver coins that had been placed over his eyes. Beneath the rose petals, the man's eyes appeared not quite closed, as though Stoveville were merely pretending he was dead. A foxy smile quirked his mouth corners.

He was not pretending to be dead, though. The man whom Lonnie had ridden all this way to deliver the money to was really, truly dead.

As the girl continued to sob quietly into her hanky, Lonnie stepped over to the other casket. His eyes had no sooner found the face of the second corpse with the puckered purple hole in the pale band around the dead man's forehead just above his eyes, than Lonnie took one loud, stumbling step backward, and said much louder than he would have liked, *"Oh, God!"*

He may have only gotten a fleeting look at the face of the man he'd inadvertently killed, back when he'd killed him, but he knew that he was getting a much longer look at him here, in his casket. This man had a pink, sunburned face and shaggy brown mustache and goatee, but now his face looked waxy behind the burn. His eyes were also covered with coins.

To Lonnie's right, the girl stopped sobbing. She sniffed, cleared her throat, and said, "Who're you?"

Her voice had sounded far, far away. Lonnie's mind was spinning so fast that it took him nearly fifteen seconds after he'd turned toward the girl to realize that the face peering at him from behind the black lace veil was beautiful. Lightly freckled and tanned behind the mourning veil, with expressive hazel eyes and a straight, fine nose.

He recognized her. He'd seen her in McGuffin's Mercantile several times, but it had only taken him one time, his first time, to have fallen head over heels in love with the girl, whom he guessed was close to his own age, maybe a little older. Of course, he'd never introduced himself or inquired about her name. There'd be no way he could have ever spoken to a girl as beautiful and self-possessed and assured as she had always seemed.

He'd admired her from afar, looking forward to each infrequent visit to town, so he could lay his eyes on her again in the mercantile and fantasize about her someday being his.

Seeing her here, with these dead men, merely added to Lonnie's confusion.

He must have been staring at her like a nitwit, because as she gazed back at him from behind her veil, her gold-blonde brows became more and more furled until she said slowly, annunciating each word clearly, as

110

though she were speaking to a half-wit, "Your name. I asked you your *name*. And what on God's green earth do you have in those *saddlebags*?"

"In what?"

The girl studied Lonnie through the veil and then turned her head slowly toward the casket containing the body of the man he'd killed. "Sorry about Willie," she said. "He was a good man, I reckon. Anyways, Pa seemed to think he was worth his salt as a part-time deputy." She paused. "How did you know him?"

"Oh, I . . . uh . . . just knew him," Lonnie said, wondering if the saddlebags were visibly leaping up and down on his shoulder from the mad beating of his heart. "Just knew him . . . that's all." He could think of little else except pulling his picket pin as fast he could, before he ran into the other deputy — the one who was still alive and would most likely recognize Lonnie. He hadn't recognized the deputy with the mole on his cheek. The boy didn't think he'd been the one with Willie.

When had Stoveville hired three deputies, and why?

"I'm sorry if he was your friend. You looked pretty shocked, seein' him there."

"Yeah." Lonnie raked his gaze away from

the man he'd killed, toward the girl. He tried not to betray the fact that he was shaking in his boots. "You're Stoveville's . . ."

"I'm his daughter. Casey. Who're you? I know I've seen you before but I can't place you. Maybe it's those big bags you're totin' around. If you're not careful, you're gonna tip over under all that weight."

"I'll manage," Lonnie said, shifting the bags on his shoulder. "I'm Lonnie Gentry."

"Ah. Your ma has an account over at the mercantile."

"That's right."

"I work there."

"I know."

Behind the gauzy, black veil, the girl's lipped quirked slightly in acknowledgment of that. Her eyes turned beleaguered once more as she shifted her head toward the coffin containing the marshal. Tears oozed out from their corners to dribble down her cheeks.

If he didn't find a way out of there soon, Lonnie thought he was going to start bawling, as well.

CHAPTER 17

Curiosity held Lonnie in that horrible room with the two dead men — Marshal Stoveville and the deputy Lonnie had killed — and Stoveville's pretty daughter.

The boy cleared his throat and asked Casey, "How did . . . how did your pa . . . ?"

The girl sniffed. "Figured everybody knew by now. The bank in Golden was robbed. Pa got the telegram sayin' the robbers were heading northwest. Him, two of his deputies, Willie Drake and Lou Dempsey, and a couple of other men from town rode out to cut 'em off at the southern pass. They cut 'em off, all right. But they didn't stop 'em. Pa was shot out of his saddle. Willie an' Dempsey kept after the robbers. This afternoon, Dempsey returned to Arapaho Creek with Willie shot in the head. Said they were bushwhacked by one of Dupree's gang."

Lonnie was sweating. The saddlebags were growing as heavy as a blacksmith's anvil on his shoulders. He looked from Stoveville's casket to the casket containing the man he'd killed.

The man he'd killed . . .

"What you got in them saddlebags?" Casey Stoveville asked him.

Lonnie jerked a startled look at her. His nerves were leaping like striking diamondbacks. He wondered if word about his mother and Dupree had worked its way as far as Arapaho Creek yet. It likely hadn't, or Lonnie would have been eyed with suspicion, and so far, even carrying the bulging saddlebags, he hadn't.

He turned to the gambling parlor's half-open door through which the low roar of the drinkers in the main saloon emanated. He hurried over to the door, closed it, and walked back to stand in front of the girl, the words exploding out of him like Fourth of July firecrackers detonating in his mouth.

"This here's the money them robbers stole," he told the girl, eager to remove the weight from his exhausted shoulders. Suddenly, Lonnie couldn't speak fast enough as he said, "I found it up at our old line shack on Eagle Ridge. I came here lookin' for your pa, because I figured he was the only one I could trust to unload it on, but now . . ." He let his voice trail off. "I never realized

114

he had so many deputies . . ."

The girl rose from her chair and said woodenly as she stared at the saddlebags, "He hired 'em last month, right after gold was discovered south of town . . . and a bad element started driftin' in . . . started drifting in from Denver." She looked at Lonnie, beetling her pretty brows. "How on earth did you —?"

The door burst open. Lonnie jerked his head around to see the deputy from the marshal's office, and another man also wearing a badge stride into the gambling den. Lonnie almost fainted when he realized that the second man was the other deputy from up on Willow Run.

"Yep, that's him, all right," the second deputy said, stopping about six feet from Lonnie, cocking a hip, and folding his arms across his chest. He was tall, with long arms, like an ape, and relatively short legs. His beard was thick and pewter-colored, and he had one green and one blue eye. He wore a brown bowler hat and a wool vest over a white shirt, and patched broadcloth trousers.

He sneered at Lonnie. "That there's the kid who bushwhacked Willie — why, you little *demon!*"

"*What?*" exclaimed Casey Stoveville.

Lonnie's heart dropped into his boots. At the same time, righteous indignation swept through the boy like a wildfire, and he yelled, "That ain't true an' you know it! You two was takin' potshots at me. I tried to get away and you kept comin', and then I dropped my rifle in the stream, and . . ."

Lonnie let his voice trail off. The deputy he'd seen in the marshal's office, Chase, and the second deputy, Lou Dempsey, were coming at him hard and fast, gritting their teeth, eyes fiery. Behind them, the other men from the saloon were pushing through the open door to get a look at what was happening in the gambling parlor.

"This little jasper killed Willie!" Dempsey shouted at the top of his lungs.

He and the deputy Lonnie knew only as Chase were all over Lonnie, grabbing his arms. Lonnie didn't know what to do. Chase and Dempsey had kill-crazy gleams in their eyes while the men crowded together in the doorway and spilling into the room behind them looked grim, grave, angry.

Lonnie jerked free of the two men's grips. Dempsey was likely lying because he didn't want anyone to know that he and Willie Drake had shot at a thirteen-year-old boy first. That would make them look stupid and inept, which both obviously were. Or, at least, Willie *had been,* before Lonnie had drilled him. Lonnie knew that no one would likely listen to his story, however. He looked wildly around for another way out of the gambling parlor.

But there was only one door, and it was filled with head-wagging townsmen holding beer mugs or shot glasses and, in some cases, burning cigars. Even if Lonnie could get to the door, he'd never get through it.

As Lonnie backed into a billiard table at the front of the room, Dempsey and Chase still coming at him, he held his arms up, palms out. He had no choice but to try to explain himself. "Hold on!" he yelled. "Let me tell it the way it *really* happened, gall-dangit!"

"Save if for the circuit judge," snarled Dempsey, gritting his teeth as he grabbed Lonnie's right arm while Chase grabbed the boy's other arm.

"That kid's Lonnie Gentry!" a man's voice thundered at the back of the room. The beefy bartender was pointing at Lonnie with one arm while planting his other fist on a broad, apron-clad hip, his face as red as a well-stoked fire. "He's Calvin Gentry's boy! Calvin's widow's been shackin' up with Shannon Dupree for over a year now!" The barman snarled like an angry mountain lion. "When he ain't been off robbin' banks, that is! Apparently, he's taken Calvin's boy down the garden path!"

The onlookers muttered their shock, eyes widening in sudden understanding.

"I thought I recognized that kid!" yelled one of the other townsmen, looking over the shoulders of several others in front of him.

Another townsman shouted, "Sure enough, I seen May Gentry ridin' with Dupree in a buggy up near Bachelor Gulch. May's kid threw in with Dupree and his thievin' killin' ways! Oh, how could ya *do it,* boy?"

"I didn't throw in with Dupree!" Lonnie screamed, trying in vain to pull his arms free of the much larger, beefier deputies. "If I threw in with him, what am I doin' here in town . . . *with the money he stole from Golden?*"

One of the townsmen stepped away from the crowd and crouched over the saddlebags that Lonnie had dropped on the floor near where Casey Stoveville was standing with her back to her father's casket. The girl appeared to be in stone-faced shock. The townsman glanced darkly up at Lonnie, frowning, then he unbuckled the strap on one of the saddlebag pouches.

He lifted the flap and dipped his hand carefully inside, looking tense, as though he was afraid the pouch was filled with rattle-snakes. Slowly, he pulled out his hand filled with a green pack of bills.

"Sure enough," the man said, staring in awe at the bills in his hand.

"Crafty," one of the other men from the crowd said, stepping forward. He was short and plump, with long, coarse gray hair tumbling down from his bowler hat. He wore a three-piece butterscotch suit with black patent half boots. "The kid's crafty, all right. Prob'ly double-crossed Dupree and stopped here for grub on his way over the mountain!"

The men around him laughed and roared their agreement.

Dempsey said, "What should we do with him, Mayor?"

The little, plump man officiously rose up on the balls of his half boots and canted his head to one side. "I don't care how young he is. Hang a killin' child and save yourself the trouble of hangin' a killin' man later! Toss him in the hoosegow. I'll cable the judge first thing in the morning, and we'll try him and hang him in the town square before the week is out!"

The crowd roared.

"Hangin's too good for that little cata-
mount!" a disembodied voice cried.

CHAPTER 18

Lonnie couldn't believe what he was hearing. He wanted to yell back at the men around him, to explain himself, but what good would it do him? They'd never be able to hear him above their own roaring.

Willie Drake must have been roundly liked. The town was out for blood. These men were only too eager to play cat's cradle with Lonnie Gentry's head!

"That don't make sense," Lonnie couldn't help saying as Chase and Dempsey began leading him across the room toward the crowd spread out in front of and around the door. "Why would I bring the money to town if I was in with Dupree?"

He'd been only talking to himself. No one could have heard him above the din.

"Hold on!" a girl's voice sounded behind him and the men holding fast to each of his arms.

Chase and Dempsey stopped and turned

Lonnie around. Casey Stoveville stood before Lonnie. Her flushed cheeks were wet with tears. Her hazel eyes were wide and bright with rage. "If you killed Willie," she said through gritted teeth, "you just as easily could've killed my pa!"

Lonnie opened his mouth to protest but before he could get a single word out, the girl cocked her right arm back and swung her balled fist forward. She bunched her lips and winced as she smashed her fist against Lonnie's left cheek.

It wasn't like any punch you'd think a girl would throw. It was a hard, crushing blow. Pain was a railroad spike hammered through Lonnie's jaw and into his brain plate. He flew backward and would have hit the floor if both deputies hadn't been hanging onto him, and kept him upright. Laughing, they turned him around and half dragged him into the parting crowd and through the door of the gambling den.

Lonnie must have passed out for a minute because the next thing he knew he was being dragged along the street, his head hanging so that he could see his boot toes carving slender furrows in the dirt and finely ground horse manure. He couldn't remember being hauled through the saloon's main drinking hall. Then he was being dragged past the General, who gave a shrill, indignant whinny when the horse saw the unceremonious way his rider was being treated.

The deputies jerked Lonnie up the steps of the town marshal's office.

"You little demon!" Dempsey snarled as he and his partner hauled Lonnie to one of the three jail cells lined up along the rear of the dimly lit office. He turned to his partner, cementing his story. "Shot Willie in the head! Never even gave him a chance. You should have seen him in action! Never seen the like! Well, you won't get no chance to grow up, kid, and that's bond!" This last was shouted as Lonnie was shoved into the cell stumbling and falling onto the cell's hard cot as the deputies slammed the cell door behind him with a rattling *clang*!

Lonnie sat up, touched fingers to his cheek, oily with blood. Chase and Dempsey stared in at him as Dempsey turned the key in the cell door's lock.

"Hah!" Dempsey laughed. "Miss Stoveville got you good, didn't she?" He glanced at Chase. "Did you see that cute little gal wind up on him?"

"Yeah, I seen her," Chase said, laughing. Lonnie found Chase staring at him critically. "Hey, you sure this kid shot Willie, Demps? He don't look like the type that would shoot a man, especially a lawman, from bushwhack."

"I didn't shoot nobody from bushwhack!" Lonnie said sharply, sitting on the edge of the cot, frustrated down to the heels of his boots. "Them two — him and Willie — bushwhacked *me,* just like I said. I ran and tried to get away, but they kept comin' . . . and shootin'."

"Don't listen to him, Chase." Dempsey tugged at his pewter beard, blinked each of his unmatched eyes in turn. It seemed like his habit to not blink each unmatched eye at the same time, and he appeared to be scowling, even when he laughed. His eyes were deeply shadowed under a heavy brow bone. "He shot at us from bushwhack when we was about to fill our canteens at a spring. I figure Dupree must have sent the kid to check their back trail. When he seen me and Willie, this yellow-toothed little devil laid in with a Winchester."

Lonnie got up and walked to the cell door. "Don't listen to him, Chase. He's lyin'!"

Dempsey glared through the bars at Lonnie. "You shut up, or I'll come in there and lay the strap to you. How would you like that?"

"You just try it!"

"All right — I will!"

Dempsey dropped his hands to his belt buckle, but before he could start unbuckling the belt, Chase swatted his partner's shoulder with the back of his hand. "Forget it. Leave him for the judge. I 'spect we'll be puttin' that gallows together before the week's out." Chase shook his head. "Too bad you an' Willie didn't know about his ma and Dupree. Could have gone right to the cabin, thrown a loop over Dupree and them other two renegades right then and there. The boy's ma, too. 'Stead of lettin' 'em lead you in circles."

Chase had the saddlebags draped over his shoulder. He turned toward the cluttered table that sat in the middle of the dingy, smelly jailhouse office. "Come on — let's see how much loot Dupree took out of the Golden bank."

Lonnie drew a deep breath and sagged back down on the edge of the cot. He probed his cheek with his fingers. Dempsey had been right. Miss Stoveville had really cut into him. He could feel a two-inch gash in the nub of his left cheek. The abrasion wasn't bleeding much, but it burned.

The cheek was the least of his concerns. He looked at the cell's three walls. There was a window in the rear wall, which was solid stone, but the window would have been too small for him to crawl through even if three stout iron bars hadn't crossed it.

Lonnie's goose was cooked.

The boy no longer even felt frustrated and angry. All he felt now was hollowed out and so tired that all he really wanted to do was sleep.

But then he thought about the General, and he looked at Chase and Dempsey, who had poured all the money packets out on the table and were staring down at all those greenbacks in shock.

"Hey, my horse needs tendin'," Lonnie said. "He needs feed and water. Get him over to a livery barn, will ya?"

He could never be so downtrodden that he did not think about the welfare of his horse.

"Shut up, kid," said Dempsey, staring down at the money. All those greenbacks piled up in packets on the table had the deputy riveted. "We'll tend your horse when we're good and ready. Hot diggity — look at all that money!"

"How much you suppose is there?" asked Chase in a hushed tone, fingering the large, dark mole on his cheek. Lonnie thought they were both going to doff their hats, get down on one knee, and cross themselves.

Even the jailed, downtrodden boy admitted there was a lot of dinero strewn about that table. That much money could buy a whole lot of things.

"Let's find out," Dempsey said, pulling a chair out from the opposite side of the table from Chase. He'd sat down and was starting to roll up his shirtsleeves when someone knocked on the jailhouse door.

The first person Lonnie thought of was Dupree, and fear grew in the boy once again.

CHAPTER 19

Dempsey and Chase leapt to their feet, drawing their pistols and clicking the hammers back.

Lonnie was glad they were on their toes. If Dupree came calling, as he was bound to do, Lonnie would be dead sooner rather than later. Lonnie didn't put it past the outlaw to storm the jailhouse and kill the deputies . . . as well as Lonnie . . . before retaking the loot. Lonnie didn't really know why it mattered how he died — by the rope or by Dupree — but it seemed to.

Maybe he didn't want Dupree to have the satisfaction.

"Who is it?" Chase called, aiming his Colt at the jailhouse door.

"Mayor Teagarden," said the voice on the other side of the door.

"Come on in, Mayor," Dempsey said, letting his pistol sag slightly in his hand though he did not uncock the weapon or holster it.

The door opened and the pudgy little man in the butterscotch suit stepped over the threshold, his fingers in the pockets of his wool vest. He grinned when he saw the money, showing one silver front tooth. "Just . . . uh . . . just wanted to make sure the Golden money was secure . . ."

"Oh, we've secured it, Mister Mayor," Chase said.

"Maybe you'd better lock it up in one of the cells for the night."

"Oh, we will, Mister Mayor," Dempsey assured the man, and grinned. "As soon as we count it. First thing in the morning, one of us'll saddle up and ride it back to Golden, get it back in the bank where it belongs. We wanna make sure it's all there. Who knows — the kid might've spent some of it or maybe hid some along the trail."

Lonnie rolled his eyes. He was too miserable to do anything else in protest of his predicament.

Mayor Teagarden strolled over to the table and stared down at the money. He whistled. "That'd sure buy someone a trouble-free life — eh, fellas? Easy street all the way. And possibly a long vacation in San Francisco to boot!" The mayor laughed, keeping his sparkling eyes on the money.

"Sure would," said Dempsey, holstering

his six-shooter. "No doubt, that's what Shannon Dupree had in mind. Not to worry, though, Mister Mayor. I'll start out for Golden first thing in the mornin', deliver these here greenbacks to the bank."

"Well, you know what, fellas?" the mayor said, rising up and down on the toes of his half boots. "I was headin' over to Golden on business tomorrow. I can throw them saddlebags in my buggy, toss a blanket over 'em to make sure nobody knows what I'm haulin', and I'll have 'em there by the end of the week."

Chase and Dempsey glanced at each other. They held each other's gazes for about three seconds, both men wrinkling the skin above their noses in silent, wistful communication.

Chase said, "Ah, no, no, Mister Mayor. We couldn't ask you to do that. Haulin' stolen money back to its rightful owner is a dangerous job. It's a job for the law. And me an' Dempsey here — with the chief marshal dead now, God rest his soul — are about the only law left in Arapaho Creek. That's a job for one of us."

"Maybe both of us," added Dempsey. "One to carry the loot, one to ride shotgun. It's a good three, four-day ride over the mountains to Golden. Who knows where

130

Shannon Dupree is about now? If the kid double-crossed that outlaw, he's probably on his way to Arapaho Creek."

"Yeah, no, sir, Mister Mayor." Chase walked over and drew the front door open as though inviting the mayor to leave. "Haulin' that loot is a job for armed lawmen. It'll be a dangerous trek over to Golden, but me and Dempsey'll make 'er, all right. That's what we get paid for, after all."

The mayor winced visibly at the proclamation. He studied the money on the table for a time, probing his silver tooth with his tongue, before he glanced at both lawmen suspiciously. "Yes, well, I suppose it would be a job for the law." He chuckled deviously and switched his gaze back and forth between the two deputies. "You boys don't let all this tinder go to your heads now, and do something — well, something *dishonorable*, now, you hear?"

Chase and Dempsey laughed as though it were the funniest joke they'd ever heard. When the mayor had strolled out through the door and Dempsey had closed the door and turned the key in the inside lock, securing the bolt, he turned to Dempsey and said, "Why, that old coot was seriously considerin' makin' off with that loot. I know he was!"

He stared at Chase, who remained standing by the table. The men stared at each other for a long time in silent conversation. Their eyes grew at once brighter and darker as malicious thoughts stole across their brains.

"Uh-oh," Lonnie thought, sitting on the edge of his cot. It wasn't hard to read these two scoundrels' simple minds.

Both deputies turned their heads to regard Lonnie through the cell's barred door. He and Dempsey said at the same time, "What about the kid?"

They turned to each other again, and Chase said with quiet menace, "Well, we're gonna have to keep him good and quiet for a long, long time."

"How we gonna do that?" Dempsey asked.

Chase glowered at Lonnie through the barred door and loosened his pistol in its holster, caressing the hammer with his thumb. "How else?"

CHAPTER 20

Lonnie stared at Chase's thumb fondling the hammer of the Colt's revolver snugged down in the man's black holster thonged to his right thigh.

Emotion heaved in Lonnie's tired brain and exhausted body, and he couldn't stop himself from running up to the door, wrapping both his hands around the bars, and yelling, "You two can't kill me! You can't steal the bank money!" He was so flabbergasted that he thought his head would explode.

Chase glared back at him from the table, lips stretched slightly back from his teeth.

Lonnie switched his gaze to Dempsey, who remained in front of the door. Dempsey wore an even more savage and cunning look than Chase. Lonnie remembered something he'd heard Dupree say once about most lawmen being a hair's breadth from being outlaws and that most *had been* outlaws at one time and likely would be again.

For some reason, it was the only thing Dupree had ever said that Lonnie had paid much attention to.

The statement had riled Lonnie. He'd wanted to yell at Dupree, "You'd like to think that, but it ain't true! Lawmen are good men! They'd never break the laws they were sworn to enforce! You just want to believe they would so you can feel better about yourself!"

Now, the boy was glad he hadn't said that. What a fool he'd have been. He could see in the eyes of these unwashed, sweaty, unshaven lawmen that they were every bit as bad as Dupree. And they'd have no more trouble killing a thirteen-year-old boy than they'd have shooting a chicken-thieving coyote.

Lonnie had been about to lay into Dempsey but he saw now he'd just be wasting his breath. He'd run into lawmen no better than the men who'd stolen the money that his trip to Arapaho Creek had been about returning.

In other words, he'd come to the end of his trail, which was what a friend of his father's had told Lonnie after his father's passing of a heart stroke in bed only four years after he'd fought so hard in the War

Between the States.

He'd come to the end of his trail . . .

The idea wasn't new to Lonnie. He himself had almost died several times in the past day. Still, to be facing the two men who were going to do the dirty deed while he himself was trapped behind bars and helpless, nearly caused him to whiz down his leg. His mouth went dry and his tongue swelled.

He switched his gaze between his two executioners, felt tears well in his eyes, and tried to get control of himself. He wouldn't break down. He wouldn't cry. He had enough sand in his hide, young as it was, to not give up that easy.

"You think we oughta do it, Dempsey?" Chase asked, still staring into the cell at Lonnie. He was opening and closing his fists slowly. His eyes were large and round and white-ringed like the General's when the horse saw a rattler or scented a wildcat on the wind. The big mole had turned black. It appeared to pulsate, like a small heart.

Chase was nervous.

Dempsey sat down at the table and started pawing through the money. "This here's more money than either you or I will ever see again, Chase. We gonna let one thieving, outlaw brat stand in our way of bein' rich?"

"I won't tell," Lonnie said weakly, still holding onto the bars of the door and staring bleakly, forlornly out. "I won't tell no one. You can take the money and go. I won't tell who took it. Besides, they'll know who took it, anyway, even if I'm not alive to tell 'em!"

"They'll know *when* we took it," Dempsey said. "If we leave tonight, head for Mexico, we'll have several hours' head start on a posse."

"It didn't help matters that you done just told him where we're goin'!" Chase chastised his partner in crime, laughing caustically as he turned away from Lonnie and moved to the table.

"Heck," Lonnie said, "where else would you go? Besides, I'll keep my mouth shut. If you leave right now, you can be in Arizona by the end of the week! No one will even find me in here until then! Lock the door! I'll keep quiet!"

"Nah," Dempsey said, spreading out the packets of banded bills. He was blinking each eye hard. "My plan is to leave a note, say Dupree came and stole the money from us, and we went after him. That'll give us several days' head start. Folks might think

136

the story's a might fishy, but they won't inform the marshal over in Camp Collins for several days, after we don't return. Hell, we'll probably be across the border by then."

Chase sat down across from Dempsey, chuckling. "Sorry, kid. I reckon there's no other way."

Anger burned in Lonnie. He squeezed the bars, trying to twist them. "You two ever killed a kid before? A thirteen-year-old boy with his whole life ahead of him? You really think you got the spleen to do somethin' that mean and low-down and just plain nasty? Why, every time you spend a penny of that there money, you're gonna remember the kid you killed so's you could make a clean break with it!"

"Shut up, kid," Dempsey growled, blinking. "Or I'll shoot you right now, tell anyone who asks that you were tryin' to escape."

Chase was counting the bills but paused to say, "And no one'll shed a tear. Not for the thievin' brat of a woman who took up with a curly wolf like Shannon Dupree."

Then he went back to counting.

Lonnie watched them for a time, stricken. Distantly, he heard them say they'd ride out at midnight, after the rest of the town had gone to bed. They'd take Lonnie out of town, shoot him, and toss him into a deep ravine where the wolves would pick his young bones clean.

Feeling choked as though by a hangman's noose, Lonnie backed up to the cot and sagged down on top of it, helpless. His only chance, he figured, was to try and make a break for it when they opened the cell door. It was a long shot but probably the only shot he'd get.

He was younger than they and fast on his feet. General Sherman was still outside. If Lonnie could get onto his horse, he'd point the General in the direction of the far hills, slap the spurs to him, and never return to the cesspool that was Arapaho Creek ever again.

A long shot, but it was the only chance he had . . .

There was a cuckoo clock on the otherwise unadorned stone wall over Stoveville's desk. At the top of each hour, a blue-headed yellow bird stepped out onto the door that opened for it, and chirped once with tooth-gnashing shrillness for each hour of the day.

The deputies must have been accustomed to the bird. They didn't seem to mind it chirping like that, like a door on rusty hinges being opened quickly several times in a row. Or maybe they were too immersed in the poker game they'd started playing with their newfound wealth after they'd finished counting the money and finding they were now each worth a little over thirty thousand dollars apiece.

They sat back in their chairs, playing poker and grinning and taking pulls from the bottle they'd hauled out of Stoveville's desk, and smoked cigars they'd found in the desk, as well. While they played, they talked over their plans for a life of leisure down in Mexico. Sometimes they sang or whistled absently or told a dirty joke while they puffed their cigars and threw back the whiskey. Occasionally, they chuckled in anticipation of midnight, when, rich men, they'd ride on out of Arapaho Creek forever.

After they'd silenced the kid, of course.

CHAPTER 21

Lonnie got so that he hated the cuckoo bird so much he'd have shot it off its perch if he'd had his rifle.

Of course, it wasn't just the bird making him nervous as a cat in an attic full of rocking chairs. He was going to die tonight, sometime after midnight, and no one would ever know how it had happened or why, and they'd never find a body to take home to his ma for burial.

His ma . . .

He wondered what had happened when Dupree had discovered his money gone.

Dupree . . .

Where were Dupree and "the boys," anyway? Lonnie almost wouldn't have minded seeing the outlaw. At least, Dupree would throw a wrench into the lawmen's plans for the boy, though Dupree's intentions for Lonnie likely wouldn't be any rosier than those of Deputies Dempsey and Chase.

At the last chirp of midnight, Lonnie's heart stopped beating. At least, it felt like it stopped. Then, as Chase and Dempsey shoved all the money back into the saddle-bags, and Dempsey headed out to fetch a couple of horses from a livery barn, Lonnie's heart turned two hard somersaults.

He looked at the small window high in the cell's back wall. He was compelled to jump up and start screaming for help through the window, but he doubted anyone would hear through the small opening and from behind the thick stone walls. Besides, Chase, who was finishing shoving some gear into a war bag for the trail ahead, would likely make good on his promise to shoot Lonnie right here and tell anyone who cared to ask that the outlaw boy had been trying to make a break for it.

Make a break for it . . .

Lonnie sat on the edge of the cot, waiting. He looked at the jailhouse's main door. As soon as either deputy opened the cell door, Lonnie would turn himself into a human arrow flying toward that outside door and freedom waiting beyond.

And, ten minutes later, that's what he did.

When Dempsey opened the cell door, Lonnie bounded off his heels and threw himself straight at Dempsey. But the last thing he saw before everything went black was Dempsey's smiling face and the cell door slamming toward Lonnie's head.

The next thing Lonnie knew, he was watching a night-dark trail slide past his outstretched fingers. His stomach and ribs ached, as though a giant were sitting on his hips. His head ached as though he'd been bludgeoned with a sledgehammer. Blinking and shaking away the cobwebs that had grown up thick as gypsum weed inside his head, he saw that what was crushing his guts against his spine was his own saddle.

Dempsey and Chase had thrown Lonnie belly-down across the General's back, and he was riding with his head hanging down the buckskin's right side while his legs and boots dangled down the General's left side. Ropes were tied around his wrists. The ropes stretched beneath the General's belly, and, while Lonnie couldn't see his ankles from his unfortunate position, he could feel that they were tied.

Tied to his wrists beneath the buckskin's belly.

He was being hauled through the night like a tied-down load of freight.

A load of human freight that would soon be nothing more than a midnight snack for the carrion eaters . . .

He turned his face to stare ahead along the trail. He could see the rumps of two horses and two jostling tails about ten yards beyond. It was a dark night but there was enough light from the stars that he could see that Dempsey was leading the General by the bridle reins. The two men rode slowly along the trail, their horses' hooves thumping dully in the well-churned dust.

Around Lonnie were dark pines reaching toward the stars. He could feel the cool, high-country air ensconcing him, making him shiver, and smell the tang of pine resin.

Vaguely, he wondered where they were. They seemed to be climbing, probably toward a southern pass. Soon the men would stop and do away with Lonnie. They were likely waiting until they were far enough from Arapaho Creek that no one in town would hear the shot, and remote enough that no one would ever find Lonnie's body.

No one but the wolves that stalked this stretch of the Never Summers.

Lonnie rode, wincing with each jarring step of his horse. He felt as though his spine was going to saw into his belly from the back side, and as though the jostling of the ride was going to pound the boy's brains to such pulp inside his skull that they'd ooze out his ears.

Finally, mercifully, the General stopped.

The misery in Lonnie's belly and head tapered off a little.

Then, not so mercifully, Chase climbed down from his horse and walked back to where Lonnie's head hung down the General's side.

"Sorry, junior," the deputy-turned-outlaw said, "but you've come to the end of your trail."

He took out a big knife and sawed through the ropes.

CHAPTER 22

When the ropes fell away from Lonnie's wrists and ankles, his first thought was to slide off his horse and to run as fast as he could. But before he could start to work himself off the General's back, he was "helped" down by Dempsey from behind.

The deputy dug his hand into the waistband of Lonnie's denim trousers, and gave a wicked pull. The boy grunted loudly as he fell from the horse like a fifty-pound sack of chicken feed. He hit the ground on his spurs and fell on his butt only to be picked up again by his collar, and thrust off the trail and away from the horses. He was so weak from his run-in with the cell door that he dropped to his knees, his head pounding.

Fear had covered him from head to toe with cold sweat.

He looked around.

They were in a clearing ringed with the arrow shapes of pine tops silhouetted against the starry sky. The quarter moon was climbing, offering wan light below the level of the trees but beginning to dim the stars. A flame-shaped mountain was silhouetted against the moon's violent glow, straight ahead of Lonnie.

The air was cool enough up here that Lonnie could see his breath. The chill didn't stop him from sweating. It just made the perspiration colder as it dripped down from between his shoulder blades to cause his shirt to cling to his lower back.

He thought he could see a cabin about a hundred yards ahead and on his right. The moonlight touched its flat roof. Abandoned, no doubt. For some reason it made this clearing feel all the emptier, lonelier. A wolf's howl emanating from somewhere on that black, velvet, flame-shaped mountain added menace to the emptiness and loneliness.

So this was where he would take his last breath. He'd wondered about his end on cold winter nights when he hadn't had enough work the previous day to tire him out. So, here it was.

From behind he could hear boots crunching grass and sage branches raking trouser cuffs. Chase's voice said in a drunken slur, "Get up, kid. Move out there a ways."

"What's the matter, Chase?" Dempsey said, also dragging his words though not as badly as Chase. His tone was slightly mocking. "Don't want him to be too close when you put a bullet in him?"

"I don't care how close he is," Chase snarled at his partner. "I don't want the shot to scare the horses."

"Oh, good thinkin'," Dempsey said with the same note of mockery.

"Hey, you wanna do it?"

"I would do it," Dempsey said, "but we flipped for it, remember? You lost."

Lonnie's heart turned another couple of somersaults as he looked around again and saw that even if he could bring himself to run — his boots felt as though they'd been filled with dry mud — he couldn't see any sheltering tree within fifty yards. All that was out here were trees and the cabin that was way off across the clearing.

Chase pressed the barrel of his pistol against the back of Lonnie's head. "Come on, kid. Get movin'. You're only drawin' this out."

Lonnie climbed wearily to his feet. Sweat dripped under his arms. He heard his voice quiver as he said, "I'm gonna come back and haunt you two. I'm gonna come back and haunt you two until you get heart strokes and die like my pa died — in your *beds!* And then you're both gonna take that long walk down them warm, stone steps until you're in Hell shakin' hands with the *Devil!*"

That thought made Lonnie feel better.

"I said get movin'!" Chase yelled.

"No!" Lonnie spat through gritted teeth. He wheeled to face Chase and Dempsey. "If you're gonna kill me, you're gonna have to do it straight on and close up!" He balled his fists at his sides and leaned forward at the waist, his rage overwhelming him. "Come on, you yellow-livered coward!"

"Why, you . . . !" Chase clicked the hammer of his Colt back and aimed the barrel at Lonnie's forehead.

The gun barked.

The sudden explosion caused Lonnie to stumble straight back. His spurs raked the ground. He tripped and fell on his rump and found himself, apparently with his skull still intact, staring at Chase who'd given a yelp and twisted around as though a snake had bitten his leg.

Chase's revolver popped and flashed. The bullet slammed into the ground between the outlaw and Lonnie, and dust and grass blew up over Lonnie's boots.

"What in the —?"

Another thundering crash cut Dempsey off.

He yelped and threw away the pistol he'd drawn as though it were a hot skillet handle. He cursed and grabbed his right forearm.

The report of what Lonnie now recognized as a rifle sounded again, knifing across the otherwise silent clearing. This shot took Chase down, howling and kicking. There was another flash in the forest to Lonnie's left, and the bullet spanged off a rock to warm the air just off his own right cheek.

The boy threw himself belly-down and buried his head in his arms as he thought, *"Dupree!"*

The rifle crashed several more times, the shots spaced about two seconds apart, and a voice called, crisp and clear on the suddenly quiet air, "Lonnie!"

Lonnie lifted his head slightly. He blinked. He could have sworn the voice had been a girl's. Nah. His ears were ringing from fear and the clamor of the rifle.

"Lonnie, I didn't hit you, did I?"

No, it was a girl's voice, all right.

Befuddled, Lonnie lowered his arms and raised his head higher. He looked off to where the gun had flashed in the dark mass of the trees, and he said uncertainly and not loudly, "I reckon I'll be all right if you

149

hold your fire . . . whoever you are."

"It's Casey!"

"Casey?"

"Casey Stoveville. Stay where you are and keep your head down in case I have to start shooting again!"

"All right," Lonnie said, again uncertainly.

Nearby, Chase and Dempsey were moaning and groaning.

Dempsey shouted hoarsely, "Hold your fire! Hold your fire! Who in tarnation you think you're shootin' at, little girl?"

There was another hiccupping cough and a rifle flash. The bullet plumed dust in front of Dempsey, who threw his head back on the ground, covered it with his arms, and cursed loudly.

His angry screams echoed shrilly around the clearing.

CHAPTER 23

Lonnie looked toward where the shots had been fired, and he could see a pale-tan silhouette taking shape against the trees.

The crunch of footsteps grew gradually louder. Just as gradually, the pale-tan silhouette took the shape of a short, slender person walking toward Lonnie and his two moaning, groaning assailants. The pale-tan shape became a tan canvas coat that hung to thighs clad in dark-blue denim trousers and calf-high boots.

Casey Stoveville's gold-blonde hair hung down from her man's tan hat to spill across her shoulders. Her eyes caught the starlight beneath the brim of her hat, and glistened. The starlight winked off the barrel of the Winchester carbine she held in her hands, downward slanted, ready to raise in an instant again if needed.

Dempsey spat and shouted, "Who you think you're shootin' at, you fool girl? Don't you know it's me — Dempsey and Chase, your pa's deputies — out here?"

The rifle belched and flashed again.

Dempsey cursed again, shrilly, as the bullet blew dirt and rocks over him.

"Who're you calling a fool girl, you dung beetle?" Casey said as she stopped about ten feet from the two men writhing on the ground near Lonnie. "I heard all about your big plans for the stolen money through the jailhouse door."

"Hey, that's my rifle!" Lonnie said, recognizing the carbine in the girl's hands.

"Thanks for letting me borrow it out of your saddle sheath," Casey said. "It came in right handy. I would have requested help from some of the men in Arapaho Creek, but when I got to thinking about it, I could think of nary a one I could trust any more than I could trust my father's deputies."

She glanced at Lonnie. "Are you all right?"

Lonnie sat up and brushed his sleeve across his dirt-pelted face. "I'll live."

"Pa taught me how to shoot but it's been a while since I've had a practice session," she said.

"You did all right," Lonnie said.

"Sorry about your cheek."

"Like I said, I'll live."

Casey took another step forward, aiming

152

the carbine at Chase and Dempsey while saying to Lonnie, "Get their guns." She raised her voice to the outlaws: "If either of you makes any sudden moves, I'm gonna cut loose with this Winchester again, and I'm close enough now to do some damage."

"You already shot us up, you fool girl!" This from Chase.

"If I hear one more 'fool girl' out of either one of you, you'll never say it again . . . or anything else."

The two deputies glanced at each other and didn't say anything.

Lonnie gained his feet. He walked cautiously over to Dempsey and Chase. Both of their revolvers were on the ground, glistening dully in the starlight. Lonnie picked them up, shoved one of the Colts behind his belt, and backed away from the men, cocking the second pistol and aiming it at the deputies.

He was still breathing hard and sweating. His vision swam. He was giddy to be alive after hovering so close to death.

He never wanted to get that close again.

Dempsey and Chase didn't look too badly hurt, despite their caterwauling. They looked as though Casey's bullets had mostly grazed their arms and legs. They were hurting, but neither one looked as though death were imminent. Not that Lonnie cared about either one of the scalawags.

Casey said, "Get up, both of you. Head on over to the horses."

"I don't think I can get up," Chase said. "You drilled a bullet through my thigh, you foo . . . I mean, Miss Casey."

Lonnie had to smile at that as he kept his pistol aimed at the pair.

"Much better," Casey said. "I like that. But if you can't stand, I'm going to shoot you where you sit. So you best get to your feet any way you can, and haul your fool self over to your horse."

"If you got these two covered, I'll fetch the mounts," Lonnie said.

"I got 'em," Casey said assuredly. "My horse is tied in the trees behind me."

Lonnie depressed the Colt's hammer and headed back toward the trail. The horses were spread out a good ways apart, having spooked at the shooting. General Sherman was nearest Lonnie, so Lonnie swung up onto the General's back and rode ahead to gather Chase and Dempsey's horses.

When he'd retrieved Casey's chestnut filly from the trees behind her, he rode out to where Chase and Dempsey had gotten to their feet and stood with their hands up, heads down, like schoolboys who'd been caught turning frogs loose in the girls' privy.

"They probably have some handcuffs in their saddlebags," Casey said.

Lonnie swung down from the General's back and rummaged around in Chase's saddlebags. He'd just wrapped his hand around something that felt like metal, when Casey screamed.

Lonnie whipped around.

Dempsey had lunged at the girl. As the outlaw, who was two heads taller than Casey, and twice as wide, fought the girl for the rifle, the carbine exploded.

Flames lapped skyward.

Dempsey ripped the rifle out of the girl's hands and clubbed her with the rifle's rear stock. Casey groaned and fell hard, rolling once, dust rising around her. Meanwhile, Dempsey cocked the carbine and swung toward Lonnie.

Lonnie had already drawn one of the two Colts he'd taken off the deputies. Without so much as thinking about it, he raised the weapon in both hands, clicked the hammer back, and aimed at Dempsey's murky shadow.

The pistol leaped and roared in Lonnie's hand.

Dempsey grunted and stepped straight back, his dark shadow hard to see against the line of black trees behind him. Dempsey lowered Casey's carbine, and flames stabbed from the barrel as the outlaw triggered the weapon into the ground. Dust flew up around his ankles.

Dempsey took another step back and dropped like a felled tree.

Lonnie clicked the Colt's hammer back and swung the pistol at Chase who had started to lunge toward Lonnie.

"You want some o' this?" the boy asked the deputy-turned-outlaw.

Chase jerked back, holding his hands up, palm out. He shook his head back and forth. "Nope, I sure don't."

CHAPTER 24

"I figured you probably didn't," Lonnie told Chase, grinning boldly. It felt good to be the one in control.

Lonnie looked at Dempsey, who was writhing on the ground, spurs ringing as they scratched the gravelly turf.

The spurs stopped ringing. Dempsey stopped writhing. Lonnie kept his pistol aimed at the fallen deputy. He rolled his eyes toward Casey, who was climbing to her feet with a grunt.

"You all right?" he asked the girl.

She was rubbing her right shoulder. "Yeah," she said, staring awfully down at the unmoving Dempsey. "Is . . . is he dead?"

"I don't know. Why don't you check? Don't worry, I'll cover you." To Chase, Lonnie said, "My trigger finger itches somethin' awful, so you best hold yourself real still. If you even think about tryin' what your friend tried, you'll end up like him."

"Kid," Chase snarled, "you got no respect for your elders."

"Only them that deserve it. I've run into precious few o' them."

Casey stood over Dempsey. "He looks dead to me," the girl said, her voice quaking slightly. It was also a little higher pitched than before. "Yeah, I'm pretty sure he's dead. I don't wanna touch him."

"That's all right," Lonnie said. "He looks dead to me, too."

Casey turned to Lonnie, her chest rising and falling sharply as she breathed. She swept her thick, blonde hair out of her face as she said, "Yep, you blew his lamp out, all right."

"Congratulations," Chase said. "That's your second lawman in two days."

"You wanna be my third?" Lonnie asked him, aiming the Colt at him.

Chase took another fearful step back, shaking his head. "Nope, I sure don't, kid."

Later, when they were riding back toward Arapaho Creek, Lonnie turned to Casey riding her chestnut filly beside him. "What're we gonna do with this fella?" He canted his head toward Chase riding ahead of them.

Casey had secured the deputy's own

handcuffs to the man's wrists behind his back while Lonnie had held his carbine on him. Now the lawman-turned-outlaw rode slouched in his saddle, sullen and silent. He occasionally grunted from the pain of his injuries, and spat to one side in frustration, but that was the extent of Chase's acting out.

Casey said levelly, "Throw him in my father's jail. Only place for such a polecat as that. First thing tomorrow, I'll send a cable to the deputy United States marshal over in Camp Collins. He'll probably ride over here and see to Chase and the bank loot himself."

The girl looked at Lonnie. "Sorry you had to do that. Kill Dempsey, I mean."

"It ain't like he didn't deserve it." Lonnie didn't feel as sick in his gut about shooting Dempsey as he had about the other deputy, Willie. Dempsey had been about to shoot Casey. Still, he knew he'd never forget these past couple of days as long as he lived.

"Was he right?" Casey asked him, her voice hesitant. "About . . . you shooting Willie?"

Lonnie couldn't help feeling more than a little defensive. "I ain't no cold-blooded killer Miss Casey, if that's what you mean."

"Don't get your neck in a hump," she said,

ducking under a pine branch that bowed low over the trail. They were gradually dropping down into the canyon in which Arapaho Creek lay. Lonnie could tell they were approaching the town from the smell of the privies and the barking of a dog. "I wasn't beratin' you about it. I just wanted to know."

"Shootin' Willie wasn't what I had in mind when I started the day yesterday. If I hadn't shot him, I wouldn't be here. And neither, probably, would Dempsey and Willie. Them two would likely be headin' for Mexico about right now."

"I believe you."

Again, Lonnie looked at her riding to his left, her hair bouncing on her shoulders. So much had happened to him recently that he still hadn't quite worked his mind around the presence of a girl he'd fancied from afar. When that happened, his tongue would likely tie itself into a tight knot.

For the moment, however, he was too tired and hungry and anxious to be bashful around a pretty girl. "How come you've decided to believe me?" he asked her.

"After I got to thinking about it, I realized you wouldn't have come to town for any reason if you'd really been in with Shannon Dupree. I realized it after I left the saloon and started thinking it through. I went over to the jailhouse to talk to Chase and Dempsey, and I heard 'em talking through the door, discussing their plans. So I went home, saddled Miss Abigail here" — she patted the chestnut's neck — "and waited for them to make their move."

Casey turned to Lonnie, and a smile caused her eyes to glitter in the light of the moon kiting over the tops of the pines lining both sides of the trail. "I'm right glad they didn't decide to kill you in the jail. Otherwise, I reckon . . ."

"I'd be dead."

"Something like that," she said, gazing at him, her full, pink lips quirking a playful smile.

"I'm obliged to you, Miss Casey," he said.

Now it was happening, darn it. Casey's smile and that frank, humorous gaze through those pretty, hazel eyes were making his tongue start to thicken up, and he was having a hard time looking at her. He found it beguiling how her upper lip was a little thicker than her lower one, and how it curled up slightly, making it hard for him not to wonder what kissing her would be like, though he'd never kissed a girl before.

Casey had a very small mole about two inches beneath her right eye, and Lonnie

161

found that nearly as enticing and mysterious as her lips.

"Well, I reckon you returned the favor back in the clearing," the girl said, and Lonnie was relieved when she turned her head to stare forward along the trail.

General Sherman whickered and shook his head. Fear pricked the short hairs along the back of Lonnie's neck. He hipped around in his saddle, staring along the pale ribbon of trail curving away behind him.

"Did you hear something?" he asked Casey.

She glanced behind. "I didn't hear anything. What'd you hear?"

"Not so much me as the General."

Casey stared along their back trail and then, apparently satisfied they were alone out here, she arched a brow at General Sherman. "That stallion of yours is probably admiring Miss Abigail." She turned her head forward and said snootily, "Men."

Lonnie's heart thudded. He liked this girl even more than he'd realized. He couldn't let on, though. He wasn't sure why he couldn't, but he couldn't. Something about being smitten with her embarrassed him.

Besides, she'd think he was tough, like a man, if he pretended he wasn't interested. Wasn't that how it worked?

They rode on into the dark town, Chase in the lead. The outlaw sat sullenly in his saddle as Casey and Lonnie swung down from their horses in front of the dark, silent jailhouse. The stone building was pale in the moonlight.

Casey cast wary looks at the building, and for a few seconds, Lonnie felt his blood turn cold. Was she thinking Dupree was waiting inside? But then he realized that this was a meaningful place for the girl, since her father had likely spent a lot of time here.

It was her father's ghost she was sensing. She was remembering only a few days back, when he was alive. Lonnie felt sorry for her. He knew how hard it was to lose someone, wishing they would come back so you could see them one more time. Losing someone was like a saddle gall, only it was inside your soul where you couldn't put salve on it.

The girl didn't sob, however. Instead, she pulled her revolver out of her coat pocket, clicked the hammer back, and aimed it with both hands at Chase. "Climb down off of there, you owl hoot. Get inside."

CHAPTER 25

Chase glowered at Casey. He glanced at Lonnie, who stayed back a ways. This was the girl's territory. Lonnie would back her if she needed backing. He doubted she'd need it. She was a tough nut, and instead of pining for her father, she was trying to fill his boots.

Lonnie looked around, keeping an eye out for Dupree.

Chase said, "If you two kids think you're gonna hold me in that jail, you're soft in your thinker boxes. I'm too much for you. Let me go, and I'll ride on out of here, and you'll never see me again. Hell, you got the money!"

Casey licked her lips and there was only a slight quiver in her voice as she said quietly, "You heard me, Chase."

Lonnie held his carbine up high across his chest. He worked the cocking mechanism loudly, seating a cartridge in the rifle's action while staring threateningly at Chase. The metallic rasp was so loud that it started a dog barking somewhere to the east, and a night bird took flight, cawing.

Casey glanced at Lonnie, gave him a half smile, then turned back to Chase.

The deputy sighed, swung his right boot over his saddle horn, and leaped straight down to the ground. He groaned and fell back against his horse, his wounds grieving him.

"Galldarn it," he complained. "I'm gonna need a sawbones take a look at these wounds!"

"In the morning," Casey said, waving her gun at him.

When they got Chase inside the jailhouse and Lonnie had lit a lamp so Casey could see to open a cell, she gave the deputy an angry prod with her pistol barrel. Chase stumbled into the far right cell, cursing. He said several nasty things to Casey about her being a girl and him being a man, but he shut up when she poked the gun through the bars and stared at him over the barrel.

She had him turn around so she could remove his handcuffs. Then she ordered him to give her his badge, and when he did, Casey tossed it to Lonnie standing by the door where he could see both inside the office as well as into the street, though it was so dark he couldn't see much out there.

He was feeling spooky about Dupree. The outlaw had to be out there somewhere, waiting for the right time to make a move.

"Consider yourself deputized," Casey said.

Lonnie looked at the five-pointed tin star in the glove of his hand. It was badly tarnished, mostly gray, but the letters were clear: DEPUTY TOWN MARSHAL.

Lonnie felt himself suddenly grow an inch taller, and his shoulders felt fuller and wider.

"Oh, so you two kids are gonna play at lawdoggin' now, huh?" Chase glowered through the bars at them, chuckling caustically.

"That's right," Casey said as she reached into a pocket of her coat.

She pulled a badge like Lonnie's out of the pocket, and pinned it to her left lapel. She stared down at it. It said TOWN MARSHAL. When she gazed up at Lonnie, her eyes were shiny with tears.

"How do I look?" she asked.

Lonnie thought she looked better than anything he'd ever seen in his whole life. "You look wonderful," he blurted, and turned away as his ears started to burn with embarrassment.

Casey brushed a fist across her cheek and

hardened her voice as she turned to regard Chase, who was now slumped on his cot. "I'll be over to feed you in the morning . . . if you don't bleed to death in the meantime."

"Hey!" he yelled. "You can't leave me locked up here in the dark, bleedin' like this!"

"I'm going to do you a favor and leave the lamp on," Casey said. "And that's more than you deserve."

Chase cursed her and continued to demand a doctor.

As though she hadn't heard him, Casey followed Lonnie outside, and closed and locked the door behind her. She'd left the lamp lit on her father's desk and the orange glow flickered in the windows. Chase continued to curse and yell and to rattle his cell door.

Casey sighed and turned to Lonnie. "Big night for you, huh? I bet you're hungry."

Lonnie shrugged. "I reckon I could eat something."

"Come on," she said, dropping down the porch steps and jerking her chestnut's reins free of the hitch rack. "I'll rustle you something up, and then you can bed down in our spare room."

"You mean we're goin' to your house?"

167

Lonnie said, shocked. "I can throw down in the livery barn."

Casey swung up onto the chestnut's back. "If Dupree's here, he'll find you there." She narrowed a beautiful eye at Lonnie. "And you'll be greased for a sputtering pan, cowboy."

Lonnie looked around the dark street, suppressing a shudder.

"Come on," Casey said, turning the chestnut away from the jailhouse.

"Hold on."

Casey glanced over her shoulder at him. "Why?"

Lonnie was standing in the stirrups as he stared south along the main street. "Heard somethin'."

Actually, the General had heard something and had twitched one ear and then the other. Then Lonnie had heard it, too. He heard it again now — the murmur of distant voices. Casey must have heard it, too, because she gave a slight gasp as she whipped her head forward.

There was silence for a time, then Lonnie heard a man's low, hard voice as well as the slow clomping of approaching horses. As he stared off toward the south end of town, he saw several shadows jostling in the darkness.

"Come on!" Lonnie said, and reined the General through a break between the jailhouse and the drugstore sitting beside it.

Silently, Casey turned the chestnut after him. Lonnie looked around wildly, feeling his heart starting to beat fast again — his poor, tired heart! — and then he saw Arapaho Creek flashing beyond some cottonwoods and pines. He whistled softly to Casey and spurred the General through the trees and down a gradual slope to the edge of the willows lining the water that gurgled gently over the rocks forming the creek bed.

The boy slipped down off the General's back and tied the reins to a branch of a willow shrub.

"Do you think it's them?" Casey whispered.

"I don't know, but I think we'd best find out."

CHAPTER 26

Lonnie shucked his carbine from its saddle boot, quietly levered a cartridge into the chamber, and off-cocked the hammer. Casey followed him as he jogged up the slope, the quarter moon lighting his way back through the cottonwoods and pines.

When he'd gained the top of the slope, he turned right and tramped along the rear of several shops before slipping through a narrow break and slowing his pace as he headed toward the main street. When he reached the mouth of the alley that opened onto the street, he dropped behind a rain barrel and shuttled his gaze to the west.

Three riders were making their way toward Lonnie and Casey, who'd dropped to one knee behind Lonnie's left shoulder, so she wouldn't be seen from the street. The riders were little more than silhouettes in the darkness, their faces dark ovals beneath the brims of their hats. Starlight shone in their horses' eyes, glistened off bridle chains and off the silver trimming Shannon Dupree's gaudy Texas saddle.

Lonnie glanced anxiously at Casey and gave her arm a hard tug as he threw himself against the side of the shop on his right. Casey pressed her back to the wall beside Lonnie.

Very quietly, so that it was little louder than a breath, she said, "Is it them?"

Lonnie nodded, staring at her with wide, grave eyes. He'd have recognized that fancy saddle skirt anywhere. Both skirts of Dupree's saddle were decorated with two small, coiled silver riatas, one overlapping the other. Lonnie had heard Dupree once say that he'd won the saddle in a poker game with a Mexican cowboy from west Texas.

Dupree was very proud of that saddle.

Lonnie turned his head so that he could look between the rain barrel and the side of the shop to see the street. The clomping of the horses grew until the dark shapes of the horses and riders were passing in front of Lonnie, roughly fifteen yards away.

"Where you s'pose we're gonna find the little twerp?" one of the men said, his voice loud in the quiet night.

"I don't know, but we'll find him, all right.

I'm bettin' the money is in the marshal's office."

Lonnie hardened his jaws at the sound of Dupree's voice. Again, he wondered about his mother.

The low, rumbling voice of Fuego said, "Ain't that the jailhouse up ahead? Look — there's a light in the window."

"Well, I'll be jiggered," Dupree said.

They passed Lonnie and were following a slight curve in the street as they headed toward the marshal's office.

Lonnie turned to Casey. "Did you hear?"

She nodded as she gained her feet and began jogging at a crouch back in the direction from which they'd come. "Come on!"

"Where to?"

"The jailhouse!"

"Why?" Lonnie said, catching up to her as they gained the rear of the shops.

"We left Chase in there!"

"So what?" Lonnie said, running along behind the girl as she headed in the direction of the jailhouse. "We'd best light a shuck out of here, Miss Casey. Town ain't safe no more!"

"It'll be safer if we know where those killers head once they leave the jailhouse!" Casey paused to catch her breath, leaning forward, her hands on her knees. "I wanna know where they're headin' so I can tell Bill Barrows, the deputy US marshal over in Camp Collins. As soon as the Wells Fargo office opens, I'm sendin' that telegram."

She made an angry face, eyes flashing in the starlight. "By God, they're gonna pay for killin' my pa!"

Casey started running again, stopped, and looked back at him. "Are you comin'?"

Lonnie looked toward where they'd left the horses. He really wanted to ride and keep on riding. He never wanted to see Shannon Dupree again. The boy's life grew more and more precious to him every time he nearly lost it, and that was getting to be too many times.

He looked at Casey. She was staring at him, frowning critically. As afraid as he was, how could he run out on Casey Stoveville?

Inwardly, he groaned.

"Yeah," he said, steeling his courage. "Yeah, of course, I am."

They ran.

CHAPTER 27

There was a loud *bang!*

Running ahead of Lonnie, Casey yelped and fell. For a second, Lonnie thought she'd been shot but then he realized what the sound had been.

Dupree and the other two outlaws had busted the jailhouse door open. Lonnie could hear them stomping around in the building whose rear wall lay just ahead.

Chase's shrill voice called out, "Now, just you wait, Dupree! Just you *wait!*"

Lonnie gave Casey his hand, and he helped her to her feet. Without saying anything, they continued running to the side of the jailhouse. They pressed their backs against the rough, cool stones, one on each side of a sashed window through which flickering orange lamplight slanted out onto the dirt around Lonnie's boots.

The window was partly covered with an old, tattered flour sack curtain. There was a five-inch gap between the two flaps of the curtain. Lonnie held his hat against his chest as he rose onto his boot toes and peered through the window into the jailhouse.

By flickering lamplight, he could see Dupree stepping back from the cell in which Chase stood, the prisoner's hands wrapped around the bars. Dupree cuffed his hat back on his blond head and slacked down into Marshal Stoveville's swivel chair, facing Chase's cell.

"So you tried to make off with the money, did you, *Deputy*?" Dupree said, laughing. "But the kid got the better of you, did he?"

Fuego and Childress were standing near the open door, facing the jail cell. Fuego had a boot propped on a chair near the door and was rolling a cigarette, an elbow propped on a knee. Childress was scraping grit out from under his fingernails with a Barlow knife and grinning in that mocking way of his.

"So where's the money now?" Dupree wanted to know.

"How should I know?" Chase said, his frightened, slightly high-pitched voice echoing around the cave-like room. "That kid of yours and that girl — Stoveville's daughter — took it and lit out. For all I know, they

175

headed to Mexico!"

"That kid ain't mine," Dupree said. "Let me be clear on that. That kid is his mother's and some dead blue-belly Yankee. I never would have fathered a no-account, thieving, sneaking, little jasper like that one."

"Thieving, huh?" Chase's ironic laughter at that was short-lived. Dupree glared at him.

"Stoveville's *daughter,* you say?" the blond outlaw leader said.

"That's right. They're in it together. She's tougher'n she looks. Must take after her pa."

Lonnie glanced at Casey. She didn't return the glance. She was too busy staring through the window, her head a little lower and to the left of his own.

Fuego turned to Dupree. "They're probably over at Stoveville's place."

"Where's the Stoveville house?" Dupree asked Chase.

Chase poked his arm out of the cell door, pointing toward the jailhouse's front wall. "Two blocks south. Little frame house with a garden and a buggy shed. Big cottonwood in the front yard. Can't miss it. That's probably where they are, all right. Say, would you fellas mind turnin' me loose?"

"Turn you loose?" Childress said, chuckling and closing his knife.

Chase hesitated. "Yeah, I mean . . . why not? I ain't no deputy anymore. You got nothin' to worry about from me. I'm gettin' shed of this town first thing in the mornin'!"

"You're gettin' shed of this town right now," Dupree said.

Lonnie hadn't seen Dupree pull his gun, but now the boy saw the gun in Dupree's gloved right hand. There was a loud *pop!* and orange-red flames stabbed from the pistol's barrel in the direction of Chase.

"Oh, my *god!*" Casey screamed, and instantly clamped her hand over her mouth, as shocked and horrified by her own exclamation as by the fact that Dupree had murdered Chase in cold blood.

"Tell me I didn't do that," she whispered to Lonnie.

Lonnie turned back to the window. Dupree was staring at him and Casey through the warped glass. So were Fuego and Childress. Childress threw his arm out toward the window and shouted, "There they are!"

"Oh, yeah, you sure did!" Lonnie said, pushing Casey aside as Dupree snapped his revolver toward the window.

Bang! Bang! Bang-Bang!

The bullets crashed through the window, blowing out the glass and wooden sashes, shredding the curtains and spraying glass and wood in all directions.

"Come on, Casey — run! *Ru-un!*" Lonnie yelled, pulling the girl to her feet and then, holding her hand, lunging into a sprint back toward the rear of the building.

Beyond the jailhouse, the inky shapes of widely scattered cabins and stock pens and outhouses hunched in the darkness. Lonnie swung around behind the jailhouse as a rifle belched behind him, bullets pluming dust at his and Casey's feet. He could hear the outlaws yelling, hear the thuds of their boots and the jangling of their spurs.

Lonnie had released Casey's hand. She was running only slightly behind him, almost as fast as he was, her own spurred boots ringing in sync with his own.

"This way!" Lonnie yelled, and they cut between an abandoned cabin and a small warehouse, running hard to the north.

He wanted to get back to the horses but he wanted to lose Dupree and "the boys" first, because it was going to take him and Casey a minute or so to get mounted and get across the stream and into the mountains. There was a lot of open ground across the stream and a ways up onto the first ridge to the east, and open ground meant that he and the girl could be cut down by rifle fire.

Lonnie heard a hard thud. Casey groaned and fell, rolling. Lonnie stopped and ran back to her. She was sitting up and leaning forward across her knees, clutching her left ankle near the stone she'd apparently tripped over.

Lonnie saw a small stack of grayed lumber partly hidden amongst the sage they'd been running through as they'd swung to the west and the horses they'd tied by the creek. Lonnie cast an anxious look behind them. He could see the silhouettes of their pursuers coming through the tall pines and the dark cabins. They were close enough that Lonnie heard their rasping breaths and the jingling of their spurs.

"You gotta get up, Casey!" Lonnie said, wrapping a hand around her arm. "Get up and run!"

"You go! Leave me!"

"I ain't leaving you!" he yelled too loudly.

"There they are!" Childress shouted.

CHAPTER 28

Casey cursed and with a groan she pushed to her feet and continued running down the wooded slope to the west.

"Come on!" she called behind her.

"I'll be comin'!" Lonnie said, dropping to a knee and raising his rifle.

He was a little startled at how easy shooting at men had gotten to be. But it seemed just as easy for men to stalk him with the intention of killing him . . . as well as the girl he fancied.

Lonnie aimed in the general direction of the shadows dancing amongst the trees and cabins, and snapped off three quick shots, his rifle crashing loudly, the echoes leaping toward the moon. He heard one of the men yowl. The others stopped running to take cover, and Lonnie wheeled and ran after Casey.

He ran hard, pausing twice to look behind. His shots seemed to have slowed Dupree's pursuit. When Lonnie caught up to Casey, she was limping badly on her left foot.

"I wish you'd leave me," she said.

"If I leave you, they'll kill you."

"They'll kill us both if they catch us."

"They won't catch us!" Lonnie insisted, suppressing a shudder.

Lonnie awkwardly took the girl's right hand.

"What're you doing?" she said, frowning at him.

"Don't get your back in a hump," Lonnie said, pulling her arm around his neck. "I'm only helpin'."

"Oh." Casey glanced behind before glancing over at Lonnie. "Thanks."

"Don't mention it."

Lonnie led Casey down to the creek and followed it upstream. He wished they hadn't hid the horses so well, because he was really starting to sweat about finding them again when, as they followed a horseshoe-shaped bend, the General whickered.

Relief washed over Lonnie, and he led Casey through the willows to where the horses stood where they'd tied them, nervously switching their tails. He helped Casey climb onto her chestnut, and reached up to give her the bridle reins. Casey was staring back in the direction from which they'd come, looking worried.

"Awful quiet back there," she said.

Lonnie had been so relieved to have found the horses and to have gotten Casey safely onto her chestnut's back that he hadn't noticed that he hadn't heard anything behind them since he'd opened up on their pursuers with the Winchester.

He was torn. He'd wanted to shed them from his trail, but the ensuing silence was ominous. He might have hit one but he certainly hadn't hit them all.

And Dupree wouldn't stop following him and the stolen money unless the outlaw was dead. He doubted Dupree was dead. He was coming, all right. He was likely being sneaky about it.

Lonnie swung up onto the General's back and looked around. The stream glistened in the dark like a snakeskin. The willows formed a thick, ragged line along the stream bank, and a sudden, light breeze ruffled them. The swishing sounds would cover the footfalls of anyone approaching.

Lonnie looked across the stream and the dark, fir-covered ridges rising toward higher, darker mountains beyond. He glanced at Casey.

"We'd best ford the stream, head up into

the mountains. It's the only way we're gonna lose 'em."

"That's how I figured," she said, keeping her voice low. Lonnie could hear the worry in it.

"Best ride slow," he said, booting the General up along the stream bank, looking for a way off the bank and into the water. "Try to keep our noise down."

"Right."

Lonnie followed a game path through the willows and into the water. He winced at the plops of the General's shod hooves, at the hollow rushing sound of the water swirling around the horse's hocks.

He was sure that even as slowly as he and Casey were riding, they could be heard from a couple of hundred yards away on so quiet a night. And they were probably backlit by the starlight reflecting off the surface of the creek.

Ducks. They were like ducks on a millpond waiting to be shot, plucked, dressed out, and tossed into a Dutch oven . . .

The short hairs were standing up straight on the back of Lonnie's neck. As the General made his way, slipping now and then on the slippery rocks that lay beneath the water's surface, he kept an eye on the dark bank behind them, on the willows dancing in the breeze.

Nothing moved in the darkness. But he was sure that Dupree was back there somewhere. There was no way the outlaw was going to let Lonnie and Casey get far with the money he considered his own. It was also clear that not only did Dupree intend to get his money back, but he intended to kill the kid . . . or *kids* . . . who now had it . . .

It seemed as though a solid month had passed before the General finally reached the creek's opposite bank. Lonnie felt another wave of relief begin to sweep over him as the General lunged up out of the water and through the willows, Casey's filly splashing not far behind him.

The bank they'd left was about sixty yards away. Still there was no movement in the darkness back there.

Lonnie turned his head forward as a bulky figure holding a rifle stepped out from behind a fir tree.

Fuego's teeth showed in the darkness as the stocky outlaw said, "Got me a couple of thievin' urchins for the killin'!"

Fuego glanced back across the creek. "Dupree, I got 'em both over here!"

CHAPTER 29

Lonnie shouted, "Ah, go flog a boll weevil, you old dung beetle!"

He jerked back sharply on the General's reins and rammed his spurs into the stallion's flanks.

The horse gave a shrill, angry whinny as it reared hard, raising its front, scissoring hooves, kicking the rifle out of Fuego's hands and sending the stout outlaw tumbling.

"Come on, Casey!" Lonnie cried as he smacked his rein ends against the General's flanks and lunged up the slope beyond the creek through the scattered, dark columns of pines and firs.

Gunfire crackled behind him. He glanced over his right shoulder to see Casey hunkered low over her saddle, whipping her chestnut with her own reins and batting her right heel against the mount's right flank. She didn't seem able to do much with her left foot.

Beyond her, the flashes of two guns shone in the darkness on the other side of the stream. Nearer, Lonnie could see Fuego trying to regain his feet, staggering around as though drunk, likely looking for his rifle.

Lonnie had a mind to stop the General, to dismount with his rifle, and pepper the stocky outlaw with .44-caliber rounds. But he nixed the idea. He wasn't such a great hand at killing men yet, and if he got too cocky, he was likely to get filled so full of lead he'd rattle when he walked.

No, his best bet was to flee. To put as much distance as he could between himself and Shannon Dupree. Which he and Casey should be able to do, because he doubted that Dupree's men had their horses.

There were still a couple of hours before dawn. Once Dupree, Fuego, and Childress had collected their mounts, they'd have a hard time tracking Lonnie and Casey until sunup. And by then the boy hoped that he and the marshal's daughter would have put a good, safe distance between themselves and the outlaws.

He and General Sherman rode up over a hump in the steep slope, and then moved downhill from a stony outcropping. At the bottom of the hill, a relatively flat stretch of ground spread out before them in the north, toward the black wall of forested mountain beyond.

The meadow appeared purple in the darkness, mottled with lilac starlight edged in shimmering silver. Sagebrush and small, black spruces and cedars spiked up here and there.

The relatively flat stretch of ground continued for nearly a mile before it began to rise toward densely forested foothills once more. Just before the rise, another, smaller creek stretched across their path, sparkling like a pretty dress.

Lonnie stopped the General, who was breathing hard. The stallion's coat was silvery with sweat, and his lungs sounded like a bellows, his chest expanding and contracting deeply beneath the saddle.

Lonnie swung down from the General's back and loosened the saddle cinch to let the horse breathe easier. He slipped the bit from the stallion's mouth, wrapped his reins around the saddle horn, and stepped aside while the General plunged his front hooves into the creek and immediately began to drink great, slurping draughts of the likely spring-fed water.

"Hey, he'll founder!" Casey warned. She'd dismounted her chestnut and, putting only a little weight on her bum ankle, was holding her horse's bridle tight in her fist.

"What's that?" Lonnie said.

Casey jerked her chin at the General. "You're gonna let that stallion founder . . . or get colic . . . or worse. I'd think a kid from a ranch would know better than to let a hot horse drink his fill like that!"

Lonnie looked at the girl's chestnut filly, who was trying to push forward while staring hungrily at the stream, her nostrils expanding and contracting wildly, hungrily.

"You think wild horses don't take their fill when they're hot and they need it?"

Casey stared at him, incredulous.

"Let her go," Lonnie urged. "Horses need water when they're hot, and I was raised around a passel of 'em, and I've never known a single horse to founder on water. Grain, maybe. Never water. When they're hot they need water even worse than we do."

Casey stared at him. She looked at the General, then at the chestnut. She released her horse's bridle, and the chestnut plunged into the stream beside the stallion and dipped her snout into the rippling water, lapping loudly.

Without the chestnut to hold onto, Casey was having a hard time standing up. Lonnie hurried over to her, wrapped her right arm around his neck, and led her over to lean against a large rock.

"How's the ankle?" he asked.

"I think it's swelling." Casey glanced across the starlit meadow. "You think they're comin'?"

Lonnie also looked across the meadow. "Oh, they'll be comin', all right. But I figure they'll gather their horses first, and that'll take a while. And they'll have to go slow in the dark, trackin' us. This is pretty big country up here and we could be anywhere."

"What did you tell that fella to do?" Casey asked. "Flog a *boll weevil*?"

Lonnie chuckled. "Don't ask me what it means. An old fella who worked at the ranch one fall used to say it when he was mad at one of the other hands. I think he was doin' all he could to not take the Lord's name in vain, or something."

Casey laughed. "He was right creative."

Lonnie pointed at Casey's left foot. "You want me to take a look at that ankle?"

"Why? You a doctor or somethin'?"

"Not official, but I've doctored plenty of horses' feet. The General tends to go lame in his right front hock from time to time, but I used an old Indian cure, and —"

"I'm not a horse, kid."

"All right."

They were quiet for a minute, then Casey said, "Sorry. I'm feelin' a little off my feed." She turned to gaze worriedly behind them once again.

"Yeah, me too."

"You didn't lose your pa."

"I did a few years back."

"Yeah, I heard," she said. "Sorry about that."

"I suppose you feel like I had somethin' to do with your pa, on account of Dupree's been stayin' out at our place from time to time. I promise you, Miss Stoveville, I didn't have nothin' to do with it."

"Oh, hell, I know that." Casey turned her mouth corners down, lowered her eyes sheepishly. "Like I said, I'm just feelin' owly. I reckon you're caught up in this as bad as I am. Why don't you head on back to your ranch? I'll get the money over the mountains to the marshal. No point in us both going."

Lonnie thought about his mother. He felt a hard push to get back to her, to see if Dupree had hurt her, but he couldn't leave Casey. Not with killers on her trail.

"Nah, you got a bum ankle," Lonnie said. "You'll need help gettin' the money over mountains."

"Kid?"

Lonnie looked at her.

She gazed at him for a few seconds, then placed a gloved fist on a hip as she said, "I'm older than you by a significant degree. And I am not currently in the market for a sweetheart. Especially a kid from the country. You have no chance with me. None. So why don't you stop showing off and go home to your mother and let me get the money over the mountains to the marshal?"

She punctuated that with an arched brow.

CHAPTER 30

Lonnie's cheeks and ears turned so hot that for a second he thought they'd burst into flame. Showing *off?*

Embarrassment mixed with rage, and he had to suck a hot breath down before saying in as deep and calm a voice as he could muster, "I do declare you got a mighty high opinion of yourself, Miss Stoveville. Rocked me back on my heels to see your true colors so sudden-like. Now, I'd be right happy to let you take that money over the mountains to the marshal, but truth be told, I don't think you're up to it. And since my reputation's sort of tied up with them saddlebags you got on the chestnut's back, I'll be showin' off for you for the next few days, I reckon."

Lonnie drew another deep, calming breath and started walking toward the General but stopped and turned back to her. "Less'n you'd like to go on back to town and let me ride on alone, that is. I could make better time if I didn't have you taggin' along with your clubfoot."

Casey drew her own deep breath and lifted her chin, looking down her nose at him. "Yes, well, since I'm the town marshal now and you are merely my deputy, I'll be leading up this expedition, *Deputy* Gentry. Now, if you wouldn't mind, I and my *clubfoot* will be needing assistance in getting mounted."

"Yeah, I figured that," Lonnie said, and helped her into her saddle.

In a way, he was grateful for her high-hatted tone. As he'd helped her into her saddle, he hadn't felt nearly as self-conscious. He felt as cool and calm as a big, twelve-point mule deer buck in a herd of does and fawns. Because now that he'd seen who Casey Stoveville really was, he realized he'd been a fool to have set so much store by the girl!

No, he didn't like Casey Stoveville one damn bit and she'd better be able to keep up to him or he was going to leave her behind, eating the General's dust!

He was thinking all that while he tightened the stallion's saddle cinch, shoved the bit back into the General's teeth, mounted up, and continued riding east toward the black mountains rising before him, blotting out the stars.

They were pretty high in the mountains by the time the sun rose. It was cool up here. Lonnie could see patches of frost, like tufts of gray fur some wolf had shed, lying here and there about the floor of the forest they were riding through. The frost glittered like diamonds, turning clear around the edges when buttery shafts of sunlight found it.

Lonnie and Casey were climbing ever higher toward Storm Peak Pass, which was about the only way over the range to Camp Collins. At least, it was the only route that Lonnie knew. He'd been over the pass only once, when he'd accompanied one of his mother's hired men last year to push a small herd of two-year-old cattle over to sell to a buyer in Camp Collins, where they could put the cows on the railroad for shipment to Chicago.

The Storm Peak Pass trail was an old Indian hunting and warring trail. More recently, white fur trappers and prospectors had used it. Freighting outfits still used it shipping gold and silver from west to east over the divide. The pass route was shorter than swinging north or south around the Never Summers, over flatter terrain around the vast, outer bulwarks of the mountains, and then cutting east through narrow valleys.

Such a trip would add a good week's worth of travel. The Storm Peak Pass route was harder but generally shorter, if you didn't get bogged down by snow in the fall or struck by lightning in the summer.

After October first of every year, snow made the trail impassable until July of the next year.

Another, often worse hazard were outlaws. The remote, high, rugged terrain around the pass was known to hide many a wanted man. Men like Shannon Dupree and "the boys," though Dupree had likely cut around the range's southern end of his run from Golden, which lay over near Denver.

Outlaws were something Lonnie didn't want to think about. He'd had his fill of outlaws. He also preferred not to think about the area being called home to some of the largest, meanest grizzly bears anywhere in northern Colorado . . .

No, best not to think about outlaws and grizzlies. Best just to think about putting as much ground behind him as he could.

When the sun was about at its nine o'clock spot in the sky, Lonnie reined the General up at a creek that snaked through a clearing

195

surrounded by the low humps of pine-carpeted ridges.

He swung down from the stallion's back and fixed the General's rigging like before so he could freely drink from the slow-running stream. Lonnie didn't look at Casey until after she'd done the same, letting the chestnut walk into the stream to get her fill.

Lonnie hadn't looked at the girl because, one, he was mad at her for talking down to him. Two, he felt guilty for being mad at her. She'd just recently lost her pa, after all, and she was probably more alone in the world than Lonnie was. At least, he had his ma. He'd heard that Casey's ma had died when Casey had been a little girl.

She couldn't be expected to follow every word of the politeness book, he reckoned.

Now when he looked at her, he saw that she was shivering and pale. Her long, canvas coat must not be enough to keep the mountain cold out, and her ankle was likely grieving her. Lonnie also realized that Casey had tied no bedroll onto her horse, behind the saddle. She only had the money-filled saddlebags riding there. She hadn't expected to be out all night, much less heading over Storm Peak Pass to deliver the money to the marshal in Camp Collins.

Dupree's spying her and Lonnie outside the jailhouse had changed all that. Now they had nowhere to go but Camp Collins. There was no turning back.

Lonnie untied his bedroll — two wool blankets stitched together along one side to form a sack of sorts — and took it over to where Casey sat in the grass beside the stream, gently removing one of her riding boots.

"Here," Lonnie said, holding out the blanket.

"What's that for?"

"You're cold. Should have said something." She'd likely been shivering all night.

She was miffed at him, just as he was miffed at her. He could see it in her eyes. That rankled him, and he was disappointed that he could be affected again by how she felt about him.

She took the blanket and draped it over her shoulders. "Thanks, kid."

Lonnie ground his jaws at "kid."

"Don't mention it, Miss Stoveville."

He wheeled and walked away from her, not liking her again.

CHAPTER 31

Lonnie knew it was best not to worry too much about Casey Stoveville.

He was stuck with this uppity town girl, so he might as well get used to the idea. No use worrying what she thought about him, because he knew that already. He'd likely be stuck with her for the next two days, because that's how long it usually took to get over the pass. It might take him and her longer, because they might be wise to at least partly avoid the main trail and sort of skirt the sides of it.

Of course, they could head for Golden, but that was a longer ride. Lonnie wanted to get the money to the US marshal as soon as possible.

Dupree would likely look for them on the main trail, which Lonnie was hoping they'd run into soon. He wasn't sure, but he figured that he and Casey were somewhere south of it. They should be able to see it snaking over the higher ridges soon. Once on the trail for a time, they might run into a freight outfit they could buy some food from.

Food . . .

Lonnie hadn't eaten since before he'd ridden into Arapaho Creek. He realized he felt as hollow as an old stump. His belly growled at the thought of a big steak and fried potatoes smothered in steak gravy. He had trail grub in his saddlebags and cavvy sack. Soon, he and Casey would have to stop and think about getting some of that food in their bellies. This was a tough ride, and you needed a bellyful to make it.

As he looked in the direction from which they'd come, the direction from which Dupree would likely be showing himself soon, he knew he couldn't take the time to eat yet.

Steeling himself against his anger at the girl he was riding with, he moved back to the horses and led the General out of the stream. As he did, he saw Casey sitting on the bank, bathing her bare foot in the water. At the sight of her bare flesh, he turned away. A boy didn't look at a girl's ankles. Doctoring her was one thing, ogling her was another.

He glanced at her foot once more quickly,

then he reached under the General's belly to tighten his saddle cinch.

"How's it look?" he asked the girl.

"I don't think it's broken."

"If it was broke, you'd know it. Probably pulled the tendons in there."

"Thanks, Doctor," she said, pulling her sock back on.

Lonnie ground his jaws at that. She'd lost her father. Girls could be cranky for no reason, and here she had a reason and he was blaming her for it.

Still, he felt miffed at her again when he had more important things to worry about. It was just that she seemed to keep taking potshots at his pride, which he'd never realized was so tender.

Because he wanted them to get moving as soon as possible, he walked out into the creek and fetched her chestnut back onto the bank. He slipped the filly's bit back into her mouth, adjusted the bridle straps to sit evenly over her ears and then tightened the cinch beneath her belly.

"Here ya go," Lonnie said. "Miss Abigail's ready for ya."

As he turned around to face Casey, she limped up to him, wrapped her arms around his neck, drew him against her warm, supple body, and planted a semi-wet kiss on his cheek.

"Thanks," she said, sort of crossing her eyes as she smiled at him, pulling that full upper lip back slightly. Her hazel eyes and her blonde hair glistened in the high-country sunlight.

She draped the blankets he'd given her over his own shoulder.

Lonnie's heart turned a backward flip in his chest.

His ears rang.

The boy had no words with which to respond to the girl's inexplicable behavior. He stood there, lower jaw hanging to his chest, while she used a rock humping out of the creek bank to get seated on the chestnut's back.

She rode out away from the creek and called behind her, "Let's make camp soon, huh? If it's safe? I don't know about you but I'm hungry."

A cabin sat in another clearing ringed with fir-covered slopes.

It was an old, gray log affair with a shake-shingled roof missing shingles the way an old man misses teeth. The shingles that remained were as gray as the hovel's weathered logs, and they were blue-green with moss. A dented tin chimney pipe angled up out of the roof, and a rusty coffee can had been turned upside down over the end of the pipe to prevent birds from nesting inside.

The windows were shuttered. A deep, packed-dirt depression lay in the ground before the front door. Rain and snow must have collected in the depression and rotted away part of the doorsill. A backless chair sat left of the door, a rock propping up one of the front legs to level the chair on the uneven ground.

A doorless privy flanked the cabin, and to the cabin's right squatted a small log stable whose roof had collapsed. Only a few rails remained of the peeled pine log corral that surrounded the stable on three sides.

"Looks abandoned," Casey said, sitting her chestnut beside Lonnie as they inspected what appeared to be an old miner's headquarters.

Lonnie said, "Let's see if it has a stove. If so, I'll try to snare us a rabbit. Nothin' like fresh meat to fuel a long ride."

She glanced at Lonnie who kept his eyes roaming around the dilapidated buildings. "Sounds good to me. I'm so hungry my stomach thinks my throat's been cut."

Lonnie jerked a surprised look at her.

"You heard me." She smiled brashly. "I know that wasn't ladylike, but out here, who's to wash my mouth out with soap?" She pulled his hat brim down, teasing him. *"You?"*

"Nah, you can talk however you want around me, Miss Casey. I ain't no saint — that's for sure." Lonnie poked his hat back up on his forehead, and swung nimbly down from the General's back. "But I don't reckon we'd best stop here for long. You can dismount and lead your chestnut around, though. If your ankle doesn't hurt too bad, I mean. Make as many tracks as you can."

He dropped the General's reins and walked up to the cabin's front door.

Behind him, Casey frowned. "Why?"

"Just do as I say, Miss Casey. I'll tell you later."

"Hey, I don't take orders from you, kid," Casey said, and eased down from her saddle, keeping her cool gaze on him. She was miffed again. "Remember, I'm the marshal. And just because we're on the trail together, and I gave you that kiss, don't go thinking we're married!"

CHAPTER 32

The girl's fickle moods were too much of a puzzle for Lonnie. He kept his mind on what lay before him, which at the moment was the cabin door.

He tripped the steel and leather latch, which clicked. The door slackened in its frame. The leather hinges squawked. When Lonnie pushed the door open a foot, the door sagged to the cabin floor, which was nothing more than hard-packed dirt. He sidled through the opening and walked on into the cabin, which was about one quarter the size of the cabin in which he and his mother lived at the Circle G.

There was little inside the place except an old table, another backless chair, and a small sheet-iron stove in the cabin's far right corner. A wood box sat beside the stove. It had a few chunks of rotted wood and a squirrel's nest inside it.

There were a few shelves on the wall opposite where the table sat. Three airtight tins sat on the shelf. Inspecting their badly faded and water-stained labels, Lonnie saw that one held tomatoes, one held pinto beans, and the third one held sweetened apricot slices.

Lonnie's stomach growled. He salivated just thinking about chewing up a sweetened apricot . . .

He looked around once more. Obviously, judging by the lack of anything but rotted wood and the squirrel's nest in the wood box and the several layers of undisturbed dust on the table, no one had visited this place in at least a year, maybe more. Lonnie had a feeling the place had long ago been a miner's cabin. It might now serve as a line shack for an area rancher — so infrequently that Lonnie didn't think that he should feel overly guilty about confiscating the three tin cans of food.

He and Casey needed the food more than the squirrels did, and they didn't have time to cook anything.

He took all three cans down off the shelf, went out, and closed the rickety door behind him. Casey was limping around, leading the filly. She stopped and turned to Lonnie, frowning.

"What do you have there?"

Lonnie grinned. "I got pinto beans, tomatoes, and apricots!"

"Hooray!"

"Hold on, hold on!" Lonnie hurried over to where General Sherman stood ground-tied, and dropped the cans into his saddlebags.

Casey gaped at him. "Kid, you got a mean streak — you know that?"

"We can't stay here," Lonnie said, glancing back in the direction from which they'd come. "We don't know how far away Dupree is, but we have to assume he's a better tracker than I think he is and that he's only a mile or so behind us. I know he won't stop lookin' for us until he gets the loot back."

"He couldn't have tracked us in the dark."

"No, but he's had plenty of time to make up for the time he lost before daylight."

"So what're we stoppin' here for?"

"I'm thinkin' that if he's still on our trail, it'll lead him here. Now, maybe we can confuse him a little, maybe lose him for good."

"How?"

Lonnie walked over and helped her back up onto the chestnut's back. "Just follow me."

"You're enjoying playing mountain man, aren't you, kid?" she asked, glowering at him from her saddle.

Lonnie didn't let her see him blushing as he swung up onto General Sherman's back. Yeah, he was showing off. But he figured he had a good reason. If Dupree caught up to them, they were dead.

"Come on, Miss Casey," he said, booting the General northward out of the yard. "Let's make some tracks!"

The General lunged into a lope.

"Hey, wait for me, goll darnit!" Casey yelled behind him. "Don't make me regret giving you that peck on the cheek back there, Lonnie Gentry!"

Lonnie felt his lips spread a grin.

That was the first time she'd used his proper name.

CHAPTER 33

Lonnie led Casey on probably what seemed a wild-goose chase to the girl.

Without following any trail, and with no seeming rhyme or reason, Lonnie galloped the General to the edge of the clearing in which the abandoned cabin sat. He slowed the horse as they entered the forest and descended a gentle hill. About halfway down the hill, Lonnie turned General Sherman onto a deer trail that ran perpendicular to the slope before dropping gradually toward the hill's bottom.

Lonnie glanced behind to see Casey following on her chestnut filly, the girl scowling after him, her hair blowing out behind her in the wind or bouncing across her shoulders. The brim of her man's hat rippled, and the chin thong danced against her chest. Just as Lonnie had to do, she occasionally ducked under low pine boughs.

At the bottom of the slope ran a stream.

Lonnie crossed the stream and put the General up through the forest on the other side.

At the bottom of the next hill lay another stream. Lonnie glanced back once more to make sure Casey was keeping up with him. The girl was handling her horse in such rugged terrain well for a gal who spent most of her time clerking in a mercantile. But her suntanned cheeks and hands attested to her likely riding the chestnut any chance she got — maybe after work or on weekends.

Lonnie enjoyed showing off his own riding ability, but he was also glad she was able to keep up with him. If she hadn't been able to ride handily, Dupree was sure to catch up to them sooner or later.

"Where in tarnation, Lonnie Gentry, are we going?" Casey demanded behind him, as Lonnie put the General into the stream.

Instead of crossing to the other side, Lonnie rode the General right down the center of the stream, going against the current. Water splashed up over his stirrups, soaking his boots. He said nothing but kept riding. He'd explain later. Besides, he was enjoying keeping her in suspense though he knew it was a devilish thing to do. The uppity town girl deserved it.

When they'd followed the creek around several bends, Lonnie put the General up the north bank. He stopped the horse to let Casey catch up, and when she'd mounted the bank to stop the chestnut beside him, she said, "You're loco!"

"You're keepin' up right well."

"Is this a test or somethin'?"

"Yeah, somethin' like that," he said, enjoying himself. She doubted she'd be looking down her nose at him for much longer.

Lonnie chuckled and reined the General sharply away from her, but as the General lunged up another, fir-stippled slope, a pine bough swept toward him in a dark-brown, lime-green blur. The boy snapped his eyes wide in surprise and started to duck — too late.

The bough caught him across his upper chest and shoulders. He had sense enough to kick free of his stirrups so he wouldn't snap both his ankles, and then, as the horse continued trotting forward under the branch, Lonnie fell back hard and turned a backward somersault over the General's burr-prickly tail.

Lonnie hit the ground with a thump and a loud "Ghahhh!" as the air was pounded out of his lungs.

He'd landed on his back, and now he lay spread-eagle on the ground, staring up through the forest canopy at bits of blue sky and fringes of white clouds beyond the arrow-straight tops of the evergreens.

A church bell was ringing loudly from nearby, and little white birds were fluttering around in front of Lonnie's face, obscuring his vision. Only, after a moment he realized the birds were actually *inside* his head. The church bells were in the same region. He lifted his head, hearing himself grunt raspily, loudly as he tried to suck a breath back into his lungs that were having none of it.

He lay his head down and arched his back, trying again to draw a breath. As he did, Casey entered his field of vision, her pretty face staring down at him from between him and the pine tops and the small scallops of blue sky beyond her. She turned her mouth corners down and shook her head, crossing her arms on her chest and cocking one hip.

"A fool and his horse are soon parted," she said. "My father told me that when he was first teachin' me to ride."

"Wise . . . wise man," Lonnie croaked out. He tried to push himself up, but Casey set a boot on his chest and pressed him back down to the ground.

"Just lay there a minute. You got the wind knocked out of you. If you've broken anything, I'm leaving you here. You best know that, Lonnie Gentry. The bobcats can have you."

When Lonnie was finally able to draw a full breath and the tolling of the bells in his ears had died somewhat, he said, "How come you seem so fond of my name all of a sudden?"

"I don't know. It's a nice name, I reckon." Then she cracked a grin, and she laughed. "Better than you deserve, you foolish child!"

"That's more like it," Lonnie said, his ears ringing again but this time with embarrassment.

She helped him to his feet. He couldn't look at her.

"Are you all right?" she asked, kind of snootily, he thought.

He turned away from her and then stooped to scoop his hat off the ground. He muttered something under his breath though even he wasn't sure what it was.

"Are you sure you didn't break anything?" Casey asked him.

Lonnie swatted his hat against his thigh, ridding it of dirt and pine needles and little round bits of squirrel scat. His back and shoulders and the back of his head ached like holy blazes, but he didn't think anything was broken. If anything *was* broken, he figured he deserved it.

In fact, he deserved to be put down like a rabid dog for acting like such a copper-riveted fool.

He wished the ground would open up and swallow him.

"I'm all right," he grouched. "I . . . just didn't see that dang pine branch, that's all. What the heck's it hangin' so low for?"

Hearing Casey give a snort behind him, he set his hat on his head and stumbled stiffly up to where the General stood about thirty yards beyond, head lowered and eyeing his fallen rider skeptically.

"Oh, hobble your lip, General," Lonnie said, grabbing the buckskin's reins. He groaned as he heaved his aching body back up into the saddle. "Come on," he told Casey, whose amused gaze he could still feel on his back, making the back of his neck burn. "No time to dally, girl!"

He touched spurs to the General's flanks.

But he proceeded a little more slowly and carefully this time.

CHAPTER 34

Lonnie stopped the General along a deer trail running along the shoulder of a grassy mountaintop clearing, at the edge of fringe of mixed pines and aspens. He eased carefully out of the saddle, for his head ached from the braining he'd taken earlier.

Not to mention that his back and shoulders felt as though he'd been beaten with a shovel.

As Casey reined up her chestnut behind the General, Lonnie dug into his saddlebags for his spyglass, which resided in a small, deer-hide sack with a rawhide thong stitched around its mouth. Looping the thong around his neck, the boy climbed the steep slope, his boots sliding on the short, slick grass and crusted layer of dirt and pebbles. Several times he had to lean forward and push off the ground with his hands.

Near the top of the hill, he got down and

214

crawled until he could see over the top of the ridge and over another, lower, pine-carpeted ridge beyond. Beyond that ridge lay a valley with a clearing, a willow-lined creek curving around the clearing's left end.

Lonnie got out his spyglass, telescoped it, and turned the wooden ring around the brass casing, bringing the clearing below into focus. He heard Casey climbing the slope behind him, breathing hard. When he turned toward her, she got down and started crawling until she lay belly-down beside him.

"Where are we?" she asked. The breeze brushed against them, scudding cloud shadows over the top of the otherwise sun-splashed hill before them.

"Guess?" Lonnie said.

"You don't know, do you? With all that runnin' around, you got us lost! Do you know where the trail to the pass is?"

"Sure do." Lonnie was trying to get some of his pride back, which he'd lost in his tumble from the General's saddle. At least, he was trying to sound confident again, though he was beginning to learn that prideful confidence could be a dangerous thing.

Just as showing off for a girl could get you killed faster than Dupree could do it.

"Well," Casey said skeptically. "Where is it?"

Lonnie rolled over onto his back and sat up on his butt, bending his knees slightly out to both sides. He rolled his neck, trying to loosen some of the kinks, and poked his hat back off his forehead.

"See that big, dark mountain humping up there, higher than the two to either side of it? It's got some snow on the left side of the peak."

"Yeah, I see it."

"That's Storm Peak Pass. The trail to the pass is beyond that lower ridge there. We'll get to it sometime tomorrow, I think."

"Are you *sure* you know where we are?"

Lonnie kept his face plain as he held out the spyglass to her. "Have a look for yourself."

"At what?"

"The clearing down there beyond the ridge in front of us."

Casey narrowed a skeptical eye at the boy. She took the spyglass and lay belly-down again, propped on her elbows, and lifted the glass to her right eye. She twisted the canister to bring the clearing into focus.

"There's a cabin down there."

"Right. The abandoned one. See the stable beside it, the privy behind it?"

Casey lowered the glass and turned to him in disgust. "You mean we've been riding in *circles*?"

"One big circle."

Casey gave a slow blink. "Why have we been riding in one big circle, Lonnie? It's the pass we should be headed for. Remember, we're trying to get that money to the deputy marshal in Camp Collins."

Lonnie took the spyglass back from her and leaned on his elbows again, raising the glass to his eyes to examine the clearing in which the cabin hunched. "First, I wanna see if Dupree is on our trail. If he is, he should be heading for the cabin soon. He should also pick up our tracks there and head into the trees east of it, the way we went. Then he'll likely swing south."

"And then what?"

"He'll lose our trail."

"Why?"

"Because I fixed it so he would."

Lonnie lowered the spyglass. "He'll lose our tracks in the creek we followed upstream. The current has likely washed the hoofprints away by now. It would take a darn good tracker — probably no one but a good *Injun* tracker — to pick them up again where we left the water. Not the way we went. I picked the hardest ground for leavin' a print. Even if he picked up our trail where we left that first creek, it ain't likely he'll pick it up where we left the second creek . . . over them rocks. No one except maybe an Injun can track a horse over rocks."

"Okay," Casey said, nodding slowly, thoughtfully, "that was pretty smart."

Lonnie grinned as he continued appraising the clearing through the spyglass.

"I said 'pretty smart,' " Casey said. "Maybe you forgot one thing."

"What's that?"

"He likely knows where we're headed. Most folks around know about the marshal stationed in Camp Collins."

"He's figured out where we're headed, all right," Lonnie said. "Dupree's dumb and mean, but he ain't *that* stupid. But I figure as long as he ain't dodgin' our every step, he'll keep wonderin' if he's figured us right, and he won't catch up to us. Especially if we don't stick to the pass trail long but skirt the edges of it where we have to."

"How long we gonna wait for 'em?"

Lonnie shrugged. "If they're not to the cabin in an hour, I'd say they're far enough behind us we won't have to worry about 'em. They'll never catch up to us before we make Camp Collins."

"And if they reach the cabin inside of an

hour?" Casey asked.

"Then we'd best pull our picket pins, and ride. I still don't think they'll catch up to us, because they'll lose our trail, but there's no point in taking any chances."

Lonnie returned the spyglass to its pouch and rose to his knees. "Any way you figure it, we'll get to Camp Collins ahead of Dupree, and deliver the money to the marshal before them cutthroats can get their hands on it."

He removed the spyglass pouch from around his neck and gave it to Casey. "Keep an eye on the clearing. I'll be right back."

"You're orderin' me around again like we were married or something!"

"Don't get your hopes up." Lonnie rose and began walking back down the slope toward the horses. "Town girls are too snooty for this cowboy." He winked and pinched his hat brim to her.

Casey snorted.

"Where you goin'?" she called after him.

"I don't know about you, but I'm hungry."

Lonnie returned to the hill clutching the three airtight tins to his chest. Casey, who'd been watching the clearing for Dupree, lowered the spyglass and grinned. "You might just do yet, kid."

"See anything over there?" Lonnie asked as he sat down beside Casey and pulled his folding Barlow knife out of his jeans pocket. Just as he rarely strayed very far from his horse, he never went anywhere without his knife.

"Nothing."

Lonnie indicated the cans spread out between him and Casey. "Which do you want first?"

"All of 'em!"

Lonnie chuckled. "Boy, you're hungrier'n a blue-ribbon bull! I better stay back a ways so you don't eat my arm off!"

He set the point of his knife against the top of one of the tins, and punched the end of the knife with the heel of his hand. The blade ground through the lid, and Lonnie sawed it along the edge of the top of the can until he was able to pry up the lid, leaving only a small portion of it attached.

He held up the bean can to Casey. "Girls first. I didn't bring up my spoon, so I hope you're not squeamish."

"Not when I'm this hungry."

Casey scooped out a handful of beans, shoved them in a most unladylike fashion into her mouth, and chewed. Lonnie did the same and passed the can back to Casey. In a little over a minute they'd emptied the can of every last bean, and the bean juice was running down the corners of their mouths.

They shared a look and laughed at each other.

Lonnie set the point of his knife against the top of the tomato tin. "How 'bout we save the apricots for dessert?"

"Well, ain't you civilized?"

Lonnie punched the blade into the tomato can and then he and Casey were shoving the juicy, red, delicious tomatoes into their mouths like little kids going to work on a frosting bowl. They devoured the tomatoes inside of another minute, and Lonnie opened the apricot tin.

The apricots were sweet, the sugary syrup sliding down Lonnie's throat like an elixir. Suddenly, his aches and pains didn't ache half as much as they had only moments before.

He and Casey had eaten half the sugary fruit slices before Casey said, "Uh-oh."

She was staring over the next ridge and into the clearing to the west.

CHAPTER 35

Spying movement over the next ridge, Lonnie pressed the spyglass to his right eye and adjusted the focus. In the single sphere of magnified vision, he watched three horseback riders trot their horses from left to right, heading for the cabin.

He continued to adjust the glass's focus until he could more clearly see that the lead rider was Shannon Dupree, by the blond hair hanging down beneath the brim of the lead cutthroat's brown Stetson, and by the blond, brushy mustache residing above his mouth.

Dupree rode standing up in his stirrups and staring toward the cabin. The hard set of his shoulders told Lonnie the man was wary, cautious. Dupree cast several quick glances at the ground beside his horse, obviously following Lonnie and Casey's tracks, which they'd made about two hours earlier.

The blond outlaw rode with his right hand

on the butt of his Colt revolver positioned for the cross draw on his left hip.

Behind Dupree rode Fuego with Childress bringing up the rear. Both men held rifles across their saddlebows.

Lonnie's heart thudded as he watched the three stop their horses in front of the cabin, Fuego swinging his head from left to right as he inspected the ground where Casey had led the chestnut, trying to confuse the sign a little, make it look as though Lonnie and Casey had spent more time there than they actually had and were not very far ahead of their stalkers.

Anything they could do to confuse the outlaws was in their best interest, Lonnie thought.

"Let me see," Casey said, holding out her hand for the glass.

Lonnie gave it to her. She trained it on the clearing, then lowered it, and looked at Lonnie. Her eyes were wide, her face a little pale.

"Well, now we know," she said. "They're on our trail."

"I didn't doubt it much. At least we know for sure. Let's finish these apricots."

Lonnie pinched out one of the dark-yellow chunks of fruit, and dropped it into his mouth.

"You go ahead," Casey said, lifting the spyglass once more. "I'm not so hungry anymore."

Lonnie said, "Yeah, me, neither."

Not wanting to waste the food, Lonnie ate the last two apricots and gathered up the cans. The mountains didn't need his trash.

He and Casey rose carefully. There was no way they could be seen up here without Dupree training a spyglass or pair of binoculars on them, but Lonnie felt a cold rush of fear return to his veins. He sensed the same thing in Casey as they slipped and slid back down the hill to their horses.

Lonnie dropped the empty tins into his cavvy sack, tightened and rearranged the General's rigging, and swung up into the saddle. He looked at Casey as she did the same, limping only slightly now on her ankle.

"Don't worry, Casey," he said. "They won't be able to track us. I made sure of that."

"Maybe not, kid, but they're still behind us, and that makes me not to want to waste a whole lot of time if you get my drift . . ." She looked around at the maze of pines and mountains rising around them. "My gosh — awfully big country out here. I think I just realized that." She looked at Lonnie.

"I'm startin' to feel a little queasy. Which way?"

"The pass trail's northeast, so I reckon we'll head northeast," Lonnie said, reining the General to the left and into a stand of pines covering the downslope of the mountain shoulder they were on.

They rode down the mountain to the bottom and then climbed the mountain beyond it. This mountain was higher but the climb was more gradual, and they crossed a creek and a clearing to a windy, treeless knob. Here they rested the horses as well as themselves, and Lonnie couldn't resist casting another look through his spyglass along their back trail.

He wasn't surprised to see no sign of Dupree. Even if Dupree was able to find the tracks Lonnie had tried so hard to hide from the outlaws, the outlaws would still be a long ways behind their quarry.

The fact that Dupree was still after him, however, caused Lonnie's chest to tighten and his breath to grow shallow. Just knowing a man who wanted him dead was following him, maybe only a mile away as the crow flies, with Lonnie's blood on his mind . . .

He and Casey continued riding, crossing one more steep, windy ridge and dropping down the other side as the giant, golden ball of the sun tumbled behind western ridges. They set up camp along another creek that wended along the bottom of the narrow valley that formed a trough between pine-studded ridges.

Lonnie used the twine he kept in his saddlebags along with a hook he'd fashioned from a baling needle that he kept in a sewing kit, also stowed in his saddlebags, to rig a fishing line. He'd attached a small red button to the hook, to attract trout whenever he was out on the range and felt like a meal of fresh fish.

He found some grubs under a rotten log, and impaled a couple of these on the end of the hook and dropped the hook into the creek that was about two feet deep and so clear it didn't even return his reflection but magnified the small rocks forming a bed on the sandy bottom. He tossed the baited hook out several times, and watched it ride along the current before dragging it back and tossing it out again, hoping a fish happened by and saw the flash of the red button.

Meanwhile, Lonnie could smell the smoke from the fire that Casey was building from the wood that Lonnie had scrounged while the girl had bathed her tender ankle in the cool stream water. He glanced back to see Casey on her knees, fanning the growing flames. Blue smoke rose and glinted in the last, orange light angling into the canyon from the west.

His and the girl's gear was piled around the camp. Fortunately, since he'd figured on spending some time at the line shack on Eagle Ridge, Lonnie had packed his camping gear. His fry pan and coffeepot would come in handy for preparing a tasty, fortifying meal for him and Casey.

If any fish took his bait, that was . . .

While he tossed the bait and retrieved it, he glanced back several times at Casey tending the fire. Her long, wavy blonde hair glowed like sunlit honey in the last light. She'd tucked it out of the way behind her ears. She had a line of ash across her right, lightly tanned cheek. Somehow, that line of ash accentuated how pretty she was. And while Lonnie didn't like her sometimes when she seemed to have a secret that she was holding over him, the girl made his heart ache a little almost all of the time.

He couldn't deny the fact that he was taken with her. She was the only thing that made this current trouble tolerable — the fact that she was in it with him, and they were riding together, supporting each other.

Almost like they were married or something . . .

That thought made him wince with embarrassment, and he tried to turn his mind back to his fishing, but not two minutes later he found himself casting another look back over his shoulder toward the camp.

Casey was sitting on a rock on the other side of the fire from Lonnie, facing him. She was leaning forward, elbows on her knees, and she was looking toward him. Immediately, she jerked her head back to the fire and began prodding the flames with the long, forked stick in her hand.

Lonnie turned quickly back to the stream, his heart thudding.

Could she be thinking the same sort of things that he was thinking? That it might be kind of nice to stay together even after all this trouble was over . . . ?

Then he cursed under his breath. He was only thirteen. She was fifteen. At their ages, two years were as long as a whole century. Besides, she'd made it clear she wasn't interested in a country boy.

His heart ached harder. It was a dull ache, like two of his ribs were pushing against his ticker from opposite sides.

The fishing line tightened in Lonnie's fingers. It jerked slightly, suddenly. Lonnie jerked back on the line and then it fell slack against the water.

The fish had gotten away. But only a minute or so later a second one did not. The ten-inch red-throated trout was flopping around on the grassy bank when Lonnie caught another, much smaller trout which he threw back to let grow another year, replacing it with another one about ten minutes later that was almost a foot long.

He dressed out the fish with his Barlow knife, tossing the guts into the stream, and carried his two trophies on a single stick proudly back to the camp. Casey was tending the coffeepot, which had come to a boil on the hot coals, and when she saw the fish she arched her brows, impressed.

"Never figured you for a fisherman, Lonnie."

"A fella gets tired of beef now an' then," was all he said, and pulled his frying pan out of his cavvy sack.

He'd set both fish, still cold from the creek, into the pan, which he'd greased with lard, when General Sherman gave a testy whicker and turned to look behind him. The chestnut shook her head and stomped.

Casey gasped as she looked toward the horses.

Lonnie grabbed his rifle from where it leaned against a log, and pumped a cartridge into the chamber.

CHAPTER 36

"What are they acting so skittish about?" Casey asked, standing tensely by the fire and staring toward the horses.

Lonnie held his Winchester up high across his chest and licked his lips as he stared past the horses tied to a single rope strung between two pines. "Heard somethin'. I'm gonna check it out. You stay here."

"You think it's Dupree?"

"I reckon I'll know soon enough."

Lonnie walked out around the horses, running a hand along the General's side as he did. He walked through the forest, pine needles and bits of cones crunching softly beneath his boots. The forest floor was soft, almost like walking on a rug.

It was also eerily quiet now at twilight.

A couple of small birds flitted here and there amongst the branches. Farther off, a squirrel chittered.

Suddenly, that silence was broken by a

long, mewling, bugling sound. It sounded like someone blowing a massive bullhorn. The cry rolled up sharply and ended in a high-pitched wail that echoed. The echoes died above the top of a stony ridge looming on the valley's far side, maybe a hundred yards away.

Lonnie stared at the ridge. The short hairs pricked along the back of his neck at the eerie sound. Then relief somewhat eased the tension between his shoulders. The bugling had likely been made by an elk. Possibly a bear, which wouldn't have been good — especially if it were a *grizzly bear* —but most likely an elk. Lonnie had heard the calls before though they usually came much later in the year, when elk bugled to define their territory and to call in mates.

But sometimes, like humans, animals got confused.

The cry came again, not as loud this time. Whatever the beast was — Lonnie was almost certain it was an elk, which posed no threat to him and Casey — it seemed to be on the other side of the dark-brown sandstone ridge that he could see through the pines and up a slight rise. And, judging by the diminishing sound, the beast seemed to be moving away from the ridge.

Behind Lonnie, the General gave another

low whicker.

Lonnie turned. The General was looking back past Lonnie, twitching his ears and switching his tail. The chestnut stared ahead, seemingly no longer bothered.

"It's all right, General," Lonnie said as he walked past the horse, patting the General's rump. "Just an elk who forgot what time of year it is."

Casey looked relieved. She still stood by the fire, the orange flames dancing and the smoke rising behind her. "You're sure it's not a bear? I've heard grizzlies calling from the ridges around Arapaho Creek." She shuddered and crossed her arms on her chest. "I sure wouldn't wanna come face-to-face with a big grizzly bear out here, Lonnie."

Lonnie leaned his rifle against the log. "I'm pretty sure it's an elk," he said. "Besides, it's in the next valley over. A big ridge between us and him."

"If you say so."

Lonnie glanced once more toward the ridge. He wished he could be absolutely certain that what he'd heard hadn't been a grizzly, but he wasn't. As he set to work looking for mushrooms to slice into the frying pan with his fish, however, he forgot about the bugling.

Night sank slowly into the valley, and soon there was only a little faint, emerald light in the sky beyond the pine tops. Coyotes called distantly, and the creek chuckled over its stony bed. The fish fried slowly in the lard with wild mushrooms he'd sliced, and two corn cakes he'd whipped together from his possibles, and the fire gave off a pleasant warmth as the air grew sharp with a mountain chill.

An almost intoxicating tranquility had descended with the darkness and the stars kindling in the sky straight above.

Lonnie and Casey sat on opposite sides of the fire, which they kept small in case Dupree was closer than Lonnie figured he was to this valley. Lonnie's mind grew slow and peaceful as he ate the tender, flakey fish and mushrooms and nicely browned cake, and washed the food down with frequent sips of the hot, black coffee.

"You catch right good fish, Mister Lonnie Gentry," Casey said as she gathered up their tin plates, wooden handled forks, and coffee cups, and carried them over to the creek for cleaning.

"Why, thank you, Miss Casey."

"Don't mention it," she said back over her shoulder.

While she was gone, Lonnie gathered

more fallen branches from the trees along the creek. He didn't want to make the fire too large, so that Dupree or anyone else skulking around the valley at night might see it. If he were alone, he'd probably let it die out altogether. But Casey probably wasn't as accustomed to sleeping out in the high-and-rocky as he was, and the mountains got cold this high. There might even be a little frost on the ground come morning.

For her, he'd try to keep the fire small. He should probably try to stay awake and keep watch for Dupree, but he was dead-dog tired. It was a weariness he could feel making his deepest bones and muscles ache. He'd probably never make it through the night without nodding off. If he did, he'd probably fall off his horse tomorrow along the trail somewhere, and break his neck.

When he returned to the fire with a second armload of wood, Casey was already curled up in Lonnie's bedroll, which he'd insisted she use. He'd even arranged pine boughs for her, to soften the cold, hard ground. His coat was good enough for Lonnie. She lay on her side, knees drawn up halfway to her belly. She'd left her boots on, and they poked out from beneath the blankets. Her blonde hair spilled prettily across her saddle. Already she appeared cold, for she'd drawn one of the two blankets halfway over her face that the fire's orange flames caressed lovingly.

Seeing her so peaceful made Lonnie even more tired. He quietly set a couple of small branches on the fire, then walked off to tend to nature. He came back, spread out some pine boughs for a makeshift mattress, in front of his saddle, on the side of the fire opposite Casey, and slacked down onto one of the fragrant branches. He scrunched himself deep inside his heavy wool mackinaw, whose collar he pulled up around his cheeks.

Lonnie lay staring up through the treetops at the stars for a time. Dupree was a constant worry nibbling at the edges of his mind. He was glad he wasn't alone. He'd spent many nights alone out on the Circle G range over the past couple of years, when his mother had deemed him old enough to do so. Some late afternoons he was too far away to bother riding all the way back to the cabin at night when he'd only have to saddle up and ride out as far again in the morning. Sometimes he'd sleep out alone in a canyon or at the old line shack.

The first couple of times he'd been a little frightened, lying awake and making mountains out of the molehills of every night sound he heard. The slightest rustle of some burrowing creature would become a stalking, red-eyed wolf in his mind. But he'd quickly gotten accustomed to sleeping out in the mountains alone, and had even come to enjoy it.

He didn't think he'd enjoy it tonight, however. Or maybe that's because three killers were stalking him, and maybe because he was enjoying Casey's company so much.

Thinking back, he realized she hadn't called him "kid" for several hours. Heck, a few minutes ago she'd even called him "Mister."

Lonnie smiled at the twinkling sky. He glanced across the fire at Casey. He could hear her breathing softly beneath her blankets. Lonnie's eyelids grew heavy. Weariness was like a fast-working drug. For a short time, he was vaguely aware of his own soft snores before sleep pulled him deep down into its gauzy depths, turning the world dark and empty, soothing in its silence.

He had no idea how much time had passed before that silence was shattered by Casey's ear-rattling scream.

Chapter 37

Lonnie sat bolt upright, heart thudding, as the girl's scream echoed around the dark encampment.

Only vaguely did he become aware that he had not built up the fire as he'd intended but had let it go out completely. His mind was slow to catch up to the scream, as well, and he realized, as the wail died, that Casey had screamed, *"Daddy!"*

Now, silence.

Lonnie stared across the fire, his eyes growing accustomed to the darkness relieved by starlight and a small snippet of moon angling up over the valley. Then he heard Casey sobbing. Getting oriented — at first, he'd thought he was at the line shack — he reached over to where he'd leaned his rifle against a tree, and fumbled around until he'd gotten a cartridge seated in the chamber.

He looked around, expecting to see three

shadows jouncing, trying to drag Casey out of her bedroll. He could hear little above the girl's scream still echoing around inside his head and the ratcheting thunder of his own hammering heart.

Distantly, he could hear her sobbing, and he quietly called her name.

There was no reply.

He jumped to his feet and tramped around the fire in his stocking feet, shivering fearfully and looking around in the shadows flanking her. She was sitting up, her face a pale oval framed by the messy spill of her honey-blonde hair.

"Casey, what is it?"

"Lonnie!"

He dropped to a knee, still looking around behind her. One of the horses whickered nervously, but he was sure the mount had only been frightened by Casey's scream. "Yeah, I'm here. What is it? Why'd you scream? Nightmare?"

Casey sobbed quietly. "Yeah." Her shoulders jerked as she crossed her arms on her chest and lowered her chin.

Her reply tempered the boy's own anxiety. His heart slowed, and his palms stopped sweating. He held the rifle's hammer back with his thumb, pulled the trigger, releasing the action, and eased the hammer down to the firing pin. Still holding the rifle in one hand, he placed his other hand on one of Casey's, and squeezed.

"About your pa?"

Keeping her head down, Casey nodded. She gave another sob and lifted one hand to wipe away a tear rolling down her cheek.

Her breath was ragged. "I dreamt he was calling me. I was inside our house and he was outside and calling and asking me to let him in, and I was running around the house. The house was dark and I was trying to find the door, but nothing in the house seemed to be where it should be, and it was like there was no door.

"Pa kept calling me, asking me to let him in, and I was trying to yell back at him that I was trying to let him in, but I couldn't get the words out. It was like there was a rag in my mouth. It was so frustrating! I couldn't call to him, and I was afraid that if he didn't know I was there, looking for the door, he'd go away and I'd never see him again!"

"It's all right, Casey."

She lowered her head again and said in a voice pinched with emotion: "That's when I woke up and heard myself screaming. Then I realized it was only a dream, and that Pa was gone. I'd never really heard him calling, and I'd never hear him calling me again."

Her head bobbed and her shoulders shook as she bawled for a short time.

"I'm never gonna see him again. He's gone forever, and I will live my whole life without ever seeing him again, and I want to so much that sometimes, aside from Dupree and the money, it's all I can think about!"

"Yeah, I know how that is."

She looked at him, frowning, her eyes wet with tears. "You do?"

"Sure."

"Oh," she said. "Your pa."

When Lonnie said nothing, Casey said, "It's an awful ache, isn't it?"

"Yeah, it hurts like hell. At least, I got my ma. You got somebody else who'll take care of you, Casey?"

Casey raised her knees to her chest, wrapped her arms around them. She sniffed, ran the back of her hand across her cheek again. "Pa said that if anything happened to him that I should find my aunt in Denver. Pa's sister. He said he thought she'd take me in, though I don't think he'd heard from her in a long time. Other than that — no, I don't have anyone."

Imagining how alone the girl must feel,

Lonnie felt a frightening hollowness inside him. He imagined what life would have been like without his ma and the ranch — a place to call home — and he had to suppress a shudder. He also had to force himself to not consider the possibility that he might be in the same boat that Casey was in.

"When we get this money to Camp Collins," Lonnie said, "you can come back to the ranch with me. We got an extra room. You can be part of our family — Ma's and mine."

That seemed to warm Casey somewhat. She gave him a lopsided smile. "Thanks, Lonnie. You're a good friend. I gotta keep my job in town, though — if I still have it when I get back, I mean. I have to work, so I can keep the house. If I lose the house . . . well, then I reckon I might have to consider takin' you up on your offer."

"You'll work it out so's you can keep your house. You're tough for a girl. Tough as most boys I've known."

"Thank you, Lonnie."

Suddenly, Lonnie's ears burned with shame. "Oh," he said, stammering. "I . . . I didn't mean no insult by that, Casey. I didn't mean you were like a boy. Just tough like one." His tongue felt as though it had doubled in size, and he was having trouble forming words with it. "But you're a girl. Anybody'd see that. I mean, not that I was lookin' or thinkin' about it or nothin', but —"

"Lonnie?"

He looked at her.

"Do me a favor? Fetch your bed and drag it over here by mine?"

Lonnie's heart hammered. Now his hands and feet also seemed to have doubled in size. "Miss Casey," Lonnie said, whispering so no one else could hear though he was relatively certain no one else was near. At least, he hoped they weren't. "Are you askin' me to . . . ?" The possibility seemed both wonderful and horrible.

Casey laughed. "Don't get your drawers in a twist, cowboy. I just wanna lay close to you tonight, that's all. Go on — fetch your stuff." She laughed. "Fetch, boy!"

Lonnie scrambled back around the fire. When he'd dragged his gear, including his rifle, over to Casey's side of the fire and had arranged his saddle beside hers, he lay down on the spruce branches, resting his head against the wool underside of the saddle. He lay for a time, aware of Casey lying curled beside him. He stared up at the stars splattered like baking powder across the firmament.

Finally, she scuttled up close to him, wrapped an arm around his belly, and lay her head on his chest. Lonnie stopped breathing. He wasn't sure what to do with his arms.

"Is this all right?" Casey asked softly. "I mean — it don't make you too uncomfortable, does it? I know how boys are."

"No, it's all right," Lonnie lied.

"You can put your arms around me," she said. "I'd like you to."

Awkwardly, Lonnie wrapped his arms around the girl's slender waist and shoulders. She lay warm against him. He could feel her heart beating softly against his chest.

She lifted her head, looked at him, frowning. "You aren't getting any devilish ideas, are you?"

"No!" he said, defensively.

"All right, then." Casey lay her head back down on his chest. "Good night, Lonnie. Thank you for taking the money to the marshal."

"Good night, Casey. It's no problem."

She chuckled at that, and then Lonnie did, too.

The longer he lay there, with his arms wrapped around this girl he loved, his nerves stopped sputtering, his heart stopped throbbing in his ears, and all seemed — at least, for now — right with this crazy world.

CHAPTER 38

Gradually, the sporadic chittering of a squirrel reached down into Lonnie's unconsciousness and pulled him up into the land of waking.

Before he'd even opened his eyes, he became aware that he was shivering. When he did open his eyes he saw that misty blue light had filled the valley, and fog hung over the creek like smoke. There was a thin, white patina of frost on his coat. He looked at the fire ring, humped with cold, gray ashes.

He'd been so tired that he hadn't awakened during the night to keep the fire built up, as he'd intended.

Casey was curled up tight against his back. Lonnie could feel the warmth of her face and lips pressed against his spine. She was the only warmth he could feel, but her frail body was shivering. She felt good and it was nice, being this close to her, despite the cold, and he hated to awaken her, but that's what happened when he tried to slip out from beneath her arm draped over his hip.

She groaned and removed her arm and pulled her blankets up over her head, curling into a tight ball on her side, shivering.

"I'll have the fire built up in a minute," Lonnie said, rising, shivering inside his coat.

When he'd gotten the fire going, orange flames crackling and sputtering and offering meager warmth, the gray pine smoke peppering his nose, he added a couple of good-sized logs, then took some twine from his saddlebags and went off to see about acquiring the coming night's supper. He didn't want to fire his rifle and possibly alert Dupree to his and Casey's whereabouts, so he'd either have to depend on angling for fish or using his slingshot or the snares he'd fashioned out of twine for bringing down small game, possibly even birds like doves or mountain grouse or wild turkeys.

All of these tools Lonnie carried in his saddlebags or cavvy sack everywhere he rode, because he never knew when he'd get stuck out somewhere away from the cabin and need the food-acquiring implements.

He'd seen some rabbits last night, when he and Casey had ridden up to the creek. Since rabbits usually liked to dine amongst rocks or shrubs that would shield them from the view of predators like coyotes, foxes, wolves, and hawks, Lonnie set his tree snare in the deep, green grass growing among the rocks lining the creek. He bent a springy cottonwood sapling over toward the ground, tied the long end of the snare to its crown, and pinned the snare and also the sapling to the ground with a sharp stick in which he'd cut a trigger notch, setting his trap.

It usually required several hours to gather game like this, and he should have set the trap last night, but he hadn't. So he had to hope that a rabbit, possibly even a fat squirrel, would wander into the snare between now and when he and Casey had swallowed down some breakfast and broken camp.

If not, he'd have to use his slingshot somewhere along today's trail. Lonnie had only the bare minimum of trail supplies in his gear, and he and Casey needed to eat steady meals to keep up their strength and stay alert. It took only one missed meal to cause fatigue and mental dullness, neither of which were fun when you had a full day ahead.

As he finished setting the trap, Lonnie saw strands of smoke from his fire wafting around him. The smoke smelled of pine resin, boiling coffee, and the even-better aroma of frying side pork. Instantly, his mouth began watering.

He walked back to the camp to see Casey up and fully dressed, wearing her coat and gloves against the morning chill. She was crouched over the small, black iron pan in which the side pork sizzled and popped. Lonnie's coffeepot steamed and chugged on a rock around which orange flames danced.

"Breakfast will be ready in a minute, Mister Gentry," she said, adding a couple of baking powder biscuits to the pan. "Hope you're hungry."

"I'm always hungry!"

Lonnie went over and tended the horses, giving them each a handful of grain and untying them from their picket line, so they could freely forage and drink from the creek. When he returned to the camp, Casey had set a couple of side pork sandwiches for him on a tin plate at the fire's perimeter, where they'd stay warm. The girl sat on her saddle, eating a sandwich, which she was washing down with the hot, black coffee steaming in the tin cup at her feet.

The sandwiches were delicious, as was Casey's coffee.

"Lonnie?" Casey said, picking apart her second sandwich with her hands, and frowning. "What's wrong with the horses?"

Lonnie followed Casey's gaze toward where both mounts stood facing east and shaking their heads as though at pesky blackflies. A couple of times General Sherman craned his neck to look back at Lonnie, as though he were communicating his edginess.

"I don't know," Lonnie said, setting down his empty plate and brushing crumbs from his jeans.

He picked up his rifle and walked out to stand beside the two horses. Both mounts continued to stare off toward a low, pine-covered eastern ridge, the top of which was being painted gold by the rising sun. The horses had settled down somewhat, but they continued to stand stiffly, staring with their wide, brown eyes, working their nostrils as they sniffed the breeze.

Lonnie patted the General's neck, then walked a ways out from the camp, looking around cautiously and nervously squeezing the rifle in his hands. He was relieved to find nothing even remotely suspicious anywhere near the camp. It wasn't as much of a relief as he would have liked, however. The horses could detect trouble a lot farther away than Lonnie could.

He remembered the bugling cry and

hoped again that it had been made by an elk . . .

Then he imagined Dupree's gang sneaking up on his and Casey's camp, and he returned to the fire, immediately kicking dirt on it to douse the flames.

"We best pull our picket pines," Lonnie told Casey, unable to keep the uneasiness from his voice. "I don't see nothin' out there, and horses can get cross-grained for reasons of their own, but since they both have burrs under their saddles and they ain't even saddled yet, let's light a shuck!"

When he and Casey had broken camp and saddled both mounts, Lonnie checked his snare. He wasn't surprised to see that it hadn't been sprung. He gathered up the trap to use later, stowed it in his cavvy sack, and swung up onto the General's back.

He and Casey moved out, looking around nervously. A half hour later, they were moving down through the forest stippling the same ridge that the horses had stared at before. Only, Lonnie and Casey were quartering east and hopefully away from any danger the horses had scented.

The hope was short-lived. Just when Lonnie had noted that both horses looked considerably calmer, the General suddenly pricked his ears.

A few seconds later, Lonnie heard what the General must have heard — a loud, bugling cry dripping with savage menace and which seemed to echo forever amongst the pine tops. The cry swirled wildly around Lonnie, disorienting him. It was soon joined by the echoes of cracking, breaking wood and snapping branches, and the thuds of some large, four-legged creature moving toward him.

CHAPTER 39

The General tossed his head wildly and loosed another piercing whinny.

Casey's filly, Miss Abigail, joined the stallion a half second later with her own ripping whinny. Lonnie whipped his head around to see what appeared to be a cabin-sized creature moving down the opposite, wooded slope, ahead and on his right and obscured by pines and aspens and occasional tamaracks and spruces.

Sunlight shone on the beast's cinnamon fur that rippled as it ran down the slope, mewling and snarling.

Holding his reins tight in both hands up close to his chest, Lonnie shouted, *"Bear!"*

He meant to add, though of course he hadn't really needed to, that they'd best make a hard run for it. But as though Casey's chestnut was violently offended by the word "Bear," the horse pitched suddenly off her front hooves, lifting her head and fear-sharp eyes and buffeting mane high in the air to Lonnie's right.

Casey screamed, "Lonnie!"

The boy reached for the girl, to try to keep her from falling out of her saddle, but Casey went flying backward off the chestnut's rump. The General gave a similar, sky-clawing pitch onto its rear hooves, causing Lonnie, who'd loosened his grip on his reins and was leaning too far out from his saddle, to lose the reins all together. Knowing that he was going to fall now no matter what, he kicked his boots free of his stirrups and gave a shrill curse that his mother would not have approved of but would no doubt have forgiven him for, under the circumstances.

That was a vague, short-lived thought, gone without a trace before the ground rose sharply at an angle to smack Lonnie on the shoulders and the back of his head. He cursed again as he rolled down the slope they were halfway to the bottom of, wincing as a sharp stick poked his right thigh.

When he rolled up against a thick, half-rotten log, bells tolling in his head and his brains feeling as though they were about to slither out his ears, he looked up. Casey was rolling toward him on his left, her hair and the slack of her coat flying wildly.

The girl's tumble was stopped by a slight,

flat shelf in the slope that was heavily padded with forest duff. She lay for a moment, head on the downslope, feet on the upslope, arms and legs akimbo.

The forest was spinning crazily around Lonnie. There was an old leaf in his right eye, causing that eye to burn. There was another one in his ear, and bits of leaves and pine needles in his hair. Some had fallen down the back of his coat and his shirt, raking his skin.

Despite his disorientation, he managed to gain one knee.

Casey was also climbing to her feet, leaves and pine needles falling from her tangled hair and her shoulders.

The mewling and growling continued to grow louder, as did the thuds of the running beast's four feet. Lonnie turned to see that the bear was only a few yards from the bottom of the ravine that was only about a twenty-foot gap between the steep slopes. He turned to Casey at the same time that Casey turned to him, her mouth and eyes wide, and they screamed each other's names at the same time.

Lonnie turned toward where he'd been thrown off the General's back. Both horses had fled into the ravine and were now galloping out of sight, the General leading the chestnut, both horses trailing their reins, until they were gone from view altogether.

Not only were both horses gone, but Lonnie's Winchester was gone, as well.

"General, you gall-blasted son of a worthless cayuse!"

Lonnie grabbed his hat off the ground and scrambled up the slope and over to Casey. As he did, he cast another look down the slope at the bear.

The bruin wasn't cabin-sized, Lonnie could see now that it was closer. But it was at least as large as a good-sized freight wagon. It would probably have dressed out close to a thousand pounds. Its long, shaggy, cinnamon fur was silver-tipped across the hump behind its head, forming a silver swath down its back to its broad rump.

It was now lumbering up the slope in the direction of Lonnie and Casey, shaking its heart-shaped head with one straight and one ragged, flopping ear, and opening and closing its mouth as though showing off its long, yellow, razor-edged teeth, one strategic swipe of which could very likely tear Lonnie in two . . .

The sun flashed off its large, glassy brown-black eyes, which owned the mind-numbing, cold-blooded savagery of the wild primeval. The grizzly was like the cold soul of the universe that would kill you without thinking only because, if it thought about it all, it would have regarded life as nothing more than silly ornament.

Lonnie locked gazes with the beast for a single moment, and the universe yawned at the boy. His belly tumbled into his boots. The beast's mindlessly brutal eyes silently vowed to impersonally, without malice, rip Lonnie limb from limb and to devour every inch of him and to chew his bones clean afterwards, simply because he was hungry or because his territory had been invaded, or merely because he *could.*

That gaze almost caused the boy's knees to turn to warm mud and to buckle.

Leaving both him and Casey a sure, easy meal for the charging bruin . . .

Lonnie shook himself out of the trance. Feeling a cold sweat bathing every inch of him beneath his clothes, he charged up the slope, grabbed Casey's hand, jerked her brusquely to her feet, and then turned and started running toward some rocks he'd only half taken note of.

Many of the rocks appeared to be boulders. They'd probably tumbled long ago from the ridge crest and now rested haphazardly and like giant, fossilized dinosaur eggs amongst the trees. Lonnie thought that he and Casey might be able to find sanctuary somewhere amongst those rocks though he had no idea where, exactly. Maybe they could climb one of the boulders, some of which appeared nearly as large as a two-story house.

Lonnie knew that grizzlies — and the big boy after him and Casey was surely a silvertip griz, if it was anything and not a rabbit! — could climb trees large enough to hold their weight, or could tear down the tree that couldn't hold them but which housed their prey.

Could they climb rocks, as well?

As Lonnie ran, breathing hard, he felt Casey pulling back on his hand. He turned toward her. She was limping badly.

"Casey, come on, we gotta —!"

"It's my ankle again!" she screamed as she dropped to a knee. "I'm sorry, Lonnie!"

She glanced back at the bear charging up the slope behind them. The big, shaggy, snarling beast was within seventy yards and closing fast. The bruin might have been large and ungainly, but it seemed to be running as fast as General Sherman could gallop when given his head.

The ground rumbled beneath Lonnie's boots. As the morning breeze swirled, it filled Lonnie's nose with the beast's heavy, sickly sweet fetor. It was the stink of a large, dead, vermin-infested, shaggy thing wrapped in the rotten cucumber stench of a rattlesnake den.

Casey peeled Lonnie's hand from around her wrist. "Run, Lonnie — for godsakes, let me go, and *run!*"

"Not a chance!" Lonnie hollered, crouching to drag Casey's squirming body over his shoulder.

He turned toward the upslope and amazed himself by how fast the ground seemed to be passing beneath his hammering boots. By how quickly the jumble of scattered, gray boulders was growing larger ahead and above him . . .

"Lonnie, you damn fool!" Casey screamed, punching his back with the ends of her fists.

Lonnie figured that Casey weighed maybe only ten or fifteen pounds less than he did, but with his heart's fierce pumping and the weird, powerful energy surging through his veins, the girl seemed to weigh nothing at all.

Lonnie gained the stone escarpment jutting out of the side of the slope, and without even pausing to plan his course, he headed for a narrow, dark cleft in the bulging stone wall ahead of him. If the cleft went nowhere, and was shallow enough for the bear to reach in for them, Lonnie and Casey would be bear bait.

Fortunately, while the cleft was indeed only about six feet deep, it didn't dead-end. Its ceiling opened onto more, higher rocks, and Lonnie thrust Casey up through the open ceiling and onto what appeared to be a granite ledge above them.

Lonnie could smell the bear's ghastly stench so strongly now that his eyes were watering and his lungs were contracting against it. He didn't bother to look back, because he didn't want to see what he knew he would. But in the periphery of his vision he saw the raging bull griz run up to the cleft, shutting out the light and filling the natural closet in the rocks with dark, stinky shadows and the ear-piercing echoes of its enraged roars.

The beast was so close to Lonnie that the boy could feel the heat of its dead-fish breath. He winced as one or two of the beast's razor-edged claws — as long as pitchfork tines — tore into his back with one clean swipe through his coat and his shirt.

"Ow, goddangit!" Lonnie yelped.

"*Lonnie!*" Casey screamed, looking down at him from the ledge above him. Her blonde hair hung toward him, nearly grazing his forehead. She thrust her right hand down toward him, as well.

Lonnie ignored it and leaped up for a handhold on the opposite side of the cleft from Casey. He found one, found small cracks and ledges in which to stick his boot toes, and began climbing the eight-foot wall. He climbed in a mad, horror-stricken frenzy, feeling the bruin's paws swiping at his boot heels. Lonnie hoisted himself over the edge and rolled clear of the dark cleft in which the bear's roars continued to echo so loudly that they seemed to be originating from inside Lonnie's own head.

The bear stench wafted up through the hole in the escarpment, between Lonnie and Casey on the other side of it, and for a quick second Lonnie thought of the ground giving way to vent the enraged screams of demons trapped in Hell . . .

Lonnie closed his eyes, relieved to be out of the beast's reach. Gradually, his heart slowed.

But then Casey groaned. "Oh, no, Lonnie — he's climbing up here!"

CHAPTER 40

Casey was kneeling on the escarpment, on the other side of the cleft up through which she and Lonnie had come. She wasn't looking into the hole, however, but down the front side of the escarpment.

Lonnie leaped to his feet and ran to the edge of the large mound of rock he was on, and stumbled back a step when he saw the large grizzly standing on its hind feet, snarling up at Casey.

"Casey, get back!" Lonnie shouted.

But he hadn't needed to. The bear lunged toward Casey, smashing its broad belly and shoulders against the side of the escarpment and thrusting its paws with extended black claws toward the girl, who gave a horrified scream and fell back on her rump, slapping a hand to her chest. Her pale face was mottle pink, her blue eyes sharp with mind-numbing fear.

The bear leaped up off its hind feet, trying to climb over the lip of the ridge and get to Casey, who scuttled back on her rump until she was pressing her back up against another boulder, knees drawn to her chest.

"He can't get up here, can he, Lonnie? Oh, please tell me he can't climb rock!"

Lonnie dropped to a knee to look down at the bruin shaking its head furiously. Lonnie saw that not only was one of the cross-grained beast's ears shredded, but it had three long, dark-pink scars forming pale streaks down the left side of its face, beneath the left eye, which drooped a little. More signs of a violent past. The lip of the scarp was higher here than back where Lonnie had climbed up through the cleft. It was a good three feet above the bear's head, and frustrating the bruin no end.

The beast kept lunging at the rock wall. It wasn't showing much grace, however. And, thankfully, its timing was poor. Each time it lunged at the wall, its jump was off enough to keep it from being able to hook its paws over the lip of the rock. Lonnie didn't know how much strength the bear had in its front legs — or were they arms?

Could it pull itself up over the rock if it managed to leap high enough?

In case it could, Lonnie looked around.

The escarpment continued to rise behind him and Casey — one stone ledge after another. A few cedars grew between the stone slabs that formed the scarp.

"Casey!" Lonnie called. "Climb up as far as you can! Keep climbing until you can't climb any farther!"

He had a feeling that if the bear could climb up to where he and Casey were now, it could probably climb all the way to the top of the scarp. But there was no point in the girl staying this close when she didn't have to.

Moving gingerly on her injured ankle, Casey began climbing the slabs of mossy-green rock forming the higher scarp beyond the slope that the bear was still on.

"What are you going to do?" the girl called over her shoulder, grabbing a twisted cedar, which she used to pull herself up onto the next, table-topped boulder.

Lonnie wasn't sure what he was going to do. But when he'd looked around and found a couple of loose, good-sized rocks, something occurred to him. He grabbed the rocks, returned to the edge of the lip where the bear had gotten a hold and was trying to climb, and slammed one of the rocks down hard on the beast's left paw.

The boy wasn't so sure that that had been

such a good idea.

The bruin looked up at him and loosed a bugling growl even louder than before, spittle stringing off its long, curving fangs, its eyes nearly crossing. Lonnie stepped back and slung the rock as hard as he could. It smacked the bear right above its snout that was as wide as a wheel hub and as broad as Lonnie's thigh. That only seemed to enrage the beast even more. It lunged toward Lonnie, turning its head this way and that, mouth wide, roaring.

"Lonnie, get up here!" Casey screamed above and behind him.

Something told Lonnie that the bruin was having enough trouble climbing the rock face that one more slam of a stone across its skull might discourage him, if it was possible to discourage a silvertip.

Lonnie sent the second rock hurling down toward the beast's massive head. The animal had lifted its snout toward Lonnie once more, and the rock smashed into the dead, black, leathery center of it. The beast gave another bone-jarring roar that seemed to fill the whole valley, echoing, causing the escarpment to quiver beneath Lonnie's boots. The beast appeared to jerk slightly, as though something had dawned on it. Lonnie watched in shock as the beast stepped away from the ledge, dropped to all fours, gave another, lower mewling growl, and then lumbered down through the trees away from the scarp.

Pine needles crunched and branches snapped beneath its heavy, running paws.

Lonnie staggered back away from the ledge in shock. His knees went weak, and he dropped to his butt.

Staring after the fleeing bear, Lonnie laughed with relief and said, "Casey — did you see that?"

A man's voice said with sneering menace, "You did good, kid. You did real good."

Lonnie whipped his head around. His heart jerked to life once more, and for a second he thought it would burst when he saw Shannon Dupree hunkered down on the flat-topped boulder beside Casey. The blond, yellow-eyed outlaw leader, wearing a sheepskin vest over his red-and-black-checked shirt, his hat tipped low on his forehead, had one arm wrapped around Casey's shoulders. In his other hand, he held his Winchester rifle, the barrel of which he was pressing up taut against Casey's right cheek.

Casey had gone white as a sheet. She stared dully at Lonnie. Her eyes bore into the boy with a vague, silent pleading as well as with mute apology.

Lonnie lurched to his feet, mind racing. He was still frazzled from the bear attack. To see Dupree squatting there beside Casey — it was all too surreal for his battered mind to wrap itself around, to understand.

"You did all right," Dupree said again with his usual mockery, nodding. He glanced beyond Lonnie. "But I got a feelin' it was Fuego's rifle shot that really discouraged that bruin."

Hoof clomps and the crunching of pine needles rose behind Lonnie. The boy turned, and his gut sank even lower when he saw the stocky, dark Fuego and Jake Childress ride slowly toward him, keeping a tight rein on their mounts that were tossing their heads nervously at the fresh scent of the kill-crazy bear.

Childress was leading Dupree's calico gelding. Both men rode with their rifles across their saddlebows. Fuego's eyes were dark, his mouth beneath his thick, black mustache unsmiling.

Childress was grinning, his too-close, pale-blue eyes glistening maliciously in the golden sunlight angling through the pines.

CHAPTER 41

Dupree said, "Kid, you stay right where you are, or I'll drill a hole through this pretty little miss's head. And you wouldn't want that, now, would you?"

"I ain't goin' anywhere," Lonnie said, rage burning off his mind fog. He clenched his fists at his sides, yearning for his rifle. "You hurt her, I'll kill you, you son of a —!"

"Nuh-uh!" Dupree said, grinning as he rose, making the girl rise with him but pulling his rifle away from her face. "What would your ma say about such barn talk, boy? If you ain't careful, I'm gonna tell May, and she'll wash your mouth out with soap!"

The killer had said this loudly enough that Fuego and Childress could hear. Both men chuckled now, reining their horses to a stop near the bottom of the scarp. Lonnie stood where he was, heart hammering the back side of his breastbone.

"She's still alive, then?" Lonnie asked,

knowing the jig was likely up for him and Casey, but still worried sick about his ma. "You didn't . . . you didn't hurt her?"

"I didn't *what*? Oh, wait!" Dupree said, pretending to ponder the question. "Gee, I don't remember, now. I can't remember if I held it against her that she turned my money . . . er, I mean, me *and the boys'* money . . . over to her son so's he could give it back to the very folks I'd taken it from! I mean, if I'd wanted that to happen to all my hard work . . . er, I mean, me *and the boys'* hard work . . . I'd have taken it into Arapaho Creek myself!"

"Let me go, you filthy coward!" Casey said, jerking her arm out of the man's grip.

Dupree, who stood close to six feet four inches tall, looked like a tall, blond-headed, slant-eyed ghoul grinning down at her. "You watch your tongue, too, Miss Pretty. Or I'll take a bar of soap and wash your mouth out myself!"

"Just try it!"

"All right, I will," Dupree said. "Just as soon as we get down off this rock." He chuckled and turned to Lonnie with a squint-eyed, suspicious look. "You ain't got a pistol on you — do you, boy?"

"If I had one," Lonnie said, barely able to

keep his rage in check, "I'd have used it by now."

He hadn't gotten an honest answer about his ma, and he knew he wouldn't get one. Dupree would only devil him about what he may or may not have done to her. That was the kind of man he was. All Lonnie wanted now was to find some way to get himself and Casey out of this current snare they were in.

Lonnie had thought he'd frightened away the bear, but Fuego's rifle shot had apparently done that. To Lonnie's embarrassment, the very men out to kill him had likely saved him . . . for now. The rifle's report must have been drowned by the bear's roar. He thought he'd seen the beast flinch a little. Maybe Lonnie wasn't as tough as he thought he was.

Maybe, for how smart he was feeling about brushing Dupree off his trail, this was finally the end of his line.

For himself, he stopped caring. He was plum tuckered out. He felt like an old man. But he didn't want it to be the end of the line for Casey. She was too much girl to be killed by Dupree. More girl than Lonnie had even thought before he'd gotten to know her. He'd fight for her to the very end.

Dupree said, "You think you're tough —

don't you, kid?"

"I'm tough enough," Lonnie shot back at the man.

"Lonnie, you hush now!" Casey said, casting him a desperately worried look.

To Casey, Dupree said, shoving her forward, "You go on down there with your boyfriend, Miss Pretty. I'm assumin' you came up this way, so there must be a way *down* this way, too."

Casey crawled gingerly down the boulders to Lonnie, who was waiting for her at the bottom. He took the girl's arm as Dupree followed her down, leaping from rock to rock, keeping his rifle leveled on both of them with one hand, extending the barrel straight out from his hip.

"Well, what're you waiting for?" Dupree barked, when he was standing over them both. He waved the rifle, angrily. "Let's get down off these rocks, and then we can see about the money."

Lonnie helped Casey back down the way they'd come up — through the cleft in the scarp. Getting down was considerably harder and slower than getting up had been, with the bear snapping its jaws at them. Dupree must have gotten onto the escarpment from the top of the ridge.

When they made it down and were standing outside the cleft, where Fuego and Childress were waiting, sitting on rocks, with their rifles resting across their thighs, Casey was barely able to put any weight at all on her ankle. She had an arm wrapped around Lonnie's neck, while Lonnie had his left arm wrapped around Casey's waist, holding her up.

"All right," Dupree said, stooping as he came striding out of the cleft, his face red from exertion, pressing his rifle against Lonnie's belly. "Where is it? You give me a smart answer, boy, I'll gut shoot you and leave you here for that bear to come back and finish!"

Lonnie chewed on his answer. He could not bring himself to tell Dupree where the money was.

Dupree grinned with menace, showing his long, fang-like eyeteeth and squinting his gray eyes, and loudly cocked his rifle.

"Lonnie!" Casey said. "It's over! We have to give him the money or he'll kill us!"

Lonnie knew it was true. Still, it was hard getting the words out. "It's on my horse. He ran off when the bear hit us." It was true. Lonnie had strapped the money to the stallion's back, so Casey's filly hadn't had to carry the extra weight over the rough terrain.

"Which way?"

"That way."

Dupree looked behind Lonnie and said, "Fuego."

The stocky half-breed rose from his rock, swung up onto his horse's back, and galloped away through the trees.

Childress said, "Maybe I oughta go with him."

Dupree eyed Childress suspiciously. "You stay here with me. He's too stupid to get any ideas himself. But the two of you together might concoct something." He spat to one side. "Something like a double-cross, maybe." He smiled. "I'd be lookin' for you two in Mexico."

"That's just like you, Shannon," Childress said, shaking his head sadly. "Don't got a trustin' bone in your body."

Dupree looked around. He told Childress to gather wood and build a fire. Childress looked at him crossways, and Dupree said, "I'm gonna watch these two lovebirds, make sure they don't go flyin' off together. Neither one of 'em will be out of my sight until we get the money back. So fetch the wood and build the fire before you and me get crossways!"

Lonnie wondered what he meant by "until we get the money back." What would happen once they had the money?

Foolish question. Lonnie knew very well what would happen to both him and Casey. Somehow, he and Casey had to get away.

But how were they going to do that when Casey could put no weight on her ankle, much less run?

When Childress had stomped off to fetch firewood, Dupree said, "You two lovebirds sit down and make yourselves comfortable. Try to run off, I'll tie you to a tree." He grinned at Casey in a way that seared Lonnie with raw fury. "Doesn't look like Miss Pretty's goin' anywhere, though. At least, not very fast."

Casey cursed him in a way that made even Lonnie blush.

Dupree whistled in awe at the girl's finesse with the rougher parts of the English language — the parts that hadn't made it into the dictionary and likely never would.

"You got a mouth on you, Miss Pretty!" Dupree looked at Lonnie. "Kid, you really know how to pick 'em. Where'd you find this one?"

"I'm Casey Stoveville. Marshal Stoveville was my father." Casey spit the words out like unwieldy prune pits. "Until you killed him, you butcher!"

Casey lunged toward Dupree, who took

one laughing step back as Casey fell flat on her face with an anguished groan.

"Now, you try that again, Miss Pretty," Dupree said, pressing the barrel of his rifle up against the back of the girl's head, "and this party's gonna be over for you right quick!"

Before Lonnie knew what he was doing, he was lunging for Dupree.

Dupree may have been big, but he was fast. When Lonnie was still three feet away from him, the outlaw shifted his rifle around and rammed its heavy butt into the dead center of Lonnie's belly.

Lonnie stopped in his tracks. His knees buckled as the wind left him in one loud spurt.

Holding his belly, he collapsed in agony.

CHAPTER 42

It took Lonnie a miserably long time to draw a breath into his lungs. When he finally did, he rolled over onto his back and kept breathing, enjoying the feeling of having air return to his body despite the horrible predicament that he and Casey found themselves in.

When he'd regained his wind as well as his senses, Lonnie realized that Casey had been kneeling beside him the whole time, one hand on his back and scolding Dupree venomously. For his part, the outlaw merely sat on a rock and built a cigarette from the makings sack he wore around his neck, and leisurely smoked it, a smug expression on his face.

When Childress returned with an armload of wood, Dupree continued to smoke while the other outlaw formed a ring with rocks, and built a fire inside the ring. He boiled coffee on the flames, then he and

Dupree sat around the fire, drinking coffee to which they added splashes of Old Kentucky Rye and looking downslope every now and then, expecting Fuego and the stolen money.

Lonnie was in no hurry for Fuego to return. When Dupree had what he considered to be his money back, he would have no more use for Lonnie and Casey. In the meantime, Lonnie waited for a chance to make a move on one of the outlaws.

His only hope for survival would be to somehow acquire one of the outlaws' guns, and either shoot them both — he thought he could shoot another man, now, given that it was the only chance he'd have at saving himself and Casey — or disarm them both and keep them pinned down while he and Casey rode off on their horses.

To that end, as one hour passed, and then another, and they all waited for Fuego, Lonnie kept a vigilant eye on the men and their guns. Both were drinking enough coffee and rye while they passed the time that both men left the camp several times to tend nature. Dupree always took his rifle with him, but Childress left his own Winchester leaning against the rock upon which he'd been sitting.

Only, one man always remained in camp.

When Childress was gone, Dupree stayed, drinking his spiced coffee and smoking, making any attempt Lonnie might make on Childress's rifle sheer suicide.

Lonnie had seen Dupree wield a rifle several times in the past. The man was not only good with a long gun, but he rarely missed at what he was shooting at, be it gophers or coffee cans perched on fence posts. Once, Lonnie had seen the killer shoot a hawk out of the sky for sport. That was when Lonnie started to hate the man, before he'd ever suspected him of being an outlaw.

Only a no-account vermin would shoot an animal for sport. Real men as well as real women killed animals for food only. Lonnie's father had never believed in mounting an animal's head on the wall, even if the animal had been brought down primarily for food. Doing so was disrespectful to the animal and only proved that the man who did it was a show-off, a soulless tinhorn, a fool.

That's what Dupree was. A fool. Lonnie didn't know why his mother hadn't been able to see that. It was frighteningly clear to Lonnie.

The afternoon was a tense one for Lonnie. He could tell that it was tense for Casey, as well. They sat against the same tree,

Casey massaging her swollen ankle. Occasionally they glanced at each other and exchanged wan smiles meant to be encouraging though they really only betrayed the desperation and anxiety percolating inside them both.

Sun-dappled shadows slid around the pair.

Birds piped and squirrels chattered in the branches. The breeze wisped and occasionally moaned amongst the treetops. Sometimes, there was the shrill cry of a hawk hunting high in the sky above camp.

Otherwise, the only sounds were the crackling of the fire, the chugging of the coffeepot, and the occasional murmurs of Dupree and Childress, mostly wondering aloud what was keeping Fuego. Their two hobbled, unsaddled horses munched grass nearby, hooves crunching pine needles as they moved slowly around to forage.

All afternoon, Lonnie's heart beat heavily, and his palms sweated.

Desperation was a living thing inside him, chewing away at his insides. He'd thought he was ready to die. But, now, having had some time to think about it, and to wonder what it would be like, to give up this world for the grave or whatever lay beyond it — would he see his father again, or his mother if she were dead as well? — he realized how badly he wanted to live. To breathe mountain air winy with the scent of pine, to hear a hawk screeching as it hunted, to be close enough to Casey to smell the distinct smell of the girl, to hear her breathing and shifting around beside him.

He knew he was too young to think about such grown-up things, but he thought that he wouldn't mind being married to Casey. He could see them working the ranch together and raising a passel of young'uns.

That, however, was probably not likely to happen . . .

Lonnie's heart jerked when, in the mid-afternoon, a horse whinnied down the slope behind him. Casey gasped and jerked with a start, as well. Dupree, who'd been sleeping lightly under his hat brim while Childress had been adding more wood to the fire, suddenly poked his hat back on his forehead, and stared down the slope through the pines.

"Here he comes," he said, rising from his rock and resting his rifle on his shoulder.

Lonnie could hear the thuds of an approaching horse. He glanced to Casey on his left. The girl's face was pale again, with a little pink on the nubs of her cheeks. Her face was drawn with worry, lips slightly parted. She slid a plainly frightened glance at Lonnie, and they both turned to stare down the slope where the hoof thuds continued to grow louder until Lonnie could hear the squawk of leather and the faint jingling of a bridle chain.

The stocky Fuego came into view amongst the trees. He rode up to the edge of the camp, and both Dupree and Childress stood regarding the man, frowning curiously.

"I was about ready to saddle up and go lookin' for you," Dupree growled.

"Thought I wasn't comin' back, huh? Maybe headin' for Mexico?" Fuego's dark eyes flashed mockingly. Then he shook his head. "Sorry, boss. I couldn't find that hoss nowheres. Came back because I was so far out I figured it'd get dark on me. No point in stumbling around after sundown."

Dupree's eyes widened. "No sign of it?"

Fuego shook his head. "None that I could see."

Dupree turned to Lonnie. The other two outlaws turned to the boy, as well, their eyes flat and hard. Dupree walked over and casually pointed his Winchester at the boy's forehead.

"Boy, if you lied to me, I'll kill you right now!"

"He didn't lie!" Casey yelled. "Both our horses ran that way down the ravine. Just

281

because that big idiot can't track . . ."

The girl let her voice trail off, knowing she was pushing too hard.

Fuego stared at her with flat eyes.

"I wasn't lyin'," Lonnie said. "Both horses ran that way down the ravine. Maybe they turned and ran up the other ridge. I don't know. I didn't see 'em. Had more important things on my mind when they run off. But if Mister Fuego didn't find 'em, that's what they must've done."

"How can I be sure?" Dupree said, staring menacingly down the barrel of his rifle at Lonnie. "How can I be sure you didn't hide the money somewheres along the trail. Maybe you an' Miss Pretty knew me an' the boys was closin' on you, and you didn't want us to catch you with it. Maybe you figured if we caught you without the money we wouldn't kill you, and you could go back for it later."

Dupree blew a caustic snort. "Well, you figured wrong, boy."

Lonnie made a hard effort to stifle his shaking. He raked his gaze from the round maw of the rifle, and said, "How do you figure killin' me an' Casey is gonna get your money back?"

"It ain't," Dupree said, smiling coldly and pressing the rifle barrel against Lonnie's chest, over his heart. "But it'll make me feel a whole lot better." He grinned again. "Best pray, boy. Best pray real hard!"

CHAPTER 43

Lonnie stared up at the outlaw, speechless. Sweat dribbled down the sides of his face to drip from his chin and dampen the front of his shirt. Even Casey had been rendered speechless by what appeared the dead certainty that Dupree was about to pull his rifle's trigger, and kill Lonnie.

The boy's shoulder was touching the girl's. He could feel Casey breathing as hard as he was.

There was a long silence as Dupree stared down at Lonnie with those snake-like eyes of his.

Finally, Childress said, "No point in killin' him yet, Shannon." The lanky outlaw was nibbling a weed. "Kid had a point. Killin' him ain't gonna get us the money. Let's get the money first, then we'll talk about what we're gonna do with him and the girl."

"Only one thing to do with 'em, either way," Fuego said. "They know all about us.

Can't let 'em live."

"Well, I for one would like to consider the situation a little longer," Childress said. "I don't know — killin' kids. I ain't never done that before. Mighty tall order. Maybe we could take 'em with us down to Mexico, set 'em free at the border."

"Travel all that way with a couple of howlin' brats?" Dupree said, still staring at Lonnie. He shook his head.

"Sounds like a good idea to me," Lonnie said after he'd tried to swallow the hard knot in his throat. "We wouldn't be no trouble. None at all. In fact, we could set up and tear down camp for you fellas."

Of course, Lonnie had no hankering to do any such thing. He was trying to buy him and Casey some time.

"Yeah," Casey said. "We could do that. And I can cook, too. No point in killin' us. The law would be extra mad, track you extra hard, if you killed a couple of kids."

Dupree looked at her in that way of his that burned Lonnie deep in his bones. The outlaw lifted his rifle and off-cocked the hammer. He laughed and then said, "We'll track the horses tomorrow, spend the night right here. Let's eat — I'm hungry as a wolf."

While the outlaws laid out their gear,

forming a proper camp, Lonnie was sent out to snare a rabbit and gather firewood. Dupree had seen how handy Lonnie was with a rope snare. The outlaws weren't worried that Lonnie would try to run away. They knew he'd stay with Casey. How far could he get on foot, anyway, before they ran him down again?

Lonnie didn't think he'd be able to snare anything before good dark, but he set his trap in the brush well away from the camp. He gathered enough wood for the night, and had built up the fire and put a fresh pot of coffee on to boil. Then they set him out in search of water. There was a small stream at the bottom of the ravine, so he walked down the slope and filled the men's canteens after taking a long drink himself. A high shriek rose from the direction in which he'd set his snare. Lonnie strode over to find that he'd caught a big jack. He wrung the frightened beast's neck, and brought him back to the fire.

Dupree chuckled and glanced at Fuego and Childress. "Told you the kid was half Injun."

Then he grabbed the rabbit out of Lonnie's hands and set to work, dressing it out, skinning it, and chopping it up for the pot in which beans and bacon bubbled on the fire. Meanwhile, Lonnie gave Casey one of the canteens he'd filled.

She took a long drink. The outlaws didn't seem to mind she was drinking their water. They'd already settled in for the night, drinking their coffee laced with rye and laying out a poker game while a pot bubbled and splattered on the fire. They were distracted, not overly worried about their captives.

That was fine with Lonnie. He hoped they'd stay distracted, so he could make a play for one of their guns.

The men ate but they didn't offer any food to Lonnie or Casey, despite Lonnie's having snared the rabbit to add to their otherwise thin stew. They acted as though the two weren't even there, sitting about ten feet back from the fire. That, too, was all right with Lonnie. He hadn't eaten since breakfast, but he wasn't hungry. He supposed that having been in almost constant jeopardy since he'd awakened that day had something to do with that.

The men ate, and Dupree ordered Lonnie to scrub their dishes. Lonnie didn't see that he had much choice, so he took the utensils down to the stream, and cleaned them. When he returned to the fire, Dupree ordered him to refill their coffee cups and to add a good portion of whiskey to each. The men were sitting on rocks and throwing playing cards down on the ground between them, calling, bluff, and raising.

Lonnie vaguely thought with an inward smirk that it would be nice if one of them drew a "Dead Man's Hand." He wasn't sure what that was, exactly, but he knew it was a poker hand.

He added more wood to the fire, then sat back down with Casey. The men were getting drunker and talking louder, and the fire was burning loudly, too, so he figured they wouldn't hear him and Casey conferring. Still, he kept his voice low as he asked, "How you holdin' up?"

"I'm doin' all right, Lonnie. How're you doin'?"

"I'm all right. How's your ankle?"

"It's feelin' better now. It's not broke or nothin'. I just have to stay off it for a while. I reckon I'll be doing that real soon, huh?" She'd dragged her voice out ironically, and gave Lonnie a droll look.

What she'd said and the way she'd said it struck Lonnie as funny, and he couldn't help chuckling. That got Casey chuckling, then, too, and they both had to cover their mouths and hold their noses to keep from rolling out the loud guffaws.

Still, Dupree heard them, and he turned to scold them. "You two shut up over there. Go to sleep. I'll be over to tie you up in a minute, so you don't run off in the night."

That sobered them, reminding them of the fix they were in.

They both sat back against the tree. A minute later, Casey slid her hand across the ground and closed it over Lonnie's, and squeezed it. He squeezed hers back. When he looked at her, she was looking down at their entwined hands, her eyelids low. A couple of tears were dribbling down her cheeks, flashing in the umber firelight.

"It'll be okay, Casey," Lonnie said.

She didn't say anything, but dipped her head a little and bit her upper lip as she continued to squeeze his hand.

Lonnie kept an eye on the outlaws' rifles, but they were keeping the long guns close to them. Lonnie was beginning to think of a way he could get his hands on one later, after the outlaws had gone to sleep, when the three men began to confer amongst themselves in low, guttural tones. They seemed to be discussing something of gravity.

Dupree and Fuego glanced over at Lonnie, raked their drink-bright eyes across Casey, then Childress looked at Lonnie and said something to his partners.

Dupree threw his cards down, and rose with a grunt, saying, "No — it's gotta be done. Might as well do it now as save it for the mornin'."

Dupree stooped to fish around inside one of his saddlebags, pulling out a small coil of rope. Neither Childress nor Fuego said anything as Dupree staggered around the fire. Lonnie could smell the alcohol reek of the man as he stood over his two captives, his heavy shoulders rising and falling as he breathed.

The sick feeling in Lonnie's belly got worse.

Dupree dropped to a knee and began wrapping the rope around both of Casey's ankles.

"Gonna tie you up, girl. You'll be goin' with us in the morning."

Casey looked sharply at Lonnie.

"What do you mean 'I' am?" Casey asked, her shrill voice quaking with trepidation. "What about Lonnie?"

"Don't got no more use for him. He's about as useless as his mother." As Dupree brusquely grabbed Casey's arm and rolled her onto her belly, he gave Lonnie an evil smirk, adding, "God rest the stupid woman's soul."

Lonnie looked down at the pistol jutting

up on Dupree's left hip, the walnut handle angled back toward his belly. Lonnie's heart started hiccuping and lurching every which way as he imagined making a grab for the pistol.

As Dupree began wrapping an end of the rope around Casey's wrists, hog-tying the girl belly-down on the ground, Lonnie bounded up onto his feet and lurched forward, wrapping his hand around the big Colt on Dupree's hip. The boy gave a loud grunt as he jerked the revolver free of the keeper thong and out of its holster.

Dupree cursed loudly and grabbed at the gun, almost tearing it from the boy's grip before Lonnie jerked it back away from him. As he did, Dupree growled, "Why, you cussed little *snip*!" and grabbed for his second Colt holstered low on his right thigh.

Dupree's hand was moving in a blur. He was fast. Too fast for Lonnie. The boy had no time to consider his actions, so he didn't bother.

He merely ratcheted the Colt's hammer back, took quick aim at the center of the outlaw's broad chest, and fired.

CHAPTER 44

The pistol's report sounded like a shotgun blast in the quiet night.

Smoke wafted in the air between Lonnie and Dupree, peppering the boy's nose with the smell of cordite, making his eyes water.

Dupree froze, dipped his chin to look down in shock at his lower left side. His back was angled toward the fire, so Lonnie couldn't see much of the man's front, but he thought he saw a dark hole in the flap of the man's sheepskin vest. Dupree stood a little to one side, and as Lonnie realized that his bullet must have plowed through the man's vest and merely grazed the man's left side — if he'd hit him where he'd thought he'd hit him, he wouldn't still be living much less standing — Lonnie took another step back and cocked the Colt once more.

"Why, you little dung beetle!" Dupree bellowed, lurching for Lonnie and throwing his arms up as he thrust his left boot forward and sideways.

The boot swept Lonnie's feet out under from him. As Lonnie became airborne, he inadvertently triggered the Colt straight up at the stars that glowed dully beyond the firelight.

"Lonnie!" Casey screamed as Lonnie's old friend, the ground, came up to greet him once more without ceremony.

Again, Lonnie's wind was pummeled from his battered lungs, and he lay on his side, legs scissored, groaning and trying with little success to suck air back into his chest. He looked at his right hand, which was thrown high over his head and lying against the ground. The Colt lay several feet beyond it, half buried in the finely churned dirt and pine needles.

Dupree was holding his hand against his side as he stepped over to Lonnie.

"No!" Casey cried from where she lay belly-down on the ground, wrists tied to her ankles behind her back.

"Kid, I thought this was gonna be hard for me," Dupree savagely barked, bending at the waist to glower down at Lonnie still trying to suck a clean breath. "But it just got a whole lot easier."

He slanted his Colt down at Lonnie,

clicked back the hammer.

The gun barked. Only, it didn't flash or stab flames toward Lonnie. And it hadn't really so much *barked* as made a *pinging* noise, and gave off a spark somewhere up near the cylinder.

"Ach!" Dupree yelped, tossed the gun away as though it were a hot potato.

Dupree grabbed the hand that had been holding the gun and looked at it with a curious mixture of outrage and befuddlement. "What the *hell?*" he yelled, lifting his head to cast his demon-eyed gaze into the woods behind Lonnie.

In the sudden silence that followed, a mild voice owning the soft twang of a Southern accent said, "Now, that ain't no way to treat a young'un an' you know it, sir."

Both Fuego and Childress were standing. They both reached for their rifles at the same time. The pistol in the woods barked two more times.

In the periphery of Lonnie's vision, he saw the flash of the flames in the darkness of the downslope trees, and he also saw, to his other side, both Fuego and Childress lose their hats. Each hat leaped off its owner's head, one after the other, and flew back behind them in the darkness beyond the fire.

Losing their hats seemed to take all the

sap out of the two outlaws' demeanors. They left their rifles where they were, and tensed, stared fearfully across the fire and into the darkness beyond Lonnie and Dupree, who was still standing where he'd been standing before, clutching his hand to his belly and grunting painfully, grinding his jaws.

The strangely slow, mild voice rose again from the forest. "Anyone reaches for another shootin' iron, they're gonna acquire a third eye — one they can't see out of — right quick. Now, ya'll stay where you are so I can keep these old hog legs quiet."

Boots crunched pine needles until the figure appeared at the edge of the firelight — a lanky gent whose clothes seemed to hang on his gaunt, bony frame. The battered and torn Confederate gray cavalry hat was tipped low over the craggy, severe-featured face that Lonnie had seen somewhere before, though he couldn't remember exactly where. The stranger held not one pistol but two old-model, cap-and-ball pistols in his gloved hands. One pistol was aimed at Dupree, the other was angled in the general direction of Fuego and Childress.

The stranger looked down at Lonnie. "Son," he said, "you got the galldarnedest worst luck of any shaver I ever known. Can you stand?"

"Can I what?" Lonnie said tightly, still unable to take a full breath.

"Can you stand? You know — get up and walk around? I'm thinkin' you should do that if you can." The man turned his head to one side and spat out a long stream of chaw onto a rock. "The girl, too — if'n she wants to ride out of here."

The severe-featured face belonged to the old Confederate — at least, Lonnie figured he was in his forties or so, maybe even older — who'd saved Lonnie's bacon back before the boy had reached Arapaho Creek.

Dupree winced against the pain in his bloody hand, and let his eyes bore into the lanky gent holding the old-model pistols on him. "You know who you're messin' with here, Grayback?"

"No," the mild-voiced stranger said while Lonnie climbed to his feet. "But I gotta feelin' you're gonna tell me."

"Shannon Dupree!" The tall, blond outlaw held out his bloody right hand clutched in the other one. "And it's my hand you just shredded with that old horse pistol, Grayback!"

The bearded stranger's severe brows drooped over his deep-set, dark-blue eyes, and he shook his head as he said, "Dupree, huh? Well, I do apologize. Don't recollect the name. It's a tall one, huh?"

"A hell of a lot taller than you, my soon-to-be-dead Rebel friend!"

"That's no way to talk to a man bearin' down on you. Now, I could understand you talkin' that way if *you* was the one holdin' the pistols, but you ain't." The Confederate glanced at Lonnie, who, standing, was still trying to drag a breath deep into his lungs. "Boy, I ain't gettin' any younger and neither is this night, and I got your horses waitin', so I sure would appreciate it if you'd take that big-talkin' Yankee's knife out of his boot and use it to cut that girl loose."

Lonnie's eyes brightened when he turned to regard the stranger. "You got our horses?"

The stranger gave a slow dip of his chin. Switching his gaze from Casey to Dupree, he pursed his lips and shook his head. "That's no way to treat a girl, neither. Tyin' her up such as that. What was you thinkin', Yankee? You think she's a calf for the brandin'? Why, I never seen the like! Boy, take his knife and cut her loose! Don't worry — if he so much as twitches, I'll give him a pill he can't digest!"

Lonnie looked at the knife handle sticking up out of Dupree's right boot. He crouched down and slipped the bowie knife out of the sheath sewn into the boot. Lonnie didn't look at Dupree while he did, though he could feel the outlaw's devil eyes boring into his back.

Knife in hand, Lonnie hurried over to Casey, and sawed through the ropes, freeing her wrists from her ankles. Casey rolled over, flinging the ropes away with a grunt. Lonnie tossed away the knife, leaned down, and wrapped his right arm around Casey's waist, helping the girl to her feet.

"You two young'uns head on back behind me. You'll see your horses there with mine, ole Stonewall — the big cream. Steer clear of Stonewall, as he'll tear your shirt, you get close, as he can smell Yankees from ten miles away!" The old Confederate chuckled at that. "Mount up and ride north along the bottom of that ravine. I'll catch up to you as soon as I've made sure we won't have no shadowers."

Lonnie glanced once more at Dupree, who was eyeing him darkly, then Lonnie helped the girl into the trees. They headed downslope together. As they did, the General gave a bugling whinny, and Lonnie grinned broadly. The big buckskin had scented its owner, or maybe had heard his voice, and that had been the General's vigorous greeting. Another whinny followed the General's, and Lonnie saw the cream standing about ten feet away from where the General stood with Casey's chestnut, about fifty yards down the slope.

The outlaws' horses were tied straight south of the camp, up higher on the slope and nearer the rocks capping the ridge crest.

"Hey, you big chicken," Lonnie greeted the buckskin, which gave its young rider a vaguely sheepish look and then bobbed its head unctuously. "Thanks for runnin' out on me. I really appreciate that."

Both the stallion and the roan were tied to one tree while the Confederate's stallion, named after an opposing general, was tied to another tree several yards away. As Lonnie helped Casey up onto the chestnut's back, he saw with relief that the second pair of saddlebags, containing the money, were still draped over the General's back, where Lonnie had strapped them to his saddle skirt.

"Lonnie, do you know that man?" Casey asked as Lonnie untied their mounts.

"Seen him once before," Lonnie said, tossing Casey her bridle reins. "Don't ask me his name, but I reckon I've acquired a Confederate for a guardian angel. Don't that beat all?"

"Well, its beats somethin', anyway," Casey

said, glancing up the dark slope toward where the fire glowed amongst the tall, black pines.

As Lonnie stepped up onto the General's back, he looked up the slope, as well. The old Confederate stood silhouetted against the firelight, just off its far right side. Lonnie could tell Dupree by the man's considerable height. He could hear the Confederate talking, and then, as Lonnie turned General Sherman toward the downslope, he saw the Confederate's gray shadow move away from the fire and toward the outlaws' horses, which they'd tied to a picket line.

Lonnie let the General pick his own way down the slope. Casey's chestnut clomped along behind, occasionally snorting and whickering. Both horses sensed the edginess of their riders. As Lonnie touched heels to the General's flanks, urging more speed when they'd gained the bottom of the ravine, the boy jerked with a start as a pistol popped once, twice, three times.

"Git on!" he heard the old Confederate yell amidst the thudding of the outlaws' horses' hooves. "Git along there, you Yankee cayuses, or I'll shoot you and leave you to the possums!"

The horses were jostling shadows against the side of the slope, scattering as they headed straight for the bottom, dodging trees. There was one more pistol crack, and then a shrill, wild Rebel yell — *"Heee-ee-yahhhh!"* —vaulted over the still night that was as tense as a held breath.

That high-pitched, echoing yell caused the hair on the back of Lonnie's neck to stand on end. He had a feeling he'd just heard what his father and so many other Yankees had heard and what had turned their knees to mush on so many Southern battlefields during the war. Behind Lonnie, the sound of fast-moving hooves rose quickly, and then, as Lonnie and Casey followed the creek meandering along the bottom of the ravine up and over a low divide, the old Confederate on the cream stallion he called Stonewall shot past them in a streak of gray lightning.

"Come on, young'uns!" he called. "We's aburnin' moonlight!"

"Lonnie?" Casey said, as they both put their horses into lopes down a broad, grassy hill, the large, silver moon quartering over them, silvering the forest on both sides of the meadow.

"What is it?" Lonnie asked, pulling his hat low over his forehead, so it wouldn't blow off.

"Why do I have the feeling we just jumped

out of the frying pan and into the fire again?"

CHAPTER 45

Nearly an hour of hard riding later, through forest and over low divides and into this narrow canyon heavy with the smell of the creek running through it, and ferns and rich, green grass, Lonnie checked the General down.

The horse was silver with its own sweat lather. As Casey stopped the filly off Lonnie's left stirrup, Lonnie stared through the trees at what appeared to be a cabin sitting about thirty yards back from the creek. The cabin was a black silhouette against the slope rising behind it, but the starlight reflecting off the tin chimney pipe poking up out of the hovel's roof told Lonnie it was a cabin, all right.

His Grayback guardian angel had stopped his own cream stallion in front of the place, and was stepping down from his saddle. He turned toward Lonnie and Casey sitting a cautious several yards away, and he said,

"Well, come on, then. You Yankee children don't like roofs over your heads?"

Lonnie studied the man and the surroundings. He didn't know who this gent was other than he was an ex-Confederate and good with his old Confederate pistols. Lonnie had watched him kill three men as easily as swatting flies, and he'd also watched him stare down Shannon Dupree. He was a killer, all right. Lonnie knew that for sure. What else he was, Lonnie didn't know. Maybe whatever it was, was good. But maybe it was bad, too, and that's what had given the boy pause.

That's what had given Casey pause, too.

"All right, then," the stranger said, removing his stallion's bridle and slipping its saddle, rifle scabbard, and bedroll off its back. He took the gear over to what appeared to be a dilapidated lean-to stable with connecting corral, and set it on the corral's rail fence. Then he went on into the cabin, and soon Lonnie saw a wan amber light burning in one of the windows.

"Gonna get cold out here, I reckon." Lonnie continued to look around, cautious. "And it looks like the money's still here on the General's back."

"Did you count it?"

Casey knew he hadn't had time to count

304

the money. It was her way of saying they shouldn't assume they could trust this old Confederate, uncommonly good with a cap-and-ball pistol, because he'd saved their lives. But the more they both thought it through, the more they both saw it from a different angle. The man *had* saved them and he hadn't taken the loot, which he very easily could have done, so they were probably being foolish, mooning around out here like a pair of stray pups.

At least, that's the angle Lonnie saw it from, and he could tell by Casey's shrug that she'd come to that conclusion, too. They both dismounted, and stripped the gear from their horses and set it near the Confederate's. Since the stranger hadn't stabled his mount or hobbled or tied it, Lonnie figured the General and the chestnut could safely forage freely, as well. Both the General as well as the chestnut got down and began rolling, which the stranger's stallion had done, as well, rubbing the lather off their backs.

Hoping that the two stallions wouldn't fight over Casey's filly, Lonnie draped the stolen money over his right shoulder and carried his rifle in his right hand as he helped Casey over to the cabin. He knocked on the door that was so rickety it bounced and groaned in its frame. Lantern light seeped through the cracks between the planks.

"It's open an' nothin' in here's gonna bite, so come on in, and light."

Lonnie opened the door and peered inside. He'd been a little worried there might be more like the Confederate in here, but he was alone, all right, sitting at a wooden table that had seen far better days. The strange old man was lighting a porcelain-bowled pipe. He sat with one mule-eared boot hiked atop the other knee. The little monkey stove behind him rattled with a freshly laid fire, and a coffeepot was chugging on top of it.

He'd set his battered gray hat on the table. His head was long and narrow, with a bulbous forehead. His hair was gray-streaked chestnut along the sides, curling over the collar of his calico shirt, but there were only a handful of strands angling back over the top of his age-spotted dome. A worm-shaped white scar knotted his cheek only a few inches from his left ear. A bayonet wound, Lonnie silently opined as he stepped inside the earthen-floored place, which was little larger than the kitchen of his own cabin.

"This your place?" he asked the man, who

was drawing on his pipe, causing the flame in his hand to leap and flutter, sparking in his dark-blue eyes.

"It is now, I reckon. Go on and set your loot down on the floor there, and pull up a chair. I won't promise you they won't cave in under you, cause they're both older'n Jehosophat's cat, but if they do, we'll burn 'em in the stove. I'm almost out of wood, anyways."

He lifted his mouth corners with amusement as he continued to blow smoke into the air around his craggy head.

Lonnie set the saddlebags down and pulled two of the three extra chairs up from the wall. He helped Casey into one directly across from the old Confederate. Then Lonnie eased down into the chair to Casey's left.

He didn't like the way it creaked and groaned beneath his weight. When he leaned forward to place his arms on the scarred table, the chair sank precariously down in front and to the right, and for a minute Lonnie thought it would break and take him to the floor with it.

But once it was down on its shorter right front leg, it held firm.

Lonnie leaned forward on his arms. He realized he was still wearing his hat, so he took it off and set it on the table before him. He looked around quickly to see that the cabin was furnished by little more than the table and chairs and the stove and a few old fruit crates so old that the labels had faded and were nearly illegible. There was a cot on the wall to Lonnie's right, with a moth-eaten wool blanket on it. A tied bedroll lay nearby. A coffee sack served as a pillow.

The place smelled of pipe tobacco, of course, but also of old, rotting wood and mouse droppings. A rusty bull's-eye railroad lantern hung from a wire over the table, casting a watery umber light amongst the shack's heavy shadows.

Except for the gurgling coffeepot, deep silence hung over the place. The old Confederate sat sideways to the table, his right profile to Lonnie and Casey, his elbow on the table, puffing his cigar and staring toward the door. Lonnie thought of him as old, because he had an old way about him, and he was still wearing the old gray hat and uniform trousers. But here where the boy could get a good look at him, he didn't otherwise seem all that old. At least, he probably wasn't far into his forties. Not young, to be sure, but he wouldn't necessarily be considered an "old man."

Lonnie felt fidgety with all the silence. Casey was fidgeting around beside him, also uncomfortable. The old Confederate seemed to not even realize that he had company, for all the conversation he was trying to make.

Wasn't he curious about the money? He must have opened the saddlebag flaps and seen it. Or . . . maybe he hadn't. Lonnie knew that it was probably not to his own credit that he likely would have snooped through the gear, had the tables been turned.

Lonnie glanced at Casey. She returned the glance, giving her brows an incredulous arch. She was as uncomfortable as Lonnie was.

Finally, the boy cleared his throat, and to fill the silence as much as anything else, he slid his hand across the table and said, "I'm Lonnie Gentry."

The old Confederate removed the pipe from his mouth and regarded Lonnie cryptically. He looked down at the boy's open hand, then slipped his pipe into his left hand, and closed his large, gnarled, brown right hand around the boy's, giving it a squeeze. He had the grip of a strong man. He scrutinized Lonnie and Casey from beneath furled brows, hesitating, and then he said in his gravelly, heavily accented voice,

"Wilbur Calhoun."

Casey slid her own hand across the table. "Casey Stoveville. Pleased to make your acquaintance, Mister Calhoun."

Calhoun nodded, regarding the girl curiously, as though trying to puzzle her out, as if maybe he didn't believe she was really whom she'd said she was.

Casey gave Lonnie a nervous, self-conscious glance, then looked around and said, by way of making conversation, "So . . . this your place?"

"Nope," Calhoun said, not bothering to explain whose it was. His mind seemed to be somewhere else as he studied Casey through a haze of wafting pipe smoke. Then he said in his slow, gravelly fashion, "Stoveville. That's the name of the marshal down to Arapaho Creek, ain't it?"

"It was," Casey said. "Marshal Stoveville was my father." She sucked her bottom lip and stared down at the table. "He was killed last week."

"You don't say," Calhoun said with interest.

His eyes flicked toward the saddlebags resting on the floor behind Casey. Lonnie knew then that the man had opened the flaps and seen the money. He was curious, but it wasn't his way to seem so. It was the

Western way to not ask questions. Lonnie's father had explained that the custom had probably come about because so many people in the West were on the run from something back east. Not all, of course, but enough to make asking too many questions dangerous. An overly inquisitive sort might just get drilled with a .44 slug — if he asked the wrong question of the wrong person, that was.

Lonnie wanted to clear the issue of the money up fast, so the old Confederate didn't get the wrong idea.

"The money's stolen, Mister Calhoun. It was stolen out of the bank over in Golden. It was stolen by the men you met tonight. That big, tall one — the blond-headed one with the devil's eyes — he's Shannon Dupree. He's courtin' my ma." The boy lowered his voice in shame, staring down at the hands he was entwining on the table. "Leastways, he was. He . . ." He cleared his throat, having trouble explaining the horrible facts of the situation. "He . . . or one of the other two — the half-breed Fuego or Childress — killed Casey's pa after they got over on the west side of the Never Summers, and Marshal Stoveville formed a posse out of Arapaho Creek to go after 'em."

Calhoun suddenly looked interested. He'd

turned toward the table now, laid a rigidly veined hand down on the rough aspen boards while he held the pipe in his mouth with the other one. "How'd the two of you come to be packin' all that money?"

"Let's just say my ma didn't want it around the cabin," Lonnie said.

"Ah." Calhoun nodded, smiled shrewdly. "She was tryin' to save that curly wolf from himself, that it?"

"That's about the size of it."

"That'll happen. Sometimes women see what they wanna see in a man, whether it's there or not. Men do the same with women." Calhoun added that last sentence with a wry snort, as if he knew plenty enough about the topic. He puffed his pipe and pondered what he'd been told. "Where you two headed?"

Casey said, "To Camp Collins. We're gonna turn the loot over to the deputy United States marshal there. Figure he'll return it to the bank over in Golden."

"You figure to ride all that way," Calhoun said, scowling his dismay, "with Shannon Dupree on your trail?"

Lonnie said, "You sound like you heard of him before, Mister Calhoun."

"Prob'ly ain't too many around the Front Range who haven't heard of that low-down dirty dog. It's a shame your ma put such stock in that cottonmouth."

"I reckon word of him hasn't traveled all the way to the back side of the Never Summers," Lonnie said, crestfallen. "But even if it had, well . . . Ma's been lonely since my pa died."

"The Yankee?" Calhoun said with another shrewd glint in his eye.

Lonnie gave his shoulder a sheepish shrug and cut his eyes at Casey, who returned the look with a skeptical one of her own. Then she shuttled a cautious look at the old Confederate sitting across from her.

"Helkatoot!" Calhoun said, knocking the dottle out of his pipe and sweeping it off the table and onto the floor. "The war's long since over, young'uns. The past is gone. Confederates and Yankees — we're all one an' the same — Americans!"

He set his pipe down, pushed up out of his chair, and walked around the table to drop to one knee beside Casey. "Let me see that foot, little miss. What you packin' there — a break or a knot?"

"I think it's just twisted," Casey said, casting Lonnie another wary glance. "It'll be all right, Mister Calhoun. Thank you, anyway."

"Oh, come on — show the ole Reb your ankle, Miss Casey. I learned some doctorin' skills back durin' the War of Northern Aggression, there bein' few enough medicos providin' for the wounded on our side." Calhoun slapped his thigh. "Put it right up there, and let me take a gander and see what kind a hurt you're packin'."

Casey fidgeted around, embarrassed, and then finally turned in her creaky chair, facing Calhoun. She hesitated some more, and then placed her boot on Calhoun's thigh. Gently, the old soldier slid the boot off her foot, looking up at her concernedly as the girl sucked a sharp breath through her teeth, her cheeks turning crimson from the pain.

"Hurt, does it?" Calhoun asked, moving even more gently.

"A little," Casey raked out.

When Calhoun had Casey's boot off, he rolled her sock down to inspect her swollen, purple ankle. He manipulated her foot a little and then released it, sank back on his heel, and said, "Helkatoot — I've hurt myself worse gettin' out of bed! What you need to do is soak that limb in the creek out yonder. It's good and cold — spring-fed. Bring the swellin' down. Boy, help her out there. I'll start some vittles cookin', what little I got, then I'll come out and wrap some rawhide around that limb of yours. The rawhide'll shrink while it dries and give that wing the support it needs to mend."

Casey shrugged. Since it appeared good advice to her, Lonnie helped her up out of her chair. She wrapped around his neck and sort of skip-hopped over to the front door, which Lonnie opened.

Two red eyes glowed at him and Casey from the darkness outside the door.

An animal gave a deep growl.

Casey screamed.

CHAPTER 46

Lonnie slammed the door and he and Casey stumbled back.

"What is it?" Calhoun said, sliding one of his pistols out of its holster fast as lightning and smooth as silk. He clicked the hammer back and walked boldly up to the closed door.

"There's something out there — a wolf, maybe," Lonnie said.

"Wolf?"

Calhoun chuckled as he depressed his pistol's hammer, and opened the door. "Cherokee, that you?"

The two red eyes moved closer until the lamp flickering over the table showed a large, shaggy, brown-and-white collie dog holding a large, limp rabbit by the neck between its jaws. The dog was eyeing Lonnie and Casey and growling deep in its throat in more of an apprehensive, curious way than an angry one.

"Hidy, Cherokee!" Calhoun intoned. Then, to Lonnie and Casey: "Don't mind him — that's my ole collie. I call him Cherokee cause I couldn't think of nothin' else to call him when he wandered into my camp, a few years back, skinnier'n a boiled chicken. He looked like a collie dog we called Cherokee back to home in Tennessee, and I always been partial to collie dogs. Smarter'n most humans I ever known." He added with another wry snort, "Heckuva lot more loyal, too."

Calhoun turned to the dog. "Drop, Cherokee."

Cherokee opened his jaws and the rabbit rolled out from between the dog's jaws to land with a thud on the earthen floor. "Just in time, my good friend. I was fixin' to prepare supper, late as it is. Meet our guests, Mister Lonnie Gentry and Miss Casey Stoveville from out Arapaho Creek way."

The dog wagged his tail and stepped forward to sniff the newcomers, but when Lonnie leaned down to pet the animal, Cherokee gave a groan and stepped back, head and tail low.

Calhoun said, "He takes some warmin' up to, Cherokee does."

Casey looked skeptically at Calhoun. "So . . . he hunts . . . game . . . for you, Mister

317

Calhoun?"

"Sure enough. I don't like to fire no shots, so . . . I mean, I'm kinda colicky about expendin' ammunition when it's so gall-blamed hard to find way up here in the high-and-rocky, and Cherokee fell to it naturally — huntin', I mean. He eats his share and brings what he don't eat back to my camp, and, well, I reckon we got us a partnership."

Calhoun held the rabbit up by its rear legs. It was long and plump, with a charcoal coat and long, broad, mule-like ears. "That's some jack there, Cherokee. You done good, old son. I'll fry him up with some wild onions and canned tomatoes, and we'll have us a nice meal to turn in on." The Confederate rubbed his concave belly, both hipbones protruding beneath it. "Myself, I can't sleep when I go to bed with no paddin' between my ribs. You two go on out and soak that foot, and I'll get the vittles started."

"Thanks, Mister Calhoun," Casey said.

"Yeah, we appreciate the grub, Mister Calhoun," Lonnie chimed in.

"Helkatoot," Calhoun said, tossing the big jack onto the table and pulling a big skinning knife from his belt sheath. "Besides, it wasn't me that fetched it. It was Cherokee!"

"Thanks Cherokee," Lonnie said, as he and Lonnie continued on out the door.

The dog followed Lonnie and the hobbling Casey across the grassy yard toward the creek that flashed in the light of the moon kiting high over the canyon, casting shadows every which way. The dog followed closely, sniffing, mewling deep in his throat, wary of strangers. He reminded Lonnie of his master in that way.

When Casey was sitting on the creek's grassy bank, and soaking her foot in the cold spring water that gurgled pleasantly over rocks and down a beaver dam a little ways upstream, she turned to Lonnie, who'd sat down against a tree close by. She opened her mouth to speak, stopped, and glanced at the cabin.

Calhoun was moving around behind the windows, cooking supper.

She turned to Lonnie again and kept her voice low and confidential as she said, "Remember what I said about us maybe falling out of the frying pan and into the fire again?"

Lonnie glanced toward the cabin. "You think Mister Calhoun's dangerous? I think he's been livin' alone a little too long." He looked at the dog that sat a ways upstream from Lonnie and Casey, staring at the newcomers in much the way that Calhoun had while he'd smoked his pipe — wary in the way that people get when they're alone a lot, and maybe got a little mushy in the head from it. "Livin' alone with just his dog for company."

Lonnie held his hand out toward the dog, trying to lure it up to be petted. Cherokee stretched out belly-down on the ground and gave a soft cry of frustration, not sure if he should trust the boy or not. The crooked white streak angling down the top of his otherwise brown head glowed in the moonlight.

Casey shook her head. "It's not that at all, Lonnie. It took me a while to remember where I'd heard Calhoun's name before, after he introduced himself. But before he came around the table to inspect my foot, I remembered. A few months back, Pa was visited by Marshal Barrows from Camp Collins. Barrows had a wanted poster, and I saw it. It had the name . . ."

Casey paused and glanced back at the cabin once more. Lonnie could hear Calhoun whistling in there as he chopped up the rabbit's carcass on the kitchen table.

"It had the name Wilbur Calhoun splashed in big, black letters across the top of it," Casey said, whispering and shielding her mouth with her hand. "He's a *train robber!*"

"A *train robber?*"

"*Shhhh!*"

Lonnie gritted his teeth and turned to the cabin again. Calhoun was still whistling while he worked.

"A train robber?" Lonnie asked again, much lower this time.

Casey nodded. "The marshal said some prospectors had seen him camping alone in the Never Summers. Said the man had a list of train robberies as long as his leg. He'd been robbing trains since after the Civil War, and often took to remote mountains between holdups. The marshal was out lookin' for Calhoun but when he talked to Pa, he hadn't seen hide nor hair of him, but he wanted Pa to keep an eye skinned for him." She glanced back at the cabin as she added, "He said Calhoun was fast as greased lightning with his old Confederate pistols. A cold-blooded killer, with a hefty reward on his head."

She slowly kicked her foot in the water, making gurgling sounds. She turned back to Lonnie, looking grave. "And you know what else?"

"Ah, heck," Lonnie groaned. "I don't think I wanna hear any more."

Casey stopped kicking her foot in the water, and swallowed. "Just after the war, he killed his wife. That's when he came west and started robbing trains."

Lonnie stared at Casey in disbelief. He could still hear Calhoun whistling, and he could hear meat frying in a pan. "You mean, that old man in there did that?"

"Well, he probably wasn't so old back then. And did you see how easily he blew those outlaws' hats off their heads? Those weren't accidental hits. I mean, if he'd been aimin' a little lower — well, you get my drift. And he stared down Dupree like he was no more of a danger than a cottontail rabbit!"

Lonnie pondered the information as again he felt his shoulder tighten with trepidation. He glanced a couple more times back at the cabin, then he said, half to himself, "Well, I reckon that's why he's so suspicious of strangers. Probably been one step ahead of one lawman or another since the war ended. But what I don't understand is this, Casey."

"What don't you understand?"

Lonnie hooked a thumb over his shoulder, indicating the cabin. "He could have run off with that money, and he didn't. He could have run off with it *twice* now and he didn't!"

"Yeah," Casey said, slowing nodding.

"And he saved your life twice and mine once." She shook her head and resumed kicking her foot in the cold spring water gurgling along the creek. "No figuring some people, I reckon."

She turned to Lonnie. "What do you figure we should do?"

"I think we oughta pull out first thing in the mornin'." Lonnie felt something brush up against his right thigh and saw that Cherokee had hunkered down beside him, slapping his tail against the ground. "Hey, look — his dog's right friendly!"

"Yeah, but Calhoun killed his wife, Lonnie. And he's a train robber. Imagine how many innocent people he killed!"

They both pondered that while Lonnie stroked the dog's burr-laden coat that smelled a little gamey.

"What if . . ." Casey seemed to ruminate on continuing, and then she decided to go ahead: "What if he's one of those crazy killers you hear so much about, wandering the mountains looking for innocent blood to spill?"

"Innocent blood to spill?"

"Yeah, like in the stories you read about in *Policeman's Gazette.*"

"Oh," Lonnie said, nodding. "Pa used to bring them rags home from town once in a while. I wasn't supposed to, but I'd read 'em out in the barn. You think them stories are true?"

"I don't know, but I hope we don't become the makin's of one of those stories tonight, Lonnie. I sure don't. I'm not sure I want Mister Calhoun close enough to me to wrap my foot with rawhide." Casey looked at Lonnie, her eyes glinting worriedly.

"Yeah, I know what you mean. Under the circumstances, I don't think I would, neither."

The cabin door scraped open and thudded shut. "All right, young'uns," Calhoun called, striding toward the creek. "Time to doctor that foot and make you good as new again, Miss Casey!"

CHAPTER 47

Cherokee barked as his master walked toward the creek.

Casey looked at Lonnie and gasped. "What am I gonna do?"

Lonnie didn't know what to say to that. He didn't have his rifle near, if he should need it. There wasn't much he could do except sit there as Calhoun knelt down beside Casey and pulled her foot out of the water. Lonnie saw that the man was wearing both his pistols and the knife he'd dressed the rabbit with, too.

If the old Confederate should go crazy and start shooting and stabbing, there'd be nothing Lonnie could do about it.

Wilbur Calhoun didn't, however, go crazy and start stabbing or shooting. He very gently set Casey's bare foot on his thigh again. He slowly and with painstaking gentleness wrapped the back of the girl's foot and ankle halfway up to her shin with the rawhide, tying and knotting it and professing, "There — you'll be good as new in a few days, or I'll return the shoat!"

Calhoun chuckled at that. When neither Lonnie nor Casey said anything, and both seemed not to understand, the old Confederate gave them a wink and, patting the head of Cherokee who'd taken a seat close to his master, tongue lolling, said, "That's an old Southern expression. Back before the war, many folks paid for their doctoring with pigs or other animals. Maybe they still do. I wouldn't know. Been a while since I been back to the old home country."

Calhoun cleared his throat, and, rising, his old knees popping, said, "Yes, ma'am — that ankle'll be good as new in no time. Soak it once more with the rawhide on, and then come on in and get warm by the fire. The hide'll shrink up and form a cast of sorts, hold the tendons tight so they can heal." As he tramped on back to the cabin, Cherokee following close on his heels, the old Southerner said, "Come on inside, now, young'uns. Gettin' cold in this holler, and supper's on. No hominy, gallblast it, but it's a good one, just the same!"

He cackled and went on inside while the dog laid out by the front door, though Lonnie could only see his white spots in the darkness in front of the low-slung hovel.

Lonnie looked at Casey. Neither said as much, but they didn't know what to make of old Calhoun. But the smell of the man's rabbit stew and coffee had drifted out over the canyon, and Lonnie's stomach was rumbling. He and Casey hadn't eaten since breakfast, and their bellies were getting way too cozy with their backbones.

Their concerns about the man's past being overpowered by the pangs of their hunger, Lonnie climbed to his feet. He helped Casey to hers, and, arm in arm, they made their way back to the cabin, past Cherokee now curled into a tight ball near the door, and on inside to one of the best meals Lonnie could remember devouring.

Of course, most meals probably tasted that good when they sated a hunger as big and lumbering as the one Lonnie was harboring, but the old Southerner's cooking was still good. Especially given that it was composed of the bare minimum of ingredients — the rabbit, canned tomatoes, and a few wild onions. There were no spices for seasoning. The coffee was hot and black, and as Lonnie tossed the last of it back, Calhoun cleared his own plate with a thick finger and poked it into his mouth.

He looked up, shuttled his gaze from Lonnie to Casey, and chuckled. Both had already cleaned their plates. Casey looked a little sheepish, sitting back from her own nearly spotless plate and empty coffee cup, her hands in her lap.

"You young'uns get enough?" asked the old Confederate.

Lonnie stifled a belch with his fist.

Casey said, "That was absolutely heavenly, Mister Calhoun." Lonnie wanted to kick her under the table to forestall what she said next, but he didn't know the headstrong girl was going to say what she did until the words were half out of her mouth.

Casey probably didn't, either. "You're a right good cook, for a man. You ever have a woman cook for you, Mister Calhoun? I mean, besides your mother, of course . . ."

She flushed a little, vaguely ashamed, while she slid a furtive glance over at Lonnie. Obviously, she was probing the man.

"A man gets to be my age, he's usually suffered havin' a female around the place, time or two," Calhoun said with a caustic chuff, piling up the empty plates on the table before him and rising. Then he stopped, gave Casey a sly grin, and winked at her. The girl blushed. The man's jovial retort seemed to shame the girl more than a straight-out admonishment for prying so boldly into his past would have done.

"I'll wash those, Mister Calhoun," Casey said, apparently feeling the need for penance.

"And strain that injured wing? I'll say you won't. You best get to sleep, little girl. You, too, boy. I'll take care of the cleanin' up. Miss Casey, you sleep right down there on the mat. It smells a little skunky, as skunk's what was likely livin' here before me an' Cherokee moved in. But that hotroll there came with the place — some pilgrim must've forgot it — and it's fresh. The boy an' me'll sleep outside — give you plenty of peace and quiet from our snorin' — eh, boy?"

Calhoun guffawed and headed out to the creek with the plates.

Casey looked at Lonnie. "Whoops," she said.

"Good goin', girl," Lonnie said, genuinely peeved at her. "If he goes loony on me out there, I'll have you to thank."

Casey stuck out her tongue at him.

Lonnie checked on the horses, contentedly grazing. Lonnie didn't think he'd have to tie or hobble them. Calhoun had told him that the canyon, with its steep ridge walls, served as a nearly enclosed corral of sorts. Besides, the horses were tired from all the running they'd done. Calhoun had also assured Lonnie that he didn't need to worry about Dupree catching up to him and Casey here.

At least, not tonight.

Not only would the outlaws have to run their horses down first, which would take considerable time, the canyon was hidden well and virtually impossible to find on even a moonlit night to someone who didn't know it was even here. Calhoun doubted that more than a few handfuls of folks over the past couple of hundred years had known of the canyon's whereabouts, and most of them, besides the old prospector or sheepherder who'd built the place, had likely been Arapaho Indians, who'd called the Never Summers home not all that long ago. A couple of wandering bands still did.

Feeling as secure as possible given the situation, and considering what he now knew about Calhoun himself, the boy threw his gear down in the soft grass and ferns by the creek. When Calhoun was done working around the cabin, the old-timer spread out his own bedroll and saddle near Lonnie. While the old Confederate was asleep nearly as soon as his head hit the soft underside of his saddle, Lonnie fidgeted and rolled from side to side. His nerves were still popping like miniature lightning bolts inside him.

As he'd started to drift off, he'd imagine a bear's roar or the demon-like face of Dupree would reveal itself, ominously shadowed by imagined firelight.

Guns would pop and hooves would pound inside the boy's weary head.

Also, Calhoun snored. Lonnie had never heard a man snore as loudly as the old Confederate. He sounded like ripsaw trying to cleave solid rock, only louder. And the snores weren't steady and predictable, which somehow made them worse. They were as irregular as the thunder in a slowly swirling storm.

Eventually, however, the soft hand of sleep rose up out of the primordial soup of unconsciousness, and swept Lonnie away. When he awoke, it took him nearly a full minute to remember where he was and what he was doing there. He sat up suddenly, squinting at the blinding sun pillaring on and around him through the canopy of the towering firs and aspens.

He shielded his eyes against the light with his hand, and sucked a sharp breath through his teeth. The sun was not only high, but it seemed to be starting its slow shift to the west!

He blinked sleep from his eyes and looked

around, getting his bearings. Straight across the creek and beyond the trees, he could see three horses — General Sherman, Casey's chestnut, and Calhoun's cream stallion grazing in a small clearing bright with sunshine gilding the green grass. Beyond the horses and more trees rose a tall, gray crag of ridge wall maybe a thousand feet tall.

The air was warm. Not hot but warm. A light breeze blew.

There was a splashing sound, and Lonnie turned to look upstream. Calhoun was sitting on the beaver dam about sixty yards away. The old Confederate was slowly kicking his bare feet in the water and holding a willow fishing pole against his thigh, the line angling down the dam and into a dark, gently rippling pool in which a cork bobbed gently. The collie dog, Cherokee, was scrounging around on the bank, head down, tail curled over his back.

Suddenly, the dog pitched back onto his hind paws, coiling like a spring. Then, bounding high and forward, Cherokee formed a near-perfect brown-and-white arc over the grass before he slammed his front paws down on the ground, burying his head for a second in a thick patch of ferns before pulling it back up with a mouse squealing between his jaws.

The dog flipped the mouse high in the air and then plunged after it again, playing.

"Cherokee, stop tormentin' that poor creature and either eat it or leave it alone!" Calhoun beseeched the dog. The man turned his bearded face, shaded by his old cavalry hat, toward Lonnie and said, "Good mornin', sunshine!"

"It ain't mornin' no more, is it?" Lonnie asked, dreadfully. He'd wanted him and Casey to get an early start. They needed to stay ahead of Dupree and to get the loot to Camp Collins pronto.

Calhoun squinted up at the sun and then casually pulled a gold watch from the pocket of his calico shirt. "Accordin' to this old timepiece I acquired thanks to you, it's nigh onto one thirty."

"Holy moly," Lonnie said, bewildered. "Half the day is gone."

He looked around for Casey. There was no sign of the girl.

He looked at Calhoun, who was grinning at him like the cat that ate the canary.

That grin caused a cold stone to drop deep, deep down into the deep well of the boy's soul.

Casey . . .

CHAPTER 48

"What?" Calhoun asked. "You think I ate her or somethin'?"

Lonnie hadn't realized he'd called the girl's name.

Calhoun chuckled, dropped his chin as he looked toward the cabin. "There she is now."

Lonnie turned to the cabin. Casey was fully clothed but she was standing in the open doorway, staring out and blinking as though she, too, had just awakened.

"What time is it?" she asked in a sleep-gravelly voice.

Calhoun said, "Well, you're both late for breakfast *and* lunch. Now, I reckon you'll have to wait for supper. I'm tryin' to catch it right now. Ain't havin' much luck." He scowled at the cork floating in the pool. "Never was much of an angler, and that's a bonded fact."

"We gotta get movin', Casey an' me,"

Lonnie said, shrugging off his blankets and climbing stiffly to his feet.

"You'd best rest up today. You two young'uns been through a lot. Rest up the rest of the day and get a clean start in the mornin'."

"What about Dupree?" Casey said, gazing apprehensively back the way they'd ridden into the canyon.

"He's likely fetched his horses by now, and him and them other two curly wolves are most like scourin' the country for you." The old Confederate pulled in his bait, inspected the worm dangling from the hook, and tossed it and the cork back into the stream again. "He won't find you here. I went back and scratched out any sign we left last night. There's only about one time of the day a fella can see the entrance to this canyon clear, from the western valley, on account of the way the light and shadows sit, and that time's done come and gone. There's a way in from the north, but it's a long ride around. You're safe here. Tomorrow, you can ride out bright and early. You'll both have some good rest behind you, good vittles in your bellies."

Calhoun scowled down at the unmoving cork in the water, and shook his head. "Leastways, I hope you do . . ."

Lonnie shuttled his gaze upstream. He'd had visions of Dupree and Fuego and Childress riding Lonnie and Casey down last night, and those phantoms lingered, needling the boy. He went over to the cabin and helped Casey hobble out to the creek, where she sat down to bathe her foot. He found a stout branch for the girl to use as a cane to help her get around, then he rolled his blankets.

"Helkatoot," Calhoun said, retrieving his line. "If there's any fish in this stream, they ain't hungry. Never have been hungry long as I been here. This old Reb can't abide a finicky fish." He gained his feet and began walking carefully down off the beaver dam. With Cherokee dogging his heels, he strode back to the cabin bathed in midday sunshine.

Lonnie sat down on the bank near Casey, still drowsy from her long slumber, and chewed a weed stem. His dreams about Dupree would not leave him. A few minutes later, Calhoun called his stallion into the yard, and saddled him. Then the old Rebel swung up into the leather, turned the horse downstream, and galloped off, the collie dog running along behind but swerving this way and that to investigate brush clumps or to give brief chase to rabbits and squirrels.

When Calhoun had followed the stream around a wide, right-swinging bend and had disappeared amongst the firs and aspens, Casey said, "Wonder where he's goin'."

She and Lonnie jerked worried looks at each other.

Lonnie leaped to his feet and went running to the cabin. He tripped the latch and nearly tore the door off its frame, lunging inside, and stopped just over the threshold, breathing hard. Relief lightened the load of worry that had been pressing on his shoulders.

The saddlebags still sat against the front wall, near the chair Casey had occupied last night. When he'd crouched down to inspect each bag, making certain that none of the money had been removed, Lonnie walked back out to where Casey faced him on her knees, concern showing in her eyes.

"I'll be hanged if it ain't all still there," Lonnie said.

"And he didn't shoot you or knife you," Casey said, only half-ironically, staring downstream toward where the old Confederate had disappeared. "All he done to me was tend my foot, and it feels better already. Maybe he's not who I thought he was at all."

"Maybe not."

"I know that's the name I saw on the Wanted circular, though. I got a good memory."

"Well, maybe some zebras can change their stripes."

"Maybe," Casey said. "I wonder where he's goin'."

"I don't know, but I'm gonna ride back and check out the mouth of this canyon." Lonnie lifted his saddle and tied bedroll onto his shoulder. "Not that I don't believe what he said about it bein' hard to find, but I reckon it's best if we don't over trust nobody. Especially when we got Dupree and his boys shadowin' us."

"You're not gonna leave me here alone, are you, Lonnie?"

Casey turned to the girl. She looked so plump-faced and morning pretty, with a splash of freckles across her nose and the nubs of her cheeks, her hair still tangled around her ears, that Lonnie couldn't help himself.

He leaned forward and kissed her on the mouth.

Her lips were warm and pliant. When he pulled away, Casey wrapped her arms around the boy's neck, drew him to her once more, and kissed him, long and deep.

Lonnie could feel the passion in the girl's body.

He could feel it in his own, as well. It made the tips of his ears burn hot as a skillet over a stoked fire.

They released each other at the same time. Casey smiled warmly at him. Lonnie didn't know what to say. It was as though every word in the English language he'd learned over the past thirteen years had suddenly left him, until he finally managed to sputter, "I won't be gone long. Give a holler if you get scared. I'll hear and come runnin'."

He started walking over to the corral, his mind still foggy from the kiss. He paused to whistle for General Sherman, who was now grazing on the near side of the stream with Casey's chestnut.

When he'd saddled the horse, Lonnie rode upstream, in the opposite direction from which Calhoun had ridden. As he left the sunlit yard and gained the shadows of the forest he turned back to Casey, who was bathing both her feet in the stream now. She'd turned to look after Lonnie. She was smiling.

Her mouth opened and closed, and Lonnie heard her yell barely loudly enough to be heard above the thudding of the General's hooves: "I love you Lonnie Gentry!"

At least, that's what Lonnie thought she'd yelled.

He turned his head forward as the General stretched his stride into a lope. Lonnie's brows hooded his eyes. The boy was in deep thought.

At least . . . that's what he *thought* she'd said.

"Nah, couldn't be," he muttered as the General picked up a faint game trail twisting amongst the pines. He'd just heard what he'd wanted to hear. *No town girl as wonderful as Casey Stoveville could love a raggedy-heeled mountain kid like Lonnie Gentry . . .*

CHAPTER 49

Lonnie followed the game trail up a low grade through the forest, occasionally skirting the creek, for what he figured was a good mile or so. When the game path appeared to dead-end in a stand of piñon pines and juniper, near the base of a craggy, gray stone wall leaning back against the southwestern sky that bore not a single cloud, Lonnie reined the General to a halt and swung down from the saddle.

He dropped the stallion's reins, slid his rifle from its scabbard, racked a round into the chamber, just in case, and then off-cocked the hammer. He followed the game trail, littered here and there with deer and elk scat, up into the trees.

Continuing to follow the trail through the trees, Lonnie saw that it did not end at all. It meandered between junipers and pines that were not as closely spaced as they'd appeared from where Lonnie had left the

General, and continued through a broad gap in the mountain wall.

At the gap in the wall, which was maybe thirty feet wide and which Lonnie vaguely remembered riding through the night before though it had looked much different in the moonlight than it did in the full light of the sun, Lonnie stopped and dropped to one knee. He saw why this mouth to the canyon in which Calhoun's cabin sat would be so hard to find from the adjacent valley.

The game trail dropped down and away from him into the valley, quickly intersecting several other game trails. There were trees to the right and left, and a jumble of boulders inside the line of trees on the right. Shade was creeping over Lonnie from the towering rock walls on either side of him, and he could sense that this opening, which sat crookedly atop the slope he was on, probably looked like solid stone from only a few yards down the slope that dropped into the valley. He didn't want to check it out and risk being seen or leaving tracks, but he was fairly certain this was so, that few people had ever gone beyond where Lonnie knelt.

It would take a man who'd spent a lot of time traveling around these mountains to happen upon such a gap as the one Lonnie was in. A former Confederate train robber, who had a lot of time for traveling remote mountains ranges as he stayed ahead of the law, would be such a person.

Feeling better, more secure, Lonnie walked back to where General Sherman stood ground-reined, and swung up into the saddle. He turned the horse around and loped back in the direction from which he'd come.

After he'd ridden fifty or so yards, he stopped, swung down, found an aspen branch with a few dead leaves on it, and used the branch to carefully, subtly scratch out his trail but leaving the deer and elk scat and a mound of what appeared coyote dung bristling with chokecherry seeds and rabbit fur.

Lonnie tossed away the branch, mounted the General once more, and returned to the cabin.

When he'd unsaddled the stallion, he rubbed him down and curried him thoroughly, and then he gave the same treatment to Casey's chestnut. With her gimpy ankle, the girl couldn't tend the horse herself, but Casey hobbled up from the creek and sat on a corral post, watching Lonnie work. She didn't say anything more about love or anything even similar, if she ever had, but merely looked around and chewed a weed and watched Lonnie work with a warm, self-satisfied half smile on her face.

She seemed to be enjoying the day of rest from travel, as was Lonnie.

Occasionally, when they heard the breeze scrape branches together or they heard birds light from the trees, they turned to see if Calhoun was returning. When the old Confederate hadn't returned by the time Lonnie was done tending both horses and rubbing some bear grease into his and Casey's tack, the two stripped down to their underwear, and waded around in the creek, skipping stones and splashing each other playfully.

After a while, they swam in the cool, deep pool beneath the beaver dam, and then lay together on the bank, drying out in the sun.

They didn't hear the thuds of a single rider until well after the sun had gone down, filling the canyon with deep-purple shadows. Lonnie and Casey, both dry now, had dressed and were gathering wood for a fire, when Calhoun returned with a croaker sack tied from his saddle horn and hanging down over his left stirrup fender. Cherokee followed him, tongue hanging but his ears up and eyes smiling. The dog was wet and dirty, as though he'd taken several swims in the stream.

The ex-Confederate cast a bright, toothy smile toward the youngsters gathering wood near the creek, and then, whistling, stripped the tack from his horse and carried the croaker sack inside the cabin.

"What do you suppose he's got in the sack?" Lonnie asked Casey, as the boy dug a shallow hole in which to build a fire against the canyon's growing chill.

"I don't know. Why don't you go in and fine out?" Casey nudged him with her hip.

"Why don't you?"

"Chicken!"

The door to the shack opened then, and Calhoun asked Lonnie to fetch him some wood from a pile behind the cabin. Turning the outdoor fire-starting duties to Casey, Lonnie gave the girl a conspiratorial wink — he'd find out what was in the sack now — then strode around behind the cabin. He found a few pine logs under an old, moldy tarp that didn't look too soft, and split them with a mallet. When he had an armful of relatively well-seasoned wood, he took it into the cabin, stopping inside the door in shock.

On the table was a fat, dead chicken, appearing freshly killed, and two potatoes, a handful of carrots, and a large turnip. All the vegetables appeared to have been freshly harvested, as they were all still wearing a moist skin of soil though the bright orange of the carrots couldn't help but shine through the dirt. On the table was also a fresh-baked pie, a small stone crock filled with only the Lord knew what, and a loaf of crusty, dark-brown bread.

There was also a bottle on the table, with its cork resting on the table beside it. Wilbur Calhoun was crouched in front of the small stove, shoving bits of paper and kindling and feather sticks into the firebox.

"Holy moly, Mister Calhoun — where'd you get all that grub?"

Calhoun turned to Lonnie. He hesitated slightly, the nubs of his craggy, red-brown cheeks turning a tad darker, and said, "Oh, this stuff here? Oh . . . well . . . I . . . uh . . . I got me an old prospector friend living downstream a couple miles. I told him I had guests and needed some possibles, and he . . . uh . . . well, he obliged . . . seein' as how he owed me a favor or two."

The old Confederate took the wood from Lonnie and set it on the floor outside the stove's open door. "Much obliged, young'un! Run along, now! I'll call you and the pretty li'l gal when supper's ready! Hope you're hungry!"

He winked and saluted Lonnie with the bottle and took a long drink.

Lonnie headed back outside, his stomach already rumbling at the sight of all that food, and filled Casey in on the details. As it was getting colder the darker it got, they both hunkered down on either side of the fire Casey had built, and enjoyed how the fading light played on the stream, and how the smoke issuing from the cabin's stovepipe grew more and more fragrant with the smell of cooking food.

About an hour later, Calhoun called them to supper, and Lonnie had a hard time holding himself back and not running ahead of Casey, whom he had to help hobble across the yard to the cabin. Once inside, they both stopped again in shock at what the table displayed — three battered tin plates covered in thick, light-tan chicken stew colored with the white of fresh potatoes and turnips and the bright orange of fresh carrots.

Tin cups of milk sat at the head of two plates. The bread sat in the middle of the table, near the stone crock that was no longer wearing its lid so that Lonnie could tell it was filled with fresh-whipped butter!

The pie sat at the far end of the table, fairly screaming to be cut into.

"Well, I never seen such polite children-folk — waitin' to be asked to sit down to table," Calhoun said, leaning over the table to cut the bread loaf into slices. Lonnie noticed that the level of the whiskey had gone down by about a third. Calhoun laughed and beckoned. "We don't stand on form here at the Calhoun plantation, young'uns. Come on in, belly up to the bar, and get to shovelin' before it gets cold!"

There were crunching sounds, and Lonnie looked under the table to see Cherokee under there, chowing down contentedly on a big heap of chicken bones.

The old Confederate laughed again, heartily, and took another deep pull from the bottle.

CHAPTER 50

Lonnie and Casey and Wilbur Calhoun made short work of the chicken stew and bread lathered in thick, fresh-whipped butter and the apple pie dessert, while Cherokee crunched bones beneath the table.

The old Confederate had slacked off on the whiskey bottle, switching to coffee for the meal, and Lonnie was glad he had. There was a certain untethered, hell-for-leather quality about the old man's spirit, which, while charming when the man was sober, could possibly turn into something dark with too much skull pop under his belt. Lonnie didn't think consciously about this, but, having been around drunk, mean men enough times in his short life, it did occur to him instinctively, and it caused an all-too-familiar apprehension in the boy.

Men were too darn big, physically, and they wielded too much power and were too well armed for Lonnie to feel safe around them when they were drinking.

He didn't like it when, after the meal, Calhoun freshened his coffee with the stuff. Lonnie thanked the man for the wonderful meal and rose from the table, wiping his mouth with the back of his hand and excusing himself.

"Hold on, boy."

Lonnie inwardly cringed as he looked across the table at the old Confederate. Casey, having insisted her ankle was much better, was washing the dishes out at the creek. The dog, having taken to the two young strangers, had followed her out there, and Lonnie could hear her talking to the dog while she scrubbed the plates and cups and the dog scampered around the brush.

Calhoun had filled his pipe. He tamped the chopped tobacco down inside the bowl, and plucked a long stove match off the table between his thumb and index finger, so ingrained with dirt that both appeared nearly black, as did nearly all the deep-cut age lines in his skin.

"Yes, Mister Calhoun?" Lonnie said.

"Wilbur."

"Beg your pardon?"

"Sit down there, and call me Wilbur."

Lonnie didn't know what to say to that. It didn't feel right, calling a man as old as Calhoun by his first name. It didn't sound right at all. In fact, it sounded almost as bad as cursing. It sounded *worse* than cursing.

Calhoun struck the match to life atop the table. The flame chuffed and blossomed and then settled down against the end of the match, which the old Confederate held over the bowl of his pipe. "You really," he said, sucking the flame down into the bowl and blowing the smoke out the side of his mouth, "you really . . . gonna take all that loot . . . back to the marshal in Camp Collins . . . ?"

He continued to suck at the flame and blow the smoke, his gaze focused on the pipe bowl.

"Yes, sir," Lonnie said, frowning at the man, not sure what his point was. "It belongs to the bank over in Golden."

"Bank money, boy," Calhoun said, flipping the match onto the floor and turning his slightly watery, drink-bleary eyes to Lonnie over the smoldering bowl of his pipe, "is money meant to be taken by them it don't belong to."

Lonnie wasn't quite sure he'd heard the man correctly. He felt the impulse to poke his fingers in his ears, to clean the wax out of them, but then he realized that he'd heard the man correctly, after all.

"I don't know what you mean, Mister Calhoun," was all that the boy could think of to say.

"I mean, son, that whoever belongs to that money has by now forgotten about it. Leastways, they've probably written it off their books, or the bank has made up for it. Most likely, rich people own that money. Rich *Yankees*. People who ain't gonna miss it none." He paused, let more smoke billow out the side of his mouth. "Folks that got enough money to lock up in a bank got enough money to lose, is what I'm sayin'."

Calhoun stopped and regarded Lonnie levelly over the smoldering bowl of his pipe. Lonnie sat frozen, waiting for the man to continue though he really didn't want him to.

"If I was you," Calhoun continued, puffing his pipe, "I'd take that money, and I'd start a life for myself somewhere a long, long way from here. New Mexico, maybe. Or maybe *Old* Mexico. Son, the senoritas down there . . . why, they'll . . ." His bearded face gained a sheepish look, and he let his voice trail off. He'd been about to gesture in the air with his hands, but he thought twice about that, too, sitting back in his chair and returning the pipe to his mouth. "Son, what I'm sayin' is this is a dog-eat-dog world. We gotta get ahead any way we can. If that means bein' stronger than the next fella, and takin' what's his and makin' it yours — why, then, that's what you gotta do."

"That ain't how I been taught it, Mister Calhoun."

"No, of course not. They don't teach you that." The old Confederate lowered his pipe once more, squared his shoulders, and leaned forward on the table, his eyes growing large and passionate. "The so-called *Good Book* . . . our parents . . . *school marms* — they wanna keep you weak, keep you cowerin' to everybody else. Cowerin' to the ones who done figured it out and learned how to make this short life we have down here on this miserable scratch of dirt somethin' worth livin'. All for the sake of bein' *civilized.* But we *ain't* civilized, boy. We're savages. All of us is savage through an' through, and hidin' that fact is plain foolish and prideful."

Calhoun laughed without humor. "It's the toughest savage that survives. It's the savviest savage that has an easy ride. Why, hell, I rode with Jesse James for a time . . . after the war. Him and me didn't get along — we was both the same kinda savage, I reckon — so we parted ways. But Jesse — he knew what I done just told you. You see, the war was a good teacher in that regard to us Graybacks."

Calhoun knocked the dottle from his pipe out onto the table. "No, no . . . you an' that girl take that money. It's yours now. You'd be fools not to take it and make a good life for yourselves."

Lonnie stared at the old Southerner who sat blaze-eyed across from him. The old man's words had grown wings and they were flying around between the boy's ears. Lonnie's palms were slick with sweat. He looked down at the overstuffed saddlebags leaning against the wall. Thousands of dollars in those two pouches. Enough so that he could go home and turn his cabin into a nice, big place, and decorate it nice, too, like he'd seen in the catalogs at the mercantile in Arapaho Creek.

He'd give his ma a nice place to grow old in, keep her mind off men that hurt her and Lonnie. Give her enough so that she wouldn't need any such man to make her happy. Because her son would make her happy.

Make her and the baby she was carrying happy. Maybelline Gentry would be wealthy and happy in her old age. If she was still alive, that was.

If Shannon Dupree hadn't killed her . . .

Lonnie was starting to breathe hard, as though he'd run a long way up a steep hill.

If his mother was gone, Lonnie would be alone. Maybe he had Casey, maybe he didn't. If he did, they'd need a nest egg to make a fresh start for themselves . . .

Maybe Calhoun was right. Maybe he should take the money. He'd never had a dime, and he at only thirteen years old worked himself to the bone, rolled into his bed every night feeling as beaten-down as an old man. Hell, none of his three pairs of socks didn't have holes in them!

Who if not Lonnie Gentry deserved such wealth that had suddenly fallen into his lap?

The door hinges squawked. Casey had left the door partway open to let the stove heat out while she'd washed the dishes at the creek. Now she nudged it wide and stood in the open doorway, holding the freshly washed plates and cooking pans, with silverware and tin cups propped on top. She was staring at Lonnie from beneath rumpled brows. She turned her head partly to one side, and narrowed her eyes reprovingly.

"Don't you listen to him, Lonnie. Don't you dare!"

CHAPTER 51

"Now, you look here, little miss — !"

"You look here, you old train robber," Casey said, slamming the dishes and silverware down on the end of the table and casting Calhoun one of her spine-melting glares, her smooth, suntanned cheeks flushing with fury. "How dare you try putting evil thoughts in Lonnie's head!"

Before Calhoun could interrupt her, she swung toward the boy. "Don't you listen to a word of his blarney. He's an old train robber and a killer. He killed his own wife! Shot her in the back! Is this the kind of man you want to be, Lonnie?"

Lonnie sat back in his chair, feeling his lower jaw becoming unhinged. Both Calhoun's words as well as Casey's had taken manic flight between his ears. He wasn't sure what to think about it all, much less what to say.

Calhoun answered for him. "He'll make

up his own mind. Where I come from, a boy big as him's a man. Hell, I had friends as well as kin who fought for the Confederacy when they was no bigger'n Master Gentry there. I'm tellin' it the way this old world works, and you oughta listen, too, little miss!"

Casey stomped her good foot down hard on the floor. "Stop calling me 'little miss!' Why, you're nothing but a common outlaw. A ne'er-do-well and a scoundrel. You're an old rogue wolf hidin' up here from them tryin' to exterminate you. My pa worked hard to run your ilk to ground so the West could grow and become a civilized place — a place folks who lived here could feel proud calling their home!"

"Yeah, well, how'd that work out for your pa? What'd it get him 'cept an early grave?" Calhoun slapped a big hand down hard on the table. "I'm tellin' it right — you two best take that money and carve a life out of this miserable rock while you can. Laws and whatnot — why they're written by the scared and the weak. Them laws're meant to be broken by them strong enough to carve a life for themselves without workin' themselves to the bone to do it! Only the weak follow the laws, cause only they *have to*!"

"You old fool!" Casey screamed, slapping her own hand down hard on the table. "How dare you spew your evil blather to an innocent boy?"

"He ain't so innocent. He might be young, but he's being hunted like a full-grown man. That grows a child up right fast — shows him what the world's *really* all about! And *fool* am I?"

Calhoun rose, kicking his chair back and wobbling a little, drunkenly, on his feet. For a second, Lonnie thought he was going to fall into the table. "You don't know nothin' about me, little miss! I fought hard in that war, and what did it get me? Nothin' more than graves to visit when I finally got back home with so much Yankee metal in my back — bedsprings an' screws an' nails — that I jingled when I walked. And when I finally did get home, I learned my wife hadn't been pinin' away for me half as much as she was tellin' me in the letters she wrote. Ah, hell, no — she weren't pinin' at all. In fact, she was makin' time with a rich man from town — Virgil Boatwright, the town banker's son. One afternoon I come back early from sellin' eggs and I caught 'em together!"

Lonnie had been riveted to every word both Calhoun and Casey had said. Now, staring up numbly at the old Confederate, sensing the anguish in the old Rebel's heart, he said, "That . . . that when you killed her?"

Tears dribbled down the old man's cheeks, soaking his beard. "No." His voice cracked on that, and he turned away, giving Lonnie and Casey his back.

He lifted his head and ran a hand back over the nearly bald top of his head. "I didn't kill her, though I might as well have. June's dead on account o' me. It was a mistake. I loved her. I *still* love her. I shot Boatwright! I reckon I only clipped him though I heard he died later, but before he expired he grabbed his old LeMat off the dresser . . . and . . . June moved between us . . . and he shot her in the back."

The old Confederate sobbed as he lowered his head, staggered toward the other end of the cabin, and took his face in his hands. His shoulders jerked as he cried. "There wasn't nothin' I could do for her, an' I heard a neighbor yellin' from his field, and I went crazy with shame an' fear, an' I ran. And, oh, Lord, I'm still runnin'."

Calhoun turned back toward Lonnie and Casey.

"That was the end of civilized life for me. I reckon I missed it more than I thought.

Leastways, the family part of that life. Been nice havin' you two young'uns here . . . to cook for . . . to listen to you talkin' out by the creek, sparkin' each other, fallin' in love, like me and June . . . back before the war."

Lonnie flushed. He glanced at Casey. The girl stared stony-faced at Calhoun though Lonnie could tell by a slight softening in her eyes that the man's story had reached through her anger.

"Hell," Calhoun said, chuckling though tears continued to dribble down his cheek and into his beard, "I went out and stole grub for you, didn't I?" He chuckled again.

There was a short, heavy silence, then Casey said tonelessly, "What?"

"Helkatoot," Calhoun exclaimed. "I never did no prospectors any favors. I stole that food you ate tonight. There's a little shotgun settlement, three cabins and some stables down along Eagle Creek, and I raided their garden and keeper shed, took a chicken out of their coop." The old Confederate's tone was buoyant with mockery. "Pretty darn good vittles even if they was stolen, wasn't they? Hell, those rock breakers ain't gonna miss none of it. They got more than they can eat, anyways, and a man'd be a fool to go hungry up here when he's got their chickens and gardens down there!"

He turned to Lonnie. "You see what I mean, boy? Why work like a dog when you don't have to? We're savages! All of us." He leaned forward and tapped his temple. "It's the smart savages that know how to make the plows pull for *them*!"

Lonnie couldn't move from his chair. He didn't know what to make of all he'd heard, but he knew one thing — Calhoun's story, however horrible, had been fascinating. And Lonnie wasn't sure he didn't agree with the old Confederate's life philosophy, either . . .

Why shouldn't he do what Calhoun had recommended — take the money and make a good life for himself? Why should he struggle when he didn't have to? Casey obviously didn't agree with Calhoun, but she was still under the influence of her father, the town marshal of Arapaho Creek.

Calhoun had been right: Marshal Stoveville's efforts at holding the lawbreakers at bay had been rewarded by only a premature death and an orphaned daughter.

"You go ahead and sit here and listen to this scoundrel as long as you want, Lonnie," Casey said in that same disdainfully toneless voice. "But I'm goin' to bed." She picked up the saddlebags, drew them over her shoulder with a grunt. "And I'll be pullin' out with the money first thing in the morning."

She stopped at the door to glare once more at Calhoun. "I'll be takin' it back to where it rightly belongs."

She opened the door and headed out, stepping around Cherokee who sat beyond the doorway, mewling his discomfort at the raised voices and the tension.

"Casey, hold on!" Lonnie said, rising from his chair but getting his boot hung up on a corner of the table, and tripping. He was drunk on the possibilities of a new, rich life. He made his way through the door and swerved around Cherokee. He caught up to Casey easily, as she was still hobbling on her injured ankle.

"Casey, stop!" Lonnie pleaded, grabbing the girl's arm.

She stopped and swung toward him, her eyes ablaze with anger.

"What're you gonna do when you go back to Arapaho Creek?" Lonnie asked her. "You gonna go back to work for that mercantile? You know how much you're gonna have to work to keep your house? And what if you lose it? Then, what're you gonna do?"

Lonnie knew that the frontier was a harsh, cruel place for young women without families. Casey knew it, too. Lonnie could see the fear in her eyes. Her gaze grew less angry and more pensive, and then, as though ashamed by what she was thinking, Casey swung around again and continued favoring her sprained ankle as she strode toward where the fire by the creek had burned down to faint, umber ashes.

She sat down and, keeping the saddlebags draped over her shoulder, raised a knee and wrapped her arms around it. She studied the darkness straight out across the murmuring creek for a time, and then she said softly, "So, what are you thinkin', Lonnie? What're you thinking we should do with this money?"

Lonnie sat down beside her. His mind was swimming with possibilities. He could hardly catch his breath. "We could take it back home. I could build up the ranch, and we could —"

"Get married?"

Lonnie hiked his shoulder. "Why not? You don't have nobody, and . . . and Ma . . . she might or might not be at the ranch when I get back." The horror of that possibility struck the boy like a blow. So much had happened, and he'd been so distracted trying to stay ahead of Dupree, of trying to keep himself and Casey alive, that he really hadn't allowed himself to consider what life would be like for him if his mother was dead.

If both his parents were dead, and, like Casey, he had no one.

Suddenly, he realized that Casey was staring at him sympathetically, as though she knew what he was thinking. She sighed, shook her head. "Damn you, Lonnie, for listening to that old train robber . . . and for making me actually consider doing such a low-down dirty thing."

She set the saddlebags aside, gently pulled off her boots, and rolled up in her bedroll. She turned her back to Lonnie.

Lonnie wandered off and tended nature, then he came back to the fire, built the flames up a little with pine branches. Then, he, too, curled up in his blankets. But he was too distracted with swirling thoughts about the money to fall asleep right away. Money and shame, money and shame — he was caught in a cyclone of those two conflicting ideas.

He could hear Casey over on the other side of the fire, rolling and thrashing this way and that, for a long, long time, before sleep finally claimed him.

He woke abruptly, lifting his head from his saddle. He blinked and looked around, heart pumping.

Something had awakened him. Then he realized what it had been, because he heard it again — Casey screaming from a long ways away: "Lonnie! Help me!" There was a slight pause as the girl's cries echoed around the canyon touched with the pearl light of dawn.

Then Casey screamed something Lonnie couldn't hear, because it was muffled with distance and partly drowned by the morning chirping of birds.

And then she screamed something Lonnie could hear:

"*Dupreeeee!*"

CHAPTER 52

Two hours later, after the sun had cleared the horizon but the valley in which the boy found himself was still cloaked in cool shadows, Lonnie abruptly stopped the General on the side of a sparsely wooded ridge.

He stared straight ahead, his eyes wide. His pulse hammered in his ears as he stared at something pale in the ferns and small spruce saplings growing around a deadfall tree about thirty yards away.

Lonnie couldn't move. His boots were glued to his stirrups. He could not bring himself to dismount and walk over and take a look at the pale object obscured by the brush.

He knew what he would find there if he did.

Dupree, Fuego, and Childress had killed Casey and thrown her body there like trash.

Finally, knowing that he had to confirm his suspicions, the boy climbed slowly,

366

heavily down from General Sherman's back. He dropped the horse's reins and walked slowly forward, setting each spurred boot down slowly, the lighthearted ringing of the spurs seeming to mock the boy's growing dread.

The long, pale object that he knew would be Casey, killed by Dupree, grew gradually larger before him. The boy's stomach felt as though someone had rammed a railroad spike through it. Tears were oozing over his eyes. He blinked them away, rubbed his cheek with a gloved hand, swallowed hard to keep the vomit down.

When he stepped into the ferns and saw that what lay before him was not Casey, after all, but the pale carcass of a freshly killed mule deer fawn lying with its pale belly facing Lonnie, the brown eyes regarding him blandly, the boy's knees nearly buckled with relief.

The fawn had likely been killed by a wolf or a mountain lion last night, partly eaten, and then dragged here to be chewed on later.

Lonnie turned and strode quickly back to his horse. His relief at not finding Casey dead was quickly obliterated by the growing possibility that he would still find her that way.

He looked down at the tracks of four horses. He'd cut the sign about a half a mile downstream from Calhoun's cabin, in the opposite direction from which Lonnie, Calhoun, and Casey had first entered the canyon two days ago. The tracks continued through a small notch in the ridge wall and on down the eastern side of the mountain, following a faint trail that was probably an old game path as well as a trace once used by the Arapahos for traveling from one valley to another within the Never Summer range.

Lonnie hadn't been on it long before he'd realized that it was probably an alternate route, probably an easier route than Storm Peak Pass, especially in bad weather, over the mountains to the eastern plains.

Earlier, it hadn't taken Lonnie long, once he'd shaken off the cobwebs of sleep, to realize what had happened to Casey. She must have awakened well before dawn and, deciding that she had to take the money to the deputy US marshal in Camp Collins herself, because she thought she could no longer trust Lonnie to help her, she'd quietly saddled her chestnut and ridden out alone along the stream and, not long after leaving Calhoun's cabin, into the hands of Dupree, Fuego, and Childress.

Lonnie had seen the tracks where the four horses had come together. Forming a group, they'd headed southeast. Two of the horses had been ridden close together, which told Lonnie that Casey's horse was likely being led. The girl was now Dupree's prisoner. For whatever reason, the outlaw and his two partners had taken her captive.

And, of course, they had the money, too.

Lonnie was vaguely surprised to discover that he was no longer concerned about the money. What made his heart pound until he thought it would crash through his breastbone was Casey.

As he rode down the slope and then followed a winding watercourse through a crease between heavily timbered ridges, he also reflected that as much as he might have wanted to, he couldn't have taken the bank loot any more than he could have sprouted wings and flown.

That was all clear to him now, wedged in between thoughts of getting Casey back unharmed. He was no more like Wilbur Calhoun than Wilbur Calhoun was like Lonnie Gentry — a good kid on his way to becoming a man of integrity no matter what the cost.

Lonnie wished he would have realized that last night, because it might have saved Casey's life as well as him a whole heap of trouble.

Better late than never.

Lonnie held the General to a fast pace as he followed the tracks of the four shod horses ahead of him. As he did, he looked around warily.

He wouldn't put it past Dupree to set a trap for him, to try to blow him out of his saddle from ambush. Lonnie wished that Calhoun were riding with him. The old Confederate may have been many things, most of them bad things, but he was also good with a gun, and he was trail-savvy. Lonnie wasn't too proud to admit that he could have used the old man's help now, with Casey's life on the line.

When Lonnie had raced into the cabin earlier, after he'd heard Casey's scream, he'd tried to awaken the old Confederate, but there'd been no doing. Lonnie had found not only one but two empty bottles on the floor. Calhoun had stirred and mumbled and called for June, sobbing, then rolled over and cried himself back to sleep on his bunk.

Late in the day, when the sun was tumbling over the mountains jutting up behind Lonnie, several strands of wood smoke touched the boy's nose. He checked the

General down where two shallow washes intersected, and tied the horse to an old root angling out the northern bank.

He was out of the mountains now, on the north side of the Never Summers, in a relatively flat, dry area relieved by widely spaced bluffs and low mesas. The ground was thin and sandy and not able to grow much except for short, brown grass and clumps of prickly pear and yucca. There were few trees except a light peppering of scrub cedars, junipers, and piñons.

The sky above Lonnie was a velvety lime-green. He glanced toward the Never Summers towering darkly behind him to see the glowing, crimson sun being cleaved by a high, black peak shaped like an ax blade. The sun was falling quickly behind that blade toward the west side of the range.

Lonnie climbed up out of the forking ravines, doffed his hat near the top of the bank, and stopped beneath the bank's crest. Slowly, continuing to smell the smoke, he edged a look over the top of the bank. He pulled his head down quickly, pulse quickening. He nervously licked his lips and then edged another look over the top of the bank, and held himself steady despite his nervousness.

He was staring out over a broad table of

ground rising gradually toward a low, sandstone mesa rimmed with bulging rock from which a few hardy cedars twisted. The crest of the mesa stood maybe three hundred feet above the land below it and on which a low, gray cabin and barn and corral sat behind a windmill, whose blades lazily twisted in the warm, dry breeze blowing over the mountains.

In the corral fashioned from peeled pine poles, five horses ate from a hay crib, lazily swishing their tails. Lonnie recognized Casey's chestnut.

Gray smoke curled from a stone chimney rising up the cabin's far right end. Voices emanated from inside the cabin. Mostly men's voices. Then Lonnie heard a girl's voice.

Casey's voice. She gave a harsh retort to something one of the men said.

There was a sharp *crack*! The sound of a brutal slap.

One of the men inside the cabin laughed. Then Lonnie almost kicked out of his boots with a start when he saw a slender, denim-clad female figure in a man's wool shirt appear in the cabin's open doorway, the door being propped open with rock. There was a motley-looking porch on the place, crouched on low stone pilings. The figure

372

walked out onto the porch and down the steps and into the weakening sunlight, which flashed off Casey's gold-blonde hair.

The girl limped around the side of the cabin, gathering wood from a low stack around the chimney, and carried the wood back into the cabin. She'd moved with her head and shoulders angled low with fear and defeat.

Lonnie watched the black, open doorway through which Casey had disappeared.

He watched it for a long time as he tried to calm himself down and gather his thoughts.

Then, his lips set in a hard, straight line, Lonnie eased back down the bank, shucked his Winchester from his saddle sheath, and pumped a cartridge into the chamber.

CHAPTER 53

Lonnie told himself he had to wait until dark to approach the cabin.

But that was a very difficult thing for him to do. The farther the sun dropped, and the darker the tableland got as well as the shallow wash in which Lonnie waited with General Sherman, the quieter everything got.

At least, the quieter everything except the cabin got.

Lonnie could hear Dupree and the other men talking loudly in there. Their voices gradually grew louder and louder. They were accompanied by the occasional violent jingle of coins being thrown down on a table, and the clinking of bottles. They were obviously playing poker.

Lonnie could also hear the clatter of pans. The smoke from the chimney grew thicker. The men had Casey cooking for them while they played cards and drank. Lonnie had to get the girl out of there. The more the men drank, the more dangerous they would get.

But he had to wait until dark. At least twilight. There was very little cover anywhere around the cabin, so if he tried to approach the hovel while it was still light, someone inside the cabin would probably see him, and Lonnie would acquire a two-ounce chunk of lead for his efforts. Worse, he'd let Casey down.

There was no telling what Dupree and the others might do to her after dark, when they were good and drunk. Lonnie didn't want to think about it. He wanted to get her out of there.

Lonnie sat on his butt on the bottom of the wash, his back to the bank, his rifle across his thighs. He'd unbuckled the General's latigo strap, and both ends of the strap were hanging free beneath the horse's belly. Lonnie had also let the horse drink water from his hat, and he'd fed him a handful of grain, as well. Now the horse stood only a few feet from Lonnie, facing his rider, head up, twitching his ears, listening.

The General knew something of great gravity was about to happen, and he was waiting with anticipation, as was Lonnie.

When there was only a little light left — sort of a soft blue fog touched lightly with the blush of salmon — Lonnie rose and took a long drink from his canteen. He patted the General's neck, and strode quickly along the wash. He followed the wash to the east, and when an even shallower wash intersected the main one from the north, he tramped through this lesser, feeder wash that was likely dry except during monsoons or when the snow was melting in the mountains.

This wash was choked with spindly sage, yucca, rocks, prickly pear, a few bleached bones of long-dead animals. As Lonnie had admonished himself to be mindful of rattlesnakes, he heard one give its high, eerie rattle. He stopped to see the diamondback, little thicker than a rope but as deadly as one twice its size, slither off amongst the rocks and shrubs, likely heading for its hole.

Lonnie paused to steady his nerves. Then hefted his rifle in his hands, holding it up high across his chest, and continued moving north along the shallow wash. He paused twice more to peer carefully over the crest of the wash, to see where he was in relation to the cabin, and then, ten minutes later, he ran up and over the crest of the wash toward the cabin's east wall. He ran hard, crouching low, holding his rifle in his right hand and swerving around occasional tufts of buck brush and sage.

There was only one window in the side of the shack facing Lonnie, to the right of the large, stone chimney and near the rear of the cabin. That was likely a bedroom window. No one was probably back there yet. A least, Lonnie hoped they weren't. There was a curtain over that small window but it was partly open.

Lonnie dropped to a knee and pressed his shoulder against the cabin's log wall, behind the chimney and the woodpile. He was breathing hard, sweating. It had warmed considerably when he'd dropped out of the mountains, and he'd wrapped his coat around his bedroll. His shirt was pasted to his back.

He mopped his brow with his shirtsleeve. He could hear the voices more clearly now. Mostly, he heard the more talkative Dupree and Childress. He knew Fuego was in there, however, because he'd seen the man's brown-and-white pinto. He wondered who the fifth horse belonged to.

Lonnie rose, drew another deep breath — here it goes — and started moving around the chimney. He'd gotten as far as the woodpile on the chimney's other side, when he heard someone walk out onto the stoop and come down the steps. Lonnie dropped back down to a knee with a gasp, and very slowly, quietly ratcheted back the Winchester's hammer, lifting the stock to his shoulder.

A figure came toward him, and he tightened his finger on the trigger.

Then he eased the tension when Casey stopped before him, rocked back on her heels, and slapped a hand to her shirt. "Lonnie!" she exclaimed.

She'd been too startled to whisper it. Immediately, she realized her mistake, and turned her head quickly toward the cabin.

Dupree yelled from inside, "What's out there, girl?"

Casey whipped her head and stricken gaze toward Lonnie. Lonnie's heart hammered his sternum until he almost couldn't breath. Fresh sweat broke out on his back and inside his gloves.

"Girl!" Dupree yelled. "What's out there?"

Lonnie gritted his teeth when he heard a chair scrape back across the rough wooden floor. He looked up at Casey standing over him, and very quietly whispered, "Snake."

Casey turned her chin toward the front of the cabin. "Just a snake. Shocked me's all! He's gone now!"

Lonnie was glad to hear a chair squeak as Dupree's weight settled back into it. "Well, hurry it up with that wood! You try to make a run for it, Fuego here'll shoot you. Fuego can shoot the wing off a fly at a thousand yards — can't you Fuego?"

Childress and someone else laughed, though Lonnie didn't think the someone else was Fuego.

Casey turned her anxious gaze back to Lonnie, who stood and squeezed her right hand encouragingly. "Now, tell 'em you're comin'," Lonnie said.

She frowned at him curiously, anxiously, but then she did as Lonnie had instructed.

"Sit down, now," Lonnie said. "Keep your head down."

Casey grabbed his arm, dug her fingers in. "What're you gonna —?"

"I'm gonna end this right here," Lonnie said. "Sit down and keep your head down."

"Forget the money. Lonnie, let's just run!"

Lonnie gazed straight into her eyes, hardened his jaws, and said firmly, "No."

Casey shook her head slowly, dreadfully, then she slowly sank down against the cabin wall, behind the chimney.

Lonnie turned his head forward. He pulled his hat down a little lower on his forehead, and then walked around the cabin's front corner. Keeping his head down, so that anyone looking out the door couldn't glimpse his face and see that he wasn't Casey, he moved up the porch steps, crossed the half-rotten boards of the stoop and stepped inside.

He stopped suddenly, raised his rifle to his shoulder. He aimed at Dupree, sitting at the left end of a small, rectangular table on which dirty tin plates and cups and several bottles were cluttered. Two lamps burned where they hung from nails on square-hewn ceiling support posts. The fireplace was to Lonnie's far right, but he didn't look at the small fire whose heat he could feel pushing against him.

He blinked once as he kept his gaze on Dupree, who sat back in his chair, his left boot hiked up onto his right knee. His hat was off but his longish, blond hair showed the marks of it. His left hand was wrapped with a bloody bandage. He had another bloody bandage around his ribs. He clutched his wounded hand against his belly, and he was glowering demonically at Lonnie.

The boy could tell by the deep lines carved around Dupree's eyes, and by the sweat beading his cheeks, that his wounds were grieving him.

"Hey, Squirrel!" he said. "Been waitin' on you. What took you so long?"

Fuego sat facing Lonnie on the other side

of the table, leaning forward, a cigarette smoldering in his right hand. He was absently fingering his wolf-tooth necklace with his left hand. The half-breed wasn't wearing his hat, either. Neither was Childress, who sat with his back to Lonnie, half smiling over his right shoulder at the boy, his close-set, pale-blue eyes glistening mockingly in the flickering lamplight.

They'd all settled in for the night.

Lonnie swallowed, tried to keep his voice from quavering as he said, "Toss your guns onto the table there. One fast move, and I'll drill ya."

"Balderdash!" intoned Dupree, laughing, showing all his large, white teeth. "Put the Winchester down, kid, before you get hurt." He held up his bandaged hand, which shook like a leaf in the wind. "I wanna talk to you about this hand" — he dropped his gaze to the bloody bandage around his ribs — "and about this here."

Too late, Lonnie heard a boot thud on the floor behind him. The stench of sweat filled Lonnie's nostrils. A man grunted loudly as he wrapped his big, bare, hairy arms around Lonnie's waist from behind, and, laughing, lifted the boy two feet off the floor.

Lonnie gave a loud groaning *chuff*! as the bear hug squeezed the air out of his lungs.

He inadvertently triggered the Winchester into a ceiling beam. The three outlaws at the table started laughing as they watched wood sliver and dirt sift down from the ceiling.

Lonnie have a loud, enraged yell, and swung his right boot forward before thrusting it straight back, hard, ramming his spurred heel into the kneecap of the man who was holding him above the floor.

The man bellowed loudly. The thick arms dropped away from Lonnie's waist. Lonnie dropped nearly straight down to the floor, and pivoted on his hips.

He saw the man who'd lifted him — a big, barrel-waisted hombre with a long, tangled, cinnamon beard and a thick, food-stained mustache. The man's hands appeared large as plowshares. He glared through narrowed eyes at Lonnie as he cupped one hand over his bloody left knee. He bulled forward, swinging his thick, right fist toward Lonnie, who flipped the Winchester around, and smashed the stock against the underside of the man's chin.

The man flew back out the open door, bellowing raucously. When he got his boots under him, Lonnie rammed the stock of his Winchester into the man's bulging gut. The man groaned and dropped to his knees, and

Lonnie slammed the rifle butt down hard on the back of his head, laying him out cold.

Guns roared behind Lonnie, who turned, cocking the Winchester as slugs sizzled through the air on either side of his head. Both Dupree and Fuego were standing and extending pistols at Lonnie, trying to aim around Childress. Childress was falling drunkenly back against the table.

Lonnie looked past Childress at Dupree, who was leveling his pistol on Lonnie once more, and Lonnie triggered the Winchester.

As Dupree crumpled, firing his revolver into the table, shattering a whiskey bottle, Lonnie stepped hard to his left in time to avoid a bullet triggered by Fuego, whom Lonnie shot next. Fuego groaned and clapped a hand to his left temple as he twisted around, tripped over his chair, and hit the floor with a loud *boom*!

Childress was still trying to get his revolver out of his holster. He stopped when he saw the Winchester aimed at his throat. He looked at the round maw only six inches away from him, and took his hand away from his gun, swallowed, and raised both hands in the air.

CHAPTER 54

Lonnie waved the barrel of his Winchester around in the air before him, expecting one of the other men to take another shot at him. But Dupree was lying beyond the end of the table, unmoving, his lips stretched painfully back from his teeth. Blood welled from the bullet hole in the center of the man's chest. The outlaw's cold, gray eyes stared lifelessly at the ceiling.

Dupree had robbed his last bank. Absently, Lonnie wondered what his mother would think about that, if she were still living.

Fuego lay on his side, writhing and groaning as he cupped both his hands to his bloody left temple. Childress stood with his hands raised, scowling at Lonnie.

"What're you gonna do now, kid?" Childress asked. "You think you know?"

"Yeah, I know," Lonnie said, glaring back at the man. "I know exactly what I'm gonna do."

A floorboard squawked behind Lonnie.

He swung around, but it was Casey this time. She stepped slowly over the unmoving figure of the man who'd grabbed Lonnie from behind, and into the cabin. Lonnie stepped back away from Childress, giving himself plenty of room, keeping his rifle aimed at Childress's head.

Casey looked around as though in a daze.

"Get their guns, Casey," Lonnie said. "Get every gun and knife you can find, and haul 'em all outside. Then we're gonna need some rope. Lots of rope."

When Casey had relieved the outlaws of all their weapons, and had tied Childress and the painfully grunting Fuego to ceiling support posts, Lonnie wagged his rifle at the big, unconscious man on the porch.

"Who's that?" he asked Casey.

"Fellow who runs this little outlaw camp," Casey said. She had a coil of rope on her shoulder. "They called him Hansen. An old partner of Dupree's."

"Best tie him, too," Lonnie said, stepping outside and keeping his Winchester aimed at the big, unconscious gent with the thick, bare arms. When Casey had hog-tied the man in much the same way that she'd hog-tied the others, making certain there was no way they could work lose, Lonnie walked back inside, found the saddlebags lying near the dead Dupree, and drew them over his shoulder. He swept the money from the table into one of the pouches. Now the bags felt as heavy as before.

"Best get these out of there," Lonnie said as he stepped out, resting his Winchester on his shoulder. "I'll stow 'em in the stable until morning."

Casey stood at the bottom of the porch steps. The big gent was waking up now and groaning as he lay belly-down against the porch floor, hands tied to his ankles behind his broad back.

"Oh, my head," he bellowed. "Oh, Lord o' mercy — my *head*!"

"That's the least of your troubles, partner," Lonnie said as he stepped over the man and descended the porch steps.

Casey smiled crookedly at the boy, and arched a brow. "You clean up right well. Ever think of becoming a lawman?"

Lonnie shrugged. "You all right?"

"I've seen better days," Casey said. "And I'll see more, I reckon." She paused and looked brightly up at Lonnie. "Your mother's alive, Lonnie. I heard Dupree talking to the others. I reckon even he couldn't hurt a woman with child."

Lonnie sighed and leaned back against a porch post in relief.

Casey moved closer to him, crossed her arms on her chest, and cocked her hip. She looked at the saddlebags draped over Lonnie's shoulder. "What're we gonna do with those, come mornin'?"

"Same thing we were always gonna do with 'em. Take 'em to the same place we're gonna take them two inside and that Hansen fella. To Marshal Barrows in Camp Collins."

"My pa'd be right proud of you."

Lonnie ran a hand across the saddlebags, considering. "Casey, I . . ."

"You don't have to say anything, Lonnie. I know who you are. You may have lost track for a little while. Heck, I lost track of myself. I reckon we all do from time to time. But I know who I am now. And I know exactly who you are, too."

"Oh, yeah?" Lonnie said, a little sheepish. "Who's that?"

Casey wrapped her arms around his neck and kissed him. "You're the man I love."

ABOUT THE AUTHOR

Peter Brandvold has penned over seventy fast-action westerns under his own name and his pen name, Frank Leslie. He is the author of the ever-popular .45-Caliber books featuring Cuno Massey as well as the Lou Prophet and Yakima Henry novels. Recently, Berkley published his horror-western novel, *Dust of the Damned,* featuring ghoul-hunter Uriah Zane. Head honcho at "Mean Pete Publishing," publisher of lightning-fast western e-books, he lives in Colorado with his dogs. Visit his Web site at www.peterbrandvold.com. Follow his blog at www.peterbrandvold.blogspot.com.

The employees of Thorndike Press hope you have enjoyed this Large Print book. All our Thorndike, Wheeler, and Kennebec Large Print titles are designed for easy reading, and all our books are made to last. Other Thorndike Press Large Print books are available at your library, through selected bookstores, or directly from us.

For information about titles, please call:
(800) 223-1244

or visit our Web site at:
http://gale.cengage.com/thorndike

To share your comments, please write:
Publisher
Thorndike Press
10 Water St., Suite 310
Waterville, ME 04901